The Fight in the Dog

A Shaun Mullin Story

Franklyn Blake

Contents

"Crime is a class distinction, not an ethical problem."
ORSON WELLES

"Oh Manchester. So much to answer for."
STEVEN MORRISSEY

Prologue

*C*ertain cities adapt themselves *to the ebb and flow of human needs. These are the cities that endure – London, Glasgow, Cambridge even – places that have processed the sea changes of civilization and re-emerged afresh, useful and vigorous.*

Other cities seem fixed. They wither, recede, and eventually lose all purpose. They become little more than dormitories. For cities, rebirth isn't optional. They shed their skin, or they rot.

Manchester in the twenty-first century is a city stripped of function. Its industry has all but expired. Many of the Victorian chimneys remain, along with a proliferation of large, dark stone buildings. These were formerly factories but now house, in ever-smaller boxes, brutally over-mortgaged graphic designers and trainee lawyers who do a sixty-hour week and get through it all with the help of cheap cocaine.

Coffee shops on every corner, a music festival here and there, and the inescapable sense of treading water.

A place that was once the workshop of the world now defines itself by a reputation for constant rain and a couple of football teams. It has drifted out of focus and become a backwater. Lost in the weeds, its status as a global powerhouse little more than a memory.

Having grown up in and around Manchester, the city exists in my memory as being extremely bleak.

Its name conjures concrete-coloured skies, Peterloo, Hindley and Brady, Joy Division, Blitzkrieg, IRA bombs, and a systemic poverty borne of the Industrial Revolution. All of these things belong together. In spirit, they are one and the same. We feel them that way.

This dark perception of Manchester – unflattering, given my love for the place - might say as much about me as it does the city. It is a brighter, happier place than it once was, I will concede that much – the trinkets of twenty-first-century life are as readily available here as anywhere else in the first world. And there are just enough people here who think that tables are for dancing on. It bustles along fairly cheerfully.

But Manchester is an old soul. The established wisdoms – and idiocies – of the past run through it as tangibly as the River Irwell.

There's a phrase that still does the rounds in Manchester to this day. It belongs to the post-Ward generation but has never quite become extinct:

"He's no better than he should be".

Know your place. Accept your fate. Aspiration is pointless, vulgar, misguided. And thereby humdrum lives beget humdrum lives, and on and on.

A tangible sense of misfortune at one's lot, woven into everyday life, to be suffered as an accident of geography, is the context for the career of the villain Peter Garton. He could only be a Mancunian.

The city isn't just his birthplace – it's who he is. It is his soul.'

From
'NO GOOD DEED: ME AND THE MANCHESTER MOB'
By Shaun Mullin

PART ONE

The City of Perpetual Dusk

1

In a neat corner of Manchester city centre, nestled between the stern Victorian buildings on all sides, is Canal Street. It is nominally the gay district of the city, but throws its arms wide to one and all.

On its more raucous nights, which mostly occur during warm summer weekends, this part of Manchester is a lot of fun. It feels wild, vibrant, joyously optimistic - if one can overlook the intrinsic 'end-of-days' undertone.

A dozen or so bars, clubs and pubs run alongside a narrow strip of water, between the Palace Theatre at the western edge of the street and the Law Courts to the east – exuberance at one end, justice at the other.

It is, in summer at least, a merry quarter.

But seasons change. As the days shorten the neon castles of Canal Street fade back to cold stone, as if a spell has been broken. Cinderella after the clock has struck.

This particular Monday in October was a quiet night. The month's end meant empty wallets until payday. The chill flecks of drizzle in the air were keeping people at home too - an unwanted reminder that the brighter evenings were now behind us for good. Another summer over.

But the relentless dance music persisted from the bars, as if the buildings themselves were trying their utmost to get something – anything – moving.

A few committed souls were making a defiant attempt at hedonism. It was harder to whip up the necessary energy without the mayfly revellers of high summer, but they would try.

These regulars, each one driven here by their own compulsions, were seasoned pleasure-seekers. They could spot an interloper a mile away.

On this night in particular, the imposter was a tallish, slim man in his early fifties. Raincoat, regulation shoes, straw-like hair. Bespectacled and unshaven. His feet were slightly splayed at ten-past-ten or thereabouts. There was a noticeable lean to his right-hand side and his coat was pulled up at the collar, giving him a hunkered-down look.

Something about his face suggested inquisition. His default expression was a challenge to the world, as if it were constantly asking "yeah, so what?"

Suspecting he was far more conspicuous than he had hoped to be, Shaun Mullin made his way towards the entrance of *The Twisted Melon*.

The music sounded like New Order, he thought, but probably wasn't.

He registered a faint whiff of amyl nitrate as he crossed the threshold. There were maybe a dozen patrons huddled into blurred shapes around small, half-lit tables. There was a long bar with purple lights flanking an unoccupied dancefloor.

Perching awkwardly on a high, velvet-topped stool, Shaun ordered neat whisky. Irish, a single, the cheapest available, no ice. He scoped the place, careful not to catch anyone's eye. The barman, Dean, gave him his glass.

"Been in before?" he asked.

"Not for a while" said Shaun. "When does it get busy?".

"Friday" said the barman.

Shaun smiled.

Comedian.

No further conversation was forthcoming. Dean backed off.

His patron sipped his whisky.

Shaun's inner monologue – always lively – was cranking up. He found conversations with himself to be just as entertaining as any he had with other people. So the chatter in his brain was more or less constant. These conversations did occasionally escape his mouth in whispers when he was alone, but were most often confined to the inside of his head.

He regarded the barman.

Sorry pal, you don't shave your head at your age.

You look like a convict.

Magwitch.

A bright-eyed youngster, probably a student and definitely high as the moon, danced his way to the bar – a performance wasted on an empty auditorium. He wore eyeliner.

Look at his pupils. Who does pills on a Monday for God's sake?

The kid ordered four drinks in an Estuary accent.

Students. That's who.

Dean turned around to face the optics.

The young lad glanced at Shaun, for a little longer than was comfortable.

Daddy complex. No thanks.

A minute later, the youngster departed with his drinks, shimmying as he went for the benefit of the stranger at the bar.

Shaun tipped his glass at Dean. Another two fingers of whisky. This place was intolerable. Its assault on the senses made it deeply hostile to an irregular, and Shaun was beginning to feel somewhat scattered in the mind.

The luxury items of the next 20 years will be silence, space and time.

He'd read that in an in-flight magazine on the way to Dublin, sandwiched between adverts for watches and reviews of cafes in Reykjavik. It felt like the truth.

He knew already he wouldn't find what he was looking for. Not here. Not this evening. But he decided on due diligence. He had come here, so he should see it through. He nodded at Dean, who came over.

"Do you know someone called Emlyn? Chunky feller. Comes in here."

"Called *what*?"

"Emlyn."

Dean shook his head.

Shaun brought up a photograph on his phone and tilted the screen in Dean's direction.

Dean shrugged. "I see a lot of faces." He wandered away.

Shaun thought about Emlyn, where he might be at this moment, and what may have become of him. Cities like this were well-accustomed to

9

vanishings. They were easy to effect. Perhaps Emlyn had simply decided to disappear for a while.

But probably not. The truth was rarely straightforward round here.

Shaun had become acquainted with Emlyn Parry at the boxing club down the road from where he lived. He was an odd-looking character, was Emlyn, with the physique of an Easter egg and arms slightly too short for the rest of him (not an advantage in the boxing world).

He'd gone missing three or four weeks previously, and there seemed to be no stray threads that could lead anyone to him. Emlyn's friends had asked the club members to keep an eye out and ask around.

It was well-known at the boxing club that Emlyn wasn't especially fussy about his sexual partners, or even which type of genitalia they possessed. He wasn't exactly a regular in Canal Street, but he'd been spotted here more than once in pursuit of whatever was currently floating his boat.

Shaun hoped Emlyn had not suffered the same fate as Carl.

Poor Carl.

≈

Two summers ago, at six twenty-seven on a Friday morning with the June sun already warming the air, Shaun Mullin discovered the body of a teenaged boy – fifteen years of age, half-obscured by foliage adjacent to the path that ran alongside the railway line. Eyes wide open, mouth ajar, and the needle still hanging from the crook of his left arm.

Within an hour of his discovery, Shaun had completed a sensitive but perfunctory interview at Stretford Police Station, politely rejected the offer of a referral to a trauma counsellor and secured a couple of days off from his employer, *The Manchester Herald* newspaper.

The next day Shaun was informed that the boy's name was Carl Wilks. An only child from the tightly packed terraces of Whalley Range. Carl was just a single casualty among many each year in the North-West. Boys (mainly) who had lost their way, acquiesced to the temptation in their own dark hearts, and finally been just plain unlucky.

There had been some talk of Shaun composing a feature for *The Herald* on lives like Carl's – the young victims of Manchester's heroin trade. But Shaun thought it vulgar and undignified, and he rejected the notion.

Shaun went to Carl's funeral. A well-attended affair. A middle-sized family and a knot of school-aged kids in uniform. As the ceremony ended, Shaun was approached by a woman who identified herself tremblingly as Carl's mother. She was appropriately bereft and wore whatever mourning garb she had been able to get together from the clothes she already owned. Her hands shook as they took Shaun's, her eyes glazed wet.

Aside from the plain details of what Shaun had seen, neither of them knew what to say. They came quickly to the realisation that there was little point saying anything at all. The worst of life's troubles defy language.

Shaun's social interactions with colleagues, family, and friends became, for a while, sombre affairs. People's concern for Shaun after his unpleasant discovery became an oppressive blanket of sympathy. Others seemed more reluctant to move on than he was. It was dull, he had decided, and there was nothing more objectionable than boredom.

And that may well have been the beginning of the end of the business. But as the date of the awful discovery receded, the memory of Carl Wilks' pale body refused to fade. In truth, Shaun had only glimpsed it for a moment before turning his back on the grim scene. Three seconds, perhaps. Five at most. The merest dot in Shaun's lived experience.

And yet, the image persisted day upon day. In dreams, in waking, and in faces he passed on the street. In the shadows cast by streetlamps and the reflections in store windows.

≈

As a former recreational user himself – speed as a teenager, cocaine once he was older and could afford it – Shaun had always shrugged off suggestions of 'drugs epidemics' and suchlike. Tabloid talk. And nobody knew how that worked better than Shaun did.

The problem with drugs was not that they're bad, but that they're terrific. People took them either for fun, or to escape some unpalatable aspect of their daily existence. Either was fine by him.

But in the hope of some escape from the unsettling memory of Carl Wilkes, Shaun began to scratch at the surface of some of the issues of addiction in urban centres.

Northern cities were tailor-made for proliferations of illegal drugs, of course. There was the obvious unemployment and poverty – the generally accepted causes. This, it seemed to Shaun, was coupled with an aimlessness in the collective consciousness up North. There was a low expectation in this city of what life might have to offer. It was inter-generational and hard to shift.

Homes had been thrown up on top of one another round here after the war, and every murky, badly-planned2 Council estate contained its dark, illicit nooks. Drug use had gradually become a problem of class. A distillation of what an uneven society did to its least fortunate. An extra layer of punishment, as if poverty were not enough.

In Guildford, it was a few underaged vodka and cokes. Up here, kids got 'on the brown'. Horses for courses, as it were.

By Christmas, the subject had taken hold of him. He had a tendency towards obsession whenever an area of study gripped him. This served him well professionally but would frequently obliterate his spare time for months on end. He'd bought a dozen or so books by now, and eagerly consumed their contents each evening.

Shaun's interest in the social politics of drug abuse was now keen enough to spark further investigation. He had arranged to meet a copper on the Manchester force – the brother-in-law of one of his neighbours.

Shaun knew plenty of local Officers through his work as a reporter, of course, but none of these relationships were in the 'cordial' category. He was aware he had something of a reputation in Police circles. He was, he would readily concede, obtuse in his professional dealings with them. They didn't like him much, and that was generally reciprocated.

But Kenneth Cooper wasn't cut from the same cloth as most coppers.

There was 'no side to him', as Shaun's mother used to say about folk she found agreeable. Unusually for an Officer, there didn't ever seem to be an angle being worked. His conversation had no subtext.

Shaun had always found speaking to the Police a stressful exercise, even in a social setting. A polite enquiry about what he'd been up to over the Christmas holidays always had the tone of an interrogation about it. But Ken, who was open and thoughtful, he liked.

Over a couple of pints in the Half Moon in Fallowfield, he and Shaun communicated in an easy, honest fashion.

Shaun sized up his conversational partner fairly quickly. Fundamentally unambitious, Ken had stayed in uniform for close to four decades, strolling wet pavements, watching vehicles rip along the M62 on countless freezing nights, and doing the necessary admin cheerily enough. His best years were behind him, and he seemed to find that fact perfectly tolerable. He had been a decent copper, and (as far as anyone is) a decent man. To all outward appearances, that was enough for Ken.

Ken told Shaun he had stopped giving a toss what the local paper wrote about Greater Manchester Police years ago. Tomorrow's chip-wrapper, and all that. Shaun was no threat.

They batted back and forth various theories about rising levels of drug use in the vicinity, and what might be done about it.

It was during this conversation that Ken Cooper raised the name of a drug dealer named Peter Garton. Shaun knew the name, but little more than that.

According to Ken, Peter Garton's great skill, the attribute that allowed his criminal career to flourish unimpeded, was restraint. Moderation.

Garton's cultural significance to Manchester was, secretly, quite sizeable. He was referenced (not by name) in a book about the 'Madchester' scene of the early '90s, as the man who fuelled the all-nighters at the Hacienda. The names of his mob members were known to music promoters and guitarists and actors and media poseurs. He fuelled them too, when it was still all pills and powders.

Heroin came later. And with it, a change in the necessary operating procedures – the era of grinning, loved-up clubbers came crashing to a halt. H was definitely not E.

Violence had to be done far more readily now, such were the people Garton was dealing with at either end of the supply chain. But his influence was only ever exerted from afar – there was no trace of Peter Garton at any knee-capping, beating, or kidnap. His DNA could be found only in the places you'd expect it to be.

He was clean, effective, and almost invisible.

There were other dealers in the North-West, of course. On the whole they were wealthier, noisier, and nastier than Garton. All of which meant they were easier to catch. Peter Garton was the longest-standing of all of them, the only major dealer of his generation not currently behind bars.

Greater Manchester Police knew plenty of the facts, of course. They could at various times over the years have pinned some minor crime to Garton solidly enough for a conviction in court. In the first few years after he came to their attention, they waited for something big to go down. Not a mere possession, or menaces, or handling, but a significant lead that would secure a twenty-year sentence.

It never came.

And once Garton had become part of the criminal furniture of Manchester, there emerged a conundrum for Law Enforcement. It has become known as 'the vacuum problem', and there has been many a paper written on it by students of Criminology.

In the back bar of the Half Moon, Ken leaned in towards Shaun, cradling his pint of mild.

"Any Force in the country will tell you this, Shaun. Same anywhere. With drugs, when one of the big dogs is put away, a vacuum is created. The demand for the product doesn't change, but the ability to access it is gone all of a sudden. That vacuum will be filled, without fail. Always quickly, and usually with somebody worse than what you've just got rid of. It's normally

Albanians or Turks that come in these days, and that is a significant game-changer for the Constabulary, I can promise you."

So, all things considered, certain elements at Greater Manchester Police were not desperate to curtail the activities of Peter Garton. He was the devil they knew. All he had to do was keep his head down and stay in his lane.

≈

And so, two years on from the discovery of Carl Wilks' pale, lifeless body, Shaun Mullin sat at the bar of *The Twisted Melon* in Manchester's Canal Street, looking for Emlyn Parry. No connection had yet suggested itself between Emlyn Parry, Carl Wilks, and Peter Garton. But the connection did exist. Manchester was a big place, and a small one.

As he sipped the last of his whisky, Shaun glanced at the WhatsApp message that had come through to his phone. A colleague apparently still at the office was requesting Shaun's assistance.

Ben.

He was capable and resourceful, was Ben da Silva, but was prone to crises of confidence that were often draining to be around. Especially for Shaun, who wasn't over-familiar with the concept of self-doubt. There was an alienating fussiness about Ben when he was in that mood. He became prim.

Shaun sighed.

This is what happens when they get you to manage people. I spend enough energy dealing with my own neuroses, I don't need anyone else's.

Shaun set his glass down on the bar a little more heavily than he'd wanted to, drawing a glance from Dean. He strode to the door, then out onto the pavement.

There he encountered a swirling mizzle, the sort that runs up sleeves and down necks. Shaun dipped his chin into the wind and upped his speed, making his way down Bloom Street in the direction of St. Peter's Square.

On rounding a corner onto a street of bright, late-night takeaways, Shaun was momentarily alarmed by a vast, looming silhouette on a building across the road. A tall, Golem-like creature, three stories high and on the move. It took him a second to realise this was his own profile, thrown into gigantic relief by the light from a kitchenware shop he was passing.

There were spectres everywhere. Dead-eyed boys, violated girls, psychos and sickos. Smackheads like Carl, and prossies who got in the wrong car, and old, mad tramps who wandered into something they shouldn't have. They were all here.

Shaun checked himself, decided in favour of brighter imaginings, and came eventually to a converted warehouse that was now an office block. Its façade had been blasted clean in preparation for a different class of occupant. The building had rather pointlessly been given the moniker *The Forge*, presumably for marketing purposes. Shaun regarded this as the gentrification of past suffering, a mockery of his city's history, and pursed his lips in disapproval every time he saw it.

The plastic droplet attached to his key fob met a small panel on the doorframe, and the lock withdrew itself.

2

The offices of The Manchester Herald, situated on the top floor of
The Forge, were relatively new. They felt to Shaun reminiscent of an
upmarket coffee shop – blonde wood and minuscule meeting pods where
people could catch COVID-19 from one another with great success.

How had the word 'pod' entered the parlance of office life? When Shaun
was at school, a pod was the collective noun for a group of dolphins. Now it
signified an inadequate meeting space.

The office floor itself was large enough. Thirty or so desks, overflowing
with folders, various publications, file trays and personal effects. Individual,
glass-walled offices at one end of the floor. A few framed front covers of *The
Herald* lining the walls – some of the more recent ones Shaun's work –
along with a clock that currently read 10.13pm.

The office was vacant except for a solitary, frowning figure sat behind a
desk, his olive complexion illuminated by a glow from his screen. Ben da
Silva, a neat and upright young man a touch over thirty years old, tinkered
at his keyboard with no conviction. Enthusiasm had deserted him an hour
ago. It hadn't occurred to him that when you've removed and replaced the
same comma on four occasions, it's time to go home.

As Shaun approached the office and regarded Ben through the glass wall
at one end, he wondered again where exactly Ben was from. Blackburn was
the practical answer. But his parents – Indo-European, almost certainly.
Portuguese? He'd never asked.

Shaun eased opened the door and entered.

"I've got a life, you know" he said.

"No you've not" Ben replied, as if it were an open-and-shut case.

Having removed his coat and hung it up, Shaun approached Ben's desk.

"Right, come on, let the dog see the rabbit."

He drew up a nearby chair and read the screen over Ben's shoulder. The piece read fine. Ben could write, that wasn't an issue. It was about tone with him. Some writers – many of them more talented than Shaun – found connection to a newspaper's 'voice' the hardest thing of all.

"For starters, 'Open to debate' rather than 'controversial'."

"Why?"

"Because we're not a tabloid."

"It's milky though. You're getting soft in your old age, you are."

Soft in my what? You cheeky bastard.

Ben grinned. Shaun glared, before his attention was drawn to a cardboard pizza box on the desk. The lid was open by a centimetre or so, and Shaun could suddenly smell its contents.

"What toppings did you get?" asked Shaun.

"You don't like pizza."

"I like it fine. What I don't like is paying fifteen quid for cheese on toast. But if you're daft enough…"

With this, Shaun hauled a giant slice from the box, catching the elastic cheese with his tongue before it slid off the base. Melted cheese was a force for good in the world, he thought. A perfectly accessible luxury item.

Shaun remembered these nights, at the *Express* and the *Mirror*, back when he was Ben's age. Younger, in fact. Tying himself in knots in pursuit of perfection, in the days before he had realised that perfection didn't exist, and that chasing it drove you mad.

Poor Ben. Shaun could guarantee him that the article was no better now that it had been two hours previously.

"Christ, Ben, let's not disappear any further up our own arses than we already have. It's fine. We're done. Go home."

Ben da Silva seemed unconvinced.

"Perfect is the enemy of good, young man. And this is good."

With this, Ben deferred to his superior and grabbed his jacket from a nearby coat stand.

"Any news on your mate Emlyn?" he asked.

"He's not really a mate. But no, none."

"Weird" said Ben. "Here one day, gone the next."

With this, Ben trotted off down the stairs with his jacket over his arm.

This left Shaun alone. He wandered the floor for a few minutes, stopping and sitting in various chairs, swinging round on each to get a view of his own desk. These were the vantage points others had on him. It felt like useful intel. What was he to his colleagues, he wondered? A curmudgeon long past his sell-by, or the venerable head of the clan?

How far he'd come.

And how little he'd changed.

He knew things now. He'd seen people in all their variations – human beings were beautiful and vicious and bold and repugnant, sometimes all in one skin. Life had certainly not passed him by.

But the decades were starting to concertina themselves into shorter and shorter spans in his mind. Thirty years had raced past, and it made him feel uneasy.

There had never been much doubt in anyone's mind – least of all his own – that Shaun Mullin was a born journalist. He was by nature inquisitive and intellectually serious, with a rare facility for getting people to say things they normally preferred to leave unspoken. He drew people to him, somehow. And they talked.

His career began in 1994, a few weeks after he had graduated from The University of North London with a first-class Degree. A friend alerted him to a vacancy on the night desk at *The Daily Express*, answering the phone and subbing an article here and there.

He didn't last long. The hours were savage and unsociable, which didn't help. But it was the tone of the place that he couldn't get on with. The cynicism in every interaction. The absence of loyalty to an idea, a principle, or even another human being was too hard to take for an idealistic young

kilogram of uncut cocaine in the other.

Quite why a man as cautious as Garton would allow one of his premises to be used in this way was a mystery to all. It was out of character, to put it extremely mildly. Daley had already considered the strong possibility that this was a fit-up, but the party line from upstairs was clear – he had to hit Garton with a ton of bricks.

It happened, sometimes, when there was a changing of the guard. A new Chief often felt the need to lay down a marker, and that meant a high-profile conviction. Chief Commissioner Graham Watts had been in post for only a couple of months and was pushing a strong anti-narcotics message. This became a pledge, which quickly turned into a formal set of targets. The game had changed, and nobody had read the rules to Peter Garton.

≈

The Manchester Herald was in its element for the next couple of weeks, with Shaun and Ben crafting articles and headlines alluding to 'The Invisible Kingpin', 'The Puppet-Master of Manchester's Drug Trade' and 'Peter Garton – The Most Notorious Man You've Never Heard Of'.

As news items went, it was perfect – a popular local publican exposed as the evil purveyor of the drugs that were killing our kids. It didn't get any better than this, Shaun knew, and sales of *The Herald* received a sizeable bounce for a few issues.

The name Peter Garton became for the first time common currency in pubs and shops and factories, as if Greater Manchester Police had captured Dick Turpin. Heads were shaken at how long he had been allowed to operate before being arrested. And if you listened to the general gossip, *The Angel* public house was the most successful pub in history, with every adult in Manchester claiming they used to drink in there.

But there is a strict time limit on public outrage – twenty to thirty days, in Shaun's experience. The world keeps turning regardless of who-is-doing-what-to-whom.

As time went by and daily life went by with it, the story began to lose its lustre. On remand awaiting trial, Peter Garton was out of sight once more, and gradually drifted out of mind too. Within three weeks of his arrest the front pages were reclaimed by the everyday tick-tock of a large city - Manchester United won something, and the city appointed its first woman Mayor.

The story would likely burst into life again at the trial of course, whenever that came, but for now the people of Manchester were happy to enter the name of Peter Garton to the city's honour role of grotesques, and move on without him in their midst.

From the law's point of view, Garton had become a prize, an emblem of victory for a new regime, his head on a proverbial spike outside HQ.

To Shaun Mullin, however, the general reading of Garton or his crimes was far too simplistic. *The Manchester Herald* had done nothing but scratch the surface of the Garton arrest. There were complexities left unexamined, facets of Garton's life yet to be discovered. He was oblique, and that was always interesting.

From Shaun Mullin's professional point of view, Peter Garton had mileage.

4

To the east of Greater Manchester lies the district of Clayton, a geometrically pleasing assembly of terraced houses arranged along closely packed streets. Without quite being middle-class (the broader, leafier avenues of the Cheshire towns are some way south) it is on the cusp of suburbia – there is no Waitrose, but some of the houses have gardens, loft conversions, burglar alarms.

Shaun enjoyed living here. It was easy enough day-to-day without being, for want of a better term, inauthentic. Dense, working-class neighbourhoods were all very well, and he'd lived in them exclusively since leaving his parents' home at eighteen. But there was a lot to be said, at his age, for the sound of an occasional wood pigeon and a tram station that wasn't daubed in misspelled graffiti.

Shaun Mullin loved Manchester's trams. He wouldn't suffer a word against them and tended to eulogise on the subject when drunk. They were a marvel to him. Waiting for them, watching them arrive, getting on, getting off. Maybe that's what he'd do in his dotage. Watch trams.

Tram-spotting. Is that a thing?

One Monday morning in late February, Shaun boarded the westbound tram at Clayton Mill and parked himself onto one of the only-very-slightly-padded buckets that passed for seating. When on the move, these trams sounded a little like milk floats used to in the seventies – another tick in the box, he thought.

It was one of those days that were common at this time of year, in this part of England. The sky arched out as a great silver dome, hampering the sun's attempts at illumination and giving the city the feel of it being dusk for the entire day. As the tram pulled away, the adjacent parkland was lit like a Humphrey Bogart thriller.

Shaun reached into a well-worn brown satchel he had with him and produced from it a hefty paperback. It was titled *BORN UNDER A BAD SIGN: The Childhood Psychology of Criminal Deviance.* Just a little light reading on the journey.

A solitary passenger got on at the Etihad Campus. A lad not much older than Carl Wilks had been when he died.

Shaun held a firm ambivalence to human beings in general, but had managed his more anti-social tendencies more and more successfully over time. He was patient with others to a greater degree nowadays.

But still, once in a while, he encountered an individual who seemed to bring his intolerance of human vacuity roaring back to life.

This young man was a Manchester City youth team footballer, by the look of him. He wore a flawless powder blue tracksuit, his earbuds were firmly wedged in, and he held a slightly camp little washbag under his arm. Shaun's attention was drawn immediately – as anybody's would have been – to his hair. It had been sculpted, greasily, into a fin-like peak that stuck out at a forty-five-degree angle, like a jaunty wafer on top of a flan.

The kid sat looking gormlessly out of the window, with his ridiculous hair being ridiculous, and the self-satisfied air of a bona-fide poseur.

Jesus fucking Christ. The state of it.

It's fair to say Shaun had taken against his fellow passenger. The strong and immediate aversion he felt was partly fuelled by Shaun's fierce loathing of sport – or, more accurately, men who liked sport.

Look at you. If you were made of chocolate you'd eat yourself.

Shaun then checked himself. He used to be like this all the time, about anything and everything that floated into his line of vision. It made no sense, and did him no favours. This wasn't how other people behaved. He was, in his middle age, trying to be calmer, more accepting, and less judgmental. So he began the process of shrugging it off.

The lad on the tram could well be a perfectly nice kid. Four decent

GCSEs and a doting grandmother. His choices were a symptom of his needs, and his needs were his own, and all that jazz.

Drop it. Don't be a dick.

As Shaun stood to disembark at Victoria, he glanced at the youth. The young man caught his eye. Shaun managed a dry smile as he got off the tram. It wasn't so hard.

Shaun wondered if his reaction to the youth on the train had been a sort of spasm of misplaced anxiety. An adverse psychological reaction to what he was about to embark upon.

Quite possibly. On the 'fight, flight or freeze' continuum, he'd always erred on the side of 'punchy'.

Cheetham Hill was no more than a ten-minute walk from the centre of the city. Early spring was doing its best to manifest itself, but the chill weather persisted. Shaun zipped up his jacket as he trudged up New Bury Road, heading for the ornate, russet-coloured tower he could see in the middle distance.

The tower belonged to Manchester Prison, more popularly known as Strangeways.

≈

Britain's eminent global position in the late 1800s was founded on extraordinary feats of infrastructure. We built things first, and we built them best, and other countries followed suit as well as they could. Sewers, roads and railways, public buildings, power lines, all subsidized by the limitless wealth of Empire. The totems of exploitation.

And because we built things first, they wore out first. One-hundred-and-fifty years on from Brunel, Stephenson and Dunlop, Britain's infrastructure is clapped out. Exhausted by the long years of use. It rots all around us, needing more and more life-saving surgery every year.

If ever there was a symbol of this decaying grandeur, it is Strangeways. It's hard to imagine a building so far out of its time. A sort of octagonal, snowflake-shaped arrangement of harsh, draughty buildings hidden behind

28

a Victorian industrialist's impersonation of Dracula's castle.

Quite recently, a spokesperson from Manchester City Council had expressed the view that the prison should be relocated, as the current structure was "unsuitable for the significant remodelling or expansion it would need to meet modern-day requirements." No plans had been forthcoming. The decay would creep on incrementally, day by day.

Shaun approached the pastiche Gothic façade on Southall Street and, with the pit of his stomach fizzing, pushed the buzzer by the front doors.

An intercom crackled into life.

≈

After being expertly searched, and then informed of the establishment's emergency procedures, Shaun was placed under the protection of HM Prison Officer MCR-33909, Howard Larch. As he trailed after Larch along a high, corrugated walkway, Shaun wondered just how much protection Larch might be able to offer him, given his rather inadequate physique.

The two men travelled along the underlit first-floor landing. Shaun was able to look down into the communal area below. Half a dozen lags played cards. Two men conversed with heads down, as if sharing the details of some nefarious plot or other. A shaven-headed, sweat-shirted lackey stood at a cell door, guarding against intrusion.

Then, at one end of the space, a face Shaun recognised.

Fuck.

Baynes.

Is that Baynes?

Patrick Gerald Baynes, whom Shaun had reported on three years ago or so, sat on the bottom rung of a set of metal stairs, absorbed in a magazine called *Glorious Gardens*. Baynes had for two months evaded arrest after raping and beating to death three prostitutes in the space of a Bank Holiday weekend. A switch had been flipped in his head when his wife left him and took the kids, and in fact it was she who finally shopped him.

Deborah Baynes no longer existed, legally – she was now living in Dundee under an alias in preparation for the unlikely event of her husband being released. And now, there he was, a genuine, twenty-four-carat maniac, available to be observed like a rare animal in a zoo by anyone with a day permit.

This place was Category A. There were dozens like Baynes in here – the sick and the broken. Strangeways' alumni included Harold Shipman and Ian Brady (the latter was responsible for more parental nightmares than any other human being in Manchester's history). Shaun's trepidation rose in his chest. He'd been underprepared for this experience. Brains counted for nothing here. The pre-eminent currency was reputation, and Shaun had none.

Larch threw open a door in the wall to expose a large room with flaking grey paint on every wall. Narrow windows behind mesh, high up in the walls. A table – screwed to the floor, to negate its potential use as an implement of violence – and two plastic chairs.

There, sat at the table, wearing shapeless prison-issue clothing, was Peter Robert Malcolm Garton.

Shaun had seen photos, but in the flesh Garton was genuinely imposing. A bona-fide wardrobe of a man, six-and-a-half feet tall, with a broad span across his shoulders and a neck the width of a chopped log. Shaun imagined him to have a thick rug of black hair beneath his shirt, on his chest and back, as a testament to his almost Neolithic manliness.

If you were going to earn a living by intimidation and coercion, looking like this was a decent start.

Larch positioned himself with his back to one wall, exuding an air of idle confidence that his physicality didn't warrant. Shaun was genuinely worried for Larch, mixing with men like Garton and Baynes every day.

Peter Garton gazed flatly at Shaun, eyebrows slightly raised as if he were expecting a tribute of some kind.

A moment passed before Shaun moved forward and took the second seat at the table, opposite this ogre. He dropped his satchel on the floor beside him, as insouciantly as he could. His heart thumped in his chest.

Over hundreds of interviews in his career, Shaun had come to know the following. A person's innate IQ was writ large on their face. It lived in the corners of the eyes and the muscles that controlled the tiny movements of the mouth. So he knew almost at first sight that Peter Garton's intelligence was at least the equal of his physical bulk.

Where the hell do I start?

He didn't have to. Garton spoke first. A resonant, measured voice, containing none of the brash nasality of most of his fellow Mancunians.

"I thought you'd be taller" said Garton.

"So did I" Shaun replied. "Too many fags as a kid".

Too facetious, possibly, but Shaun thought it was a good line. He worried for a moment that his self-satisfaction had shown in his face, and Garton had seen it. But he couldn't tell. Garton's face remained obelisk-blank.

"I gather you were in one of my pubs the other week. In Ancoats."

"I was. It's a good boozer."

"No it's not. What were you after?"

"A decent Guinness."

"We don't do Guinness in there."

A beat, as Shaun considered his response carefully. These were the moments that mattered. He needed to stay in the game without gaining the upper hand.

"Which is why I won't be going back."

The merest grin appeared at the corner of Garton's mouth.

Thank God.

He doesn't mind a bit of sparring. Let him be cleverer than you are.

"Speaking of cigarettes, actually…" said Shaun.

He reached down into his satchel, faux-casual, and produced a carton of Chesterfield Red cigarettes. He set them down in front of Garton. Larch moved in at once towards the table and took hold of the carton. He turned it one way then the other, making sure the cellophane was intact all the way around. Satisfied, he replaced the cigarettes and moved back to his prior position.

Garton stashed the fags beneath his chair.

There's your tribute, Pete.

Chesterfields.

Done my research.

Shaun felt a slight relaxation between the two of them. The air in the room settled around him. And, for the first time since the conversation began, he was aware of breathing out.

"Thanks for agreeing to this, Mister Garton."

Garton's brow creased slightly.

"I've agreed to nothing."

"On the phone, your Solicitor said you might be amenable to a conversation."

"My Solicitor's a cunt" announced Garton, as if this were a universally accepted view around the globe, like Everest being the highest mountain, or cows being mammals.

There followed a silence, during which both men performed an identical mental arithmetic – the sizing up of an opponent as either friend or foe. The decision to make a tactical withdrawal or push on.

Men from a certain background were highly skilled at this. They evaluated other men in a second. It was a form of safeguarding, and those who hadn't mastered it usually became unstuck sooner rather than later.

Garton grinned. His curiosity overrode any caution he felt about continuing the conversation. The obvious sincerity in Shaun, and his clear intellect, were enough for now, he had decided.

"What can I do for you, Shaun?"

Shaun glanced over to Larch. Larch glanced back.

"I just wanted to meet. Face-to-face. I've probably done ten thousand words on you the last six weeks."

"And the mugs keep printing it."

Because the mugs keep reading it.

Garton continued. "I saw your bit last week, about that kiddie murder in Stockport. Awful business."

Garton should know, thought Shaun. It was funny – people like this could cheerfully extract the fingernails from a grown man one at a time with a pair of pliers, but they were absolute Puritans when it came to violence against anyone under sixteen. They exhibited more outrage even than the pub vigilantes, the cut-their-balls-off brigade. Perhaps because men like Peter Garton knew the topology of it. They were closer to the real meaning of pain than the rest of us.

"And it's me next, is it? Big double-page spread?"

"People want to read about you. You're an interesting subject" Shaun said, trying hard not to sound as if he were flattering Garton.

Garton grinned. "Well, I'm not one to deprive the public of its fix, as we know."

Shaun measured his next words carefully, making sure he made eye contact with the giant of a man sat opposite him.

"It's not for the paper. It would be... a longer-term project."

Peter Garton leaned back in his chair and folded his arms.

Euphemism was obfuscation. Shaun knew it was a mistake. To men like this, ambiguity was a close cousin to dishonesty, and that didn't fly. Shaun knew he should have stated his intentions plainly.

But Garton had already caught up.

"A book?" he asked.

Shaun nodded.

"About what?"

"You. Your life. From your perspective."

Garton clearly found this notion ridiculous. His lips tightened and his shoulders rose an inch or two.

"So, Shaun, excuse me if I'm being thick. Can me and you call a spade a spade for a moment?"

"Of course" said Shaun.

"Given that I have no intention of offering Greater Manchester Police the slightest foothold into my comings and goings, what the fucking hell would you need me for? I mean, I can tell you about my fundraising for the Rotary Club if you like."

Here lay the crux, Shaun knew. He changed his tone, warming to his task. This was his tradecraft, and he did it very well.

"Full disclosure from me, Peter."

Shaun had kept the use of Garton's forename in his back pocket for precisely this moment. It registered as intended.

"I know Manchester. Intimately. As do you. And so I know that the one thing you can count on people to do round here is talk."

Peter Garton smiled. Shaun continued.

"Everybody knows everything. You cannot shut people up. Anything happens in Manchester, the news spreads like wildfire."

He paused, about to enter distinctly new territory.

"You're not fooling anyone with this landlord-and-local-businessman bit. It's paper-thin. Everybody knows what you are, right? Only they've never made it stick, because you're careful and not a greedy bastard. That's interesting to me. It suggests you're cut from different cloth."

Shaun paused and looked at the block of stone opposite. He wasn't sure this gambit had quite landed.

Shaun continued.

"I'd like to understand it better. So in terms of your involvement, I want you to give detail. Balance. Round things out."

No response was forthcoming. Garton scratched his chin. He then leaned forward again, causing a corresponding shift in Larch's posture. Shaun was relieved.

Lanky streak of piss is awake after all.

Shaun sensed a particular energy at play in Garton now. There was a vanity in being written about that people found hard to resist. Even, perhaps, a man as dedicated to anonymity as this one had been.

"What if I don't want to?" asked Garton.

"I'm writing the book anyway."

"I thought as much. Tabloid 101. Your version of events, not mine."

"I'll tell the truth."

"The truth?" sneered Garton. "I don't know you from the back of my arse, why would I believe that?".

He now had a sterner countenance, and his eyes had come alive. From Shaun's vantage point this was the first time he had shaken off the worn look of a man denied his liberty. This was the real-world Peter Garton.

"I'm not a hack, Peter. I'm on the level."

"Good. Because your profession's got a worse reputation than mine, if we're honest."

Garton's voice was more urgent now.

You need control, don't you Pete?

You live off it.

And you don't have it right now.

In response to Garton's raised voice, Larch shifted his focus from the far wall to the table.

"Wind your neck in, Garton" he said. It was a suggestion rather than a command, which was probably a sensible way to operate in here, especially if you were ten stone wet through.

Then Garton told Larch to fuck off.

Quietly. But nevertheless.

Oh God.

Shaun felt himself wither. His chin sank involuntarily onto his chest as if his body was suddenly keen to disappear into itself. From here to the headline 'JOURNO'S VISIT SPARKS STRANGEWAYS RIOT' was potentially a journey of about 10 seconds, he knew.

Shaun turned to Larch, who had a look of great umbrage on his face, as if he'd wandered into Strangeways that morning in the mistaken belief it was a vicarage.

Garton realised he hadn't been clear. He addressed Larch again.

"I mean literally. Fuck off. Leave the room."

Larch seemed momentarily as if he might defy the order. After all, he was the one in uniform here.

"Don't fucking test me, Larch." There was the voice of control, of easy dominance, coming from stillness. These men, the real ones, all had it.

And with that, HM Prison Officer 33909 Howard Larch walked to the door, opened it, and placed himself on the other side of it. It clanged shut.

Shaun panicked.

Where you going, you dickhead? You can't leave.

As it turned out, he could. And he had. Larch's gloopy eyes, distorted weirdly by a slight magnification in the glass, peered in through the window in the door. But he was definitely not in the room any longer.

Shaun was alone with Peter Garton.

Garton beamed at Shaun.

"Nobody here but us chickens", he said.

≈

The headquarters of Greater Manchester Police was a relatively new facility out on the Oldham Road. It had the unfortunate look of a block of timeshares in Torremolinos. Six stories of concrete cuboids in a stack, and a glazed atrium in one corner. Most City Councils made a mess of urban regeneration, of course, and this flagship building was a high-profile beacon of civic wrong-headedness.

Its occupants, however, enjoyed working in it. Perhaps there was some hidden utilitarian boon to the place once inside. Or maybe it was simply nicer than the places they'd come from – Stretford had just dealt with a rat infestation, you couldn't open the windows at Wythenshawe, and Denton hadn't had much done to it since it was an asylum. In context, HQ was an aspirational building.

In the staff canteen, Graham Daley forked the last of his chicken Parmigiana (which was very good) and slid a slice of cheesecake into position in front of him. His colleagues, fellow DIs Chinn and Pitt, were staring at empty plates. Daley didn't hurry anything, including lunch.

The three men were discussing the recent revenue figures from traffic offences. Inexplicably, they'd gone down in the previous three months. Christmas and New Year were traditionally boom time for traffic cops, but not this year. Bloody COVID, most likely.

Daley saw one of his newer Detectives making a beeline for him across the canteen floor.

Ryan Hemsley was an eager sort who hadn't been out of uniform for more than a couple of months, and hadn't made the best of starts in plain clothes. He was better known to his senior officers than was advisable.

"Oh, here we go, Hemsley's lost his hi-vis again."

Chinn and Pitt both chuckled.

Hemsley approached the table. "Sorry Sir, I've just had GMP on the blower about Shaun Mullin."

"Mullin? The journalist?" said Pitt.

"He's visiting Peter Garton" said Hemsley.

Daley raised his eyebrows. "What, now?"

"Apparently."

Pitt chipped in with "Whadda prick."

"How's he managed that?" asked Daley of Hemsley.

"No idea. I checked on the system and he's filled out the D-four-sixty. Applied two weeks ago and someone signed it off. We missed it" said Hemsley.

Daley rose from the table, his cheesecake untouched.

"Fuck's sake. This bloke's been back five minutes from London and he thinks he's Jack the Peanut."

Daley could tell Chinn had never heard this expression before. He was secretly hoping to have it spread around the station and enter the vernacular. Chinn would be using it for starters, he was sure.

As Daley marched off in the direction of the lifts, Chinn and Pitt gave Hemsley a look that seemed to suggest all of this was his fault.

There followed a rather fractious conversation on the fourth floor in Graham Daley's office, during which the signee of Mullin's request for a

Strangeways visitor's permit professed to having no memory of seeing it. But he must have seen it to have signed it. Yes, he supposed so, but he didn't remember. It was a textbook demonstration of Officer obfuscation – don't deny, but don't take the rap either.

Yes, while concurrently, no.

Daley sent the offending Officer away and called in Hemsley.

"I am not having that wanker talking to my suspect ever again, Detective."

"No Sir."

"Find out what he's playing at and gently encourage him to fucking stop it."

≈

Garton and Mullin spent six minutes alone. First, they discussed (in consciously vague terms) what had and had not happened in the lead up to the former's arrest. Nothing emerged that Shaun didn't already know.

A matter-of-fact protestation of total innocence, and the prediction that the charges wouldn't stick, as long as the law played fair, which it probably wouldn't.

Then, off the back of a question about Garton's relationships with some of the sketchier characters that frequented his pubs, there was a strange hiatus in the conversation. Shaun later reflected that it was the most authentic moment of that first, nervy meeting.

Peter Garton sighed. He looked at Shaun. And eventually, he spoke.

"Honestly Shaun. I don't get it. You've spent thirty years of your life writing about the likes of me. You must be sick of the stench in your nostrils by now, aren't you? Good Catholic boy like you."

Good Catholic boy? Where's he got that from?

"No such thing as a good Catholic. That's sort of the point" Shaun said.

"Tell me about it. Hail Mary, full of grace, the Lord is with thee."

Shaun couldn't help but take the conversation back a step, although he knew it showed weakness.

"How do you know I'm a Catholic?"

"I don't sit down with people I know nowt about."

Shaun nodded slowly. There had been no threat in the statement. It was perfunctory, perfectly explanatory.

"It's a few conversations I'm after. Nothing more than that. Half a dozen visits maybe. That's it" said Shaun.

"I could publish my own diaries instead" said Garton, with a sudden touch of whimsy in his voice. "They'd sell a few copies, don't you reckon?"

"I'd've thought so" Shaun agreed. "Didn't have you down as a diarist".

Garton sniffed, as if he'd expected this underestimation.

You've been misunderstood your whole life, haven't you, Pete?

Garton sat up a little straighter and clasped his hands in front of him on the table. He had changed tack. He now appeared to Shaun, very clearly, to want to wrap things up.

"Leave it with me."

Yes.

Garton then extended a hand, which was the size and hue of a Christmas ham. Shaun looked at it for a moment, then extended his own. As they shook, Garton whispered:

"Do not ever be tempted to fuck me over, Shaun."

There was the voice again. Shaun found himself at once acquiescent, as Larch had been.

"I've got long fucking arms, I promise you."

It was an odd phrasing, but Shaun understood its meaning perfectly well. Garton's influence could still be exerted beyond these walls. His incarceration hadn't entirely neutered his power.

≈

As Peter Garton was escorted back to his cell, he considered how useful Shaun Mullin might be to him in the coming months and years. That was his instinctive response to any experience the world presented him. How could he profit from it? What was in it for him? Nothing presented itself immediately, but he would continue to think on it. He didn't have a great deal else taking up his time, after all.

Shaun was one of the few people who could easily traverse the boundary between outside and in, between Manchester's open streets and the antique cages of Strangeways. That would be of use somehow.

Garton may have been incarcerated, but the world outside the prison walls still held his focus.

There was a loose end out there in the city. Something of his, a very valuable commodity, was in the possession of a man he knew. He needed it back. Perhaps Shaun could help with that, in exchange for interview time.

He thought it likely that his friends in blue would concoct something just plausible enough to lock him up for a significant stretch. Ten to fifteen years was his guess.

That would be reasonable recompense, he felt, for his apparent affronts to society. Prison was a transaction, a sacrifice to be made in return for indulging one's impulses to the detriment of the greater good. It was a tax on free will. And he would be out in six to nine, if he kept his nose clean.

The item currently on his mind had become a symbol of his thirty-year resistance to the forces of law, an icon of success in a city that wished him failure. It represented every risk he had taken, every challenge he had rebuffed, and every threat that had been carried out on his behalf.

His career had been shot through with difficulty and danger, and he would have his reward for that.

For Peter Garton, there was unfinished business beyond the confines of Strangeways.

5

*B*y the time Shaun had got to the Victoria tram stop at midday, the cement located in his shoulders had begun to dissipate, and the buzzing in the pit of his stomach had calmed. His meeting with Peter Garton had been an alarming, anxiety-inducing experience, and Shaun was wondering if he had the fortitude to repeat it. As a younger man, maybe. But now?

After a distracted afternoon at work, he slipped into the snug of the *Penny Whistle* at about five. It was the nearest boozer to the office, and the one he liked best. It had the odour of old wood and brass polish, and the tattiest dartboard in Lancashire.

As had been hastily arranged earlier that afternoon, Ben da Silva was there (pathetically sipping a lime and soda yet again, which was starting to get on Shaun's wick). With him was Kevin Burtenshaw from the Property section and Jamie from Advertising, who was modelling one of his extensive range of poor quality suits. Shaun wasn't keen on Jamie.

Prick looks like he's modelling for Oxfam.

Shaun sat, as Jamie went to the bar on his behalf.

"What's he like then?" asked Ben.

"He's a lot of things. Absolutely enormous for starters. Honestly, he's the size of a fucking tractor."

For the next twenty minutes or so, Shaun regaled the trio with the details of his visit to Strangeways.

In common with coppers and actors, writers are never 'off'. In the re-telling, Shaun automatically recast Larch as a crepuscular figure, a kind of uniformed Steerpike, keys jangling against his thigh as he shuffled along the

41

high walkways. He gave Baynes an aura of deep malevolence he simply didn't possess, although of course his incongruous reading material about gardening was an impactful detail, so he kept it in.

Telling stories to maximum effect was a faculty he took for granted, these days. Naturally and effortlessly, Shaun tidied up any errant parts that didn't fit the desired narrative, accentuated certain details for greater impact, and moulded the terrain of his story into perfect shape.

Then, his colleagues having been given a tale for the ages, Shaun went to buy them a drink.

Shaun set four empties down on the counter-top and waited for the Shirley to finish her current order of two pints of Best. He looked round at the men – and in here it was always men – sat at the fringes of the bar.

A couple of frail pensioners atop wooden stools were playing dominos. One-Eyed Doug sat in his usual spot by the fruit machine with a pint of Guinness, and hoicked a glob of phlegm from his throat to his mouth.

Shaun had slid in next to a tall young man who sat with his back to the rest of the pub. He glanced at the man's face, which after a genuine double-take, he found was a familiar one.

Shaun had been arrested on three occasions, most recently four years ago at a demo in central Manchester, for vandalising a municipal litter bin.

Once in the back of the Police van, he was swiftly de-arrested and sent on his way. Shaun liked to think this was because one of the Officers recognised him and figured it wasn't worth the grief – what with the pen being mightier than the baton, and all that.

But in truth, a quick check of the CCTV footage had revealed a case of mistaken identity – the miscreant wasn't Shaun at all.

This man at the bar of the *Penny Whistle* was the arresting Officer on that day, Shaun was sure of it. He had been a callow uniformed copper back then but had lost some of the softness in his cheeks since.

"Excuse me."

The man looked around awkwardly, as if he'd been expecting this

42

challenge. He had the air of a teenager whose note from his parents excusing him from PE had just been exposed as bogus.

"D'you remember me?" asked Shaun.

The man shook his head in an unconvincing denial.

"Yeah you do. You nicked me on the anti-austerity march. In the Arndale."

"Not me, mate."

The voice was reedy and weak.

It's definitely him.

Shaun played along, cheerful. "You're a copper though, aren't you?"

"No, I'm a plumber."

Shaun glanced down at the man's hands.

Plumber my arse. Never done a day's work in your life.

Something stopped Shaun from pursuing the matter. There were any number of reasons a Police Officer, sat alone with a pint and minding his own business, might not wish to divulge their status in a city centre pub. It was probably sensible, when off duty, to deny any affiliation to Greater Manchester Police in an environment such as this one.

"Sorry. My mistake."

He turned to face forward again as the man shuffled in his seat.

Shirley approached with a smile.

"Hello Shaun, love. What you having?"

A piss, as soon as possible.

"Lime and soda, please Shirl, and three IPA."

After setting the drinks down on the table in front of his chattering colleagues, Shaun marched over to the gents and pushed open the door.

He stood at the urinal and started reading an A4 poster mounted in a flimsy aluminium frame. It appeared to be advertising 'male vitamins', whatever they were. The door opened again.

Shaun's acquaintance from the bar entered and stood next to him. A silent, loaded moment passed, with neither man acknowledging the other.

"Checking the pipework for leaks?" quipped Shaun.

43

"What?"

"The pipes."

A beat. Nothing.

"You're a plumber."

"I'm not a fucking plumber Shaun, you know I'm not. I just try to be careful in these sorts of places."

The use of Shaun's name confirmed it – the Officer had come here specifically to see him. And that could only be because of his visit to Peter Garton that afternoon. They really did jab their fingers into any available crevice, Greater Manchester Police. But they worked in straight lines at least, so you could figure out easily enough what was coming next.

"Next time you could play along a bit. So I don't get my tyres slashed."

Or your face, round here.

"No problem."

Shaun looked over at the Officer, waiting for the inevitable.

"I'd like to talk to you, Shaun."

"What about?"

"Not in here. Back car park, blue BMW."

With that Ryan Hemsley zipped up his fly, ran his hands under some cold water for a second or two, and returned to the bar.

After a few minutes back at the table, in the finest tradition of old-school tabloid reporters, Shaun made his excuses and left. Ben, Kev and Jamie were happy enough to finish their drinks without him - a highly diverting discussion about holidaying in the Scottish islands was in full flow.

Ben smelled a rat in Shaun's rather odd excuse about a phone call he had scheduled for eight o'clock – he was well enough acquainted with his boss to know this was likely a lie. He lied all the time, Ben knew, but it was rarely about anything significant. He was just in the groove of making his life as easy as he could, and would say anything to swerve a potential inconvenience.

He was a good bullshitter, was Shaun, and it now occurred to Ben that it was an underrated life skill. Convenience often involved deceit, the demands of the world being as incessant as they were.

A blue BMW, less than a year old, in the car park of the *Penny Whistle* was a rarity. A diamond in shit. It may as well have had its blue lights flashing and the siren on, such was its obviousness. It certainly couldn't belong to anyone drinking in the pub that night.

As Shaun approached, the driver's side window rolled down smoothly and Hemsley perched an elbow on the sill.

"Thanks for coming out here Shaun. Not the warmest, is it?"

"Sorry, I wasn't sure if you wanted to speak to me, or whether you were just telling me about your new car."

Everyone at HQ had told Hemsley that Mullin was a smart-arse. The stories were legion.

"Do you want to get in for a minute?"

"No" said Shaun. "I'm not stopping. Your boss - "

"I wanted a quick word about Peter Garton."

Shaun ploughed on regardless of Hemsley's interjection. "Your boss, what's his name?"

"DI Daley."

"Daley. That's him. Tell him I'll be in to see him first thing tomorrow morning, would you? Might as well go straight to the organ grinder."

"It's nothing more than an informal - "

"Yeah, let's do it in a Police Station and get it done properly. We all know where we are then, don't we?"

A pause. Hemsley seemed to chew on a non-existent toffee.

"Right, yep".

This meant time out of a busy day, and paperwork, and a formality that wasn't especially helpful in regard to an unofficial 'word-in-the-ear'.

Hemsley swore Shaun gave him a little wink as he walked off, the cheeky bastard. He raised the car window, muttering under his breath as Shaun Mullin receded into the darkness.

≈

At just after nine o'clock that night, a blue Peugeot mini-cab picked its way cautiously along North Road in Clayton, and drew to a stop outside number 44. Shaun clambered awkwardly from the back seat, handed over a ten-pound note, pulled his door keys from his pocket and went inside.

As he did so, he reflected that the condition of the interior of a car was probably a good indicator of the condition of the interior of the owner's head. On that basis, his driver tonight had a very well-organised mind.

Shaun didn't drive, but conjectured that any car of his would likely contain empty crisp packets, coffee-stained seats, and at least one unpaid parking ticket.

He decided there wasn't much to do at this time on a Monday night that might be regarded as useful or entertaining. And no man in his right mind ever complained of too much sleep. Shaun took a glass of water up to his bedroom, placed it on his side table, and went to draw the curtains.

He froze. The figure of a man was stood in the street outside, a little way further off. Although he was little more than a silhouette, backlit as he was by a street lamp, there was a middle-aged shape to him.

The figure had been looking directly at the bedroom window when Shaun appeared, and had then turned and walked off in the direction of the church, crossing the street with his hands buried in his coat pockets. Shaun watched as the figure marched off into Vale Street without looking back.

It was probably no-one. Probably nothing. On any other night of Shaun's life he would have thought little of it, but his encounter with Strangeways and its inmates had knocked Shaun off kilter – Garton, Baynes, and the other monsters society keeps hidden from decent folk. They have an energy that burns itself into one's psyche.

Shaun went downstairs and checked he'd double-locked the front door.

A restless night followed, with the pillows never quite right and obstinate feet that refused to get warm.

6

Chief Commissioner of Police for Greater Manchester, Leonard Watts, enjoyed his occasional meetings with DI Graham Daley. He felt that Daley was a model of deference, displaying a clear and unequivocal respect without being an out-and-out arse-kisser.

Sadly, Daley didn't feel the same way about these encounters with the corpulent Watts, especially when they were sprung on him like this.

Now in his sixties, Watts was enjoying his status as the most senior Officer on the Force, and didn't feel the need for niceties like making appointments to see busy colleagues. And he found them more pliable to his needs when they weren't expecting him. The entire savannah as far as the eye could see belonged to him, and he would roam it in whatever way he pleased. He was the apex species, the elder-wolf with no natural predators and an intimate knowledge of his domain.

Having struck a red line through his entire morning's plans at fifteen minutes' notice, Daley led Watts into his office on the top floor of HQ, a corner room glazed from floor to ceiling on two adjacent sides. DI Chinn traipsed in dutifully behind them.

Why could Watts not just fuck off back to shaking hands with MPs and handing out prizes to cadets?

"Bit early for whisky, Len?" asked Daley.

Watts nodded. "Don't touch it 'til the yard-arm, these days."

The three men eased into the chairs at a round table at one end of the office. The chairs were plush, modern, Scandinavian-style. Watts ran his hand appreciatively across the smoothed wood of one of the arms.

"I could do a coffee though" he said.

Daley glanced at Chinn, who stood up again, pursing his lips slightly in protest. He went to Daley's desk and phoned down for three coffees and a plate of biscuits.

"Thank you DI Chinn" said Watts.

Daley looked at Watts, who was sat slightly too far back in the chair to suggest full engagement in any subsequent conversation. He had placed the fingertips of both hands so they were touching one another to create the peak of a triangle, as if he were one of the great minds in the history of policing in the middle of a profound rumination.

Once Chinn was settled again, Watts began.

"I'd like to discuss the Garton prosecution. How's it going?"

This was the sentence Daley had expected.

Watts continued. "I'm hearing conflicting reports from every Thomas, Richard and Harold, which is all rather unhelpful. Would you like to tell me where you think we're at, Graham?"

"Well..." replied Daley, despite this being the very last thing wished to discuss, "...in all honesty, we're not a lot further on than we were a couple of weeks ago."

"That was my sense" responded Watts, with an irritating air of faked prescience. "What's holding things up?"

This was a fork in the road, Daley knew instinctively. Sometimes playing for an easy life in a moment like this simply delayed the inevitable shellacking, which would be worse when it eventually came.

Daley decided quickly on full disclosure. A lancing of the boil. It wasn't that they'd made a mess of the Garton case, but try as they undoubtedly had, they simply could not uncover a trail of activities commensurate with the man's reputation. Garton was, as of right now, nigh on un-prosecutable.

"Honestly, I'm not sure how we got the charge past the CPS. It's absolute bollocks, Chief Commissioner, pardon my French."

Chinn's eyebrows rose to almost disappear beneath his hairline.

Daley continued: "If it turns out Peter Garton hid that cocaine in the cellar of his own boozer, I'll run down Rochdale High Street starkers."

"I don't think anyone wants that, Graham" said Watts.

Daley continued, leaning in a little. "What we've been trying to do is focus on the bigger picture. His finances. That's our best chance of getting him a long stretch. The cocaine... I can't see it sticking with a jury."

Chinn was alarmed at this outpouring of transparency from his colleague. The usual process when dealing with the higher-ups was to trot out a pro-forma that included "taking the matter extremely seriously" / "working hard" / "close to a breakthrough". Everyone knew Garton hadn't stowed those drugs, but this was the first time he'd heard it said out loud.

"Well at least he's off the streets for now. Leaves the field clear for evidence gathering" said Watts.

"Indeed."

"So we're working on proceeds of crime. Good" said Watts.

Daley exchanged a glance with Chinn.

"Yep."

"And?"

With a deep breath, Daley continued. "There doesn't seem to be any. Crime, or proceeds. Currently there's no drugs and no money, aside from what we got from *The Angel*. Not in significant volumes, anyway."

Watts darkened. There had to be money somewhere. It simply must exist. Garton hadn't been running a charity for the last thirty years.

But he had evidently been a very effective criminal. Many a scumbag presented himself to the world, and to the Police, as a law-abiding entrepreneur, but this kind of artifice usually fell apart once the surface was scratched at by a determined band of Officers. Not with Garton, who had avoided the usual pitfalls – ego, vanity, and greed.

Once his business model was in full swing by the late 1980s, Garton resisted expansion. He was operating at the perfect size, maximising his income without drawing undue attention to where it was all coming from. It wasn't broke, so there was no need to fix it.

Daley's team had found sixty grand in a Halifax Building Society savings account, and a slightly smaller amount at *The Angel*. That was it.

Both these hauls could be reasonably explained by a man who ran a legitimate, medium-sized enterprise whose revenues came predominantly in cash. And in fact, these 'savings' had come from pub earnings that had been accounted for with the Inland Revenue over many years. Garton had made sure they were watertight.

Daley's colleagues in Forensics had wiped six pubs for traces of drugs, and set the sniffer dogs loose in each one. There had been a few ambiguous readings in toilet cubicles that might possibly have indicated the presence of cocaine and heroin in five of the six – but these were easy to blame on customers. It was a pretty measly return, and not one that could form the basis for the prosecution of a kingpin.

The only real point of interest at any of Garton's licenced premises was the safe upstairs at *The Weavers' Tavern* in Blackley. The Police had found its door wide open and its contents – whatever they may have been – gone. A probable last-minute liberation of something valuable by one of Garton's stooges, but they couldn't possibly know what or who had been involved.

Garton's home, which Daley had high hopes for, had come back entirely evidence-free.

The conversation was moving in an unwanted direction, thanks to Daley's forthright assessment. Chinn decided to rescue his colleague.

"We've changed tack in the last few days, Chief Inspector. And we're starting to get good results in other areas" he said.

DI Chinn was up to his usual trick. He became invisible when the bad news was being delivered, and then suddenly re-materialised as a three-dimensional entity to take credit for the positives.

"Go on" said Watts.

"We've located five of his six captains."

Watts' face creased in revulsion. "Captains?"

"That's what we're calling them" continued Chinn.

"Well don't" said Watts. "It is a military nomenclature, Chinn, and it's entirely inappropriate. We're not in a war. Garton's not a General, and his underlings are not Captains. We don't want the press echoing that sort of language."

"Point taken, Sir."

This scolding was quietly pleasing to Daley, who now chimed in again.

"Regional heads, Commissioner?"

"Better" said Watts.

Daley continued before Chinn could open his mouth.

"As DI Chinn mentioned, we have locations for five of the six of these… heads. Three of them are still at their home addresses. They seem to think drawing the curtains is enough to put us off the scent, bless them. One of them has moved in with his mother in Bolton, and the fifth has taken up residence in a bed-and-breakfast in Blackpool. The local Force has eyes on."

Chinn couldn't help himself, and leapt in.

"We have a volume of evidence acquired over some months linking these men to drugs and to Garton."

Watts interjected.

"And one of these men is Craig Phillipson, do I have that correct?"

"Yes" said Daley. "Phillipson, Yardley, Rossi. It's that lot."

"It would be good to get that piece of shit off the streets" Watts said.

Chinn picked up where he'd left off.

"We think we can get at Garton through these men."

Watts nodded. "One of the bastards will blab, they always do. Five of them, did you say?

Chinn nodded.

"And what about number six?"

There was an awkward hiatus. Daley had decided to leave it to Chinn. It was his turn. Fuck him.

First to buckle under the pressure, Chinn eventually said "No idea. He's disappeared."

"Good grief, Detective Inspector. Really? Almost seven thousand Officers, and their combined efforts have resulted in 'no idea'?"

Chinn gaped for a moment.

Watts moved on.

"Do we have a name?"

"We do" said Chinn, with as positive a tone as he could muster.

After which there was a timid tap at the office door.

"Ah, coffee." said Watts.

"Enter" barked Daley.

The door opened tentatively a little way, and a Sergeant Mohammad peered in through the gap. He was, to Watt's disappointment, bereft of coffee and biscuits.

"Sorry to bother you, DI Daley. Shaun Mullin's in reception for you."

For what would likely be the only time in his life, DI Graham Daley was pleased to hear Shaun's name.

≈

After collecting him from reception, Daley led Shaun into Interview Room Two, where Chinn and Pitt were already seated. On the way there, the corridor chit-chat was stilted, Shaun believing there was no such thing as small talk with a copper. Everything and anything was evidence, as far as the Force was concerned. Best to give them as little as you politely could.

On entering, the room and its set-up immediately felt a little too formal for Shaun's liking. Too thought-through.

Relax, Shaun. It's just a chat.

Daley indicated an empty seat at the table, opposite Pitt and Chinn.

"We're going to record this Shaun, if you're alright with that."

"Why?"

"Just so we're all as clear as we can be. Problem?"

Daley was reframing this meeting. Shaun had missed a memo somewhere.

"Am I under caution, Detective Inspector?"

"Of course not."

"Then yes, it's a problem."

Daley didn't seem too bothered by this. DI Pitt agreed to take notes instead. It struck Shaun as odd, in a modern facility such as this, to see something as prosaic as a pen and paper.

Shaun sat. Daley flashed a smile.

"So, thanks for coming in."

You didn't ask me to come in. Fuck are they playing at here?

Shaun got the sense that his plan, which was centred (if he were honest) on being an awkward bugger and insisting on time-consuming due process, was quickly coming apart. He had wanted to speak to Daley directly, possibly make a statement, or at the very least have some simple record of their conversation. But the situation had escalated.

Pitt held the pen with his digits bunched oddly around it, as if he were new to the concept of writing and hadn't yet worked out the ergonomics of it.

Shaun had met Pitt before, and had found him disturbingly 'off'. He wondered if there was something askew with Pitt's biology. He had a freakishly strong jawline partially disguised by thick, Desperate-Dan stubble, and ears so large he might have borrowed them from a joke shop. His eyes were too big for their sockets. Pitt was a character who, at first sight, may have been dealt one too many chromosomes by the man upstairs.

Pitt had mentioned to Shaun during a previous encounter – at the site of a fatal road traffic accident in Denton – that he was married. The mind boggled at the kind of woman who would hitch herself to a creature like Pitt for the remainder of her days. None of anyone's business really, of course - who really knew the springs and cogs of someone else's marriage? Perhaps he was a good listener and an enthusiastic lover, and that was enough for Mrs. Pitt.

"Ok Shaun" said Daley. "We wanted a chat about your visit to Peter Garton at the end of last week. What was the purpose of the meeting?" Shaun was aware that, in terms of the law, 'mind your own fucking business' was a perfectly legitimate response. But something in the room told him not to waltz down that particular avenue as breezily as he may usually have done.

You've nothing to hide.

"I'm writing something. I need some background."

Daley sneered at this. 'Background'. He knew who Garton was. They all did. No amount of journalistic revision could disguise his character.

"A feature. Well" said Daley, lightly. "I hope you got what you needed, because you won't be going back I'm afraid."

"Why not?"

"Maybe after he's convicted. But it's just too risky pre-trial, Shaun. We'll be blocking all future applications. Sorry."

This was predictable, and unfortunate. Shaun didn't like it, but in truth he was in sympathy with DI Daley to a degree. It was a difficult issue to manage for the Police, visits to a remanded prisoner. There were too many variables around who came in from the outside world, and why.

There was no point pushing back. Shaun was aware of the need for caution in his dealings with these three Officers right now. He bit his lip.

Then Chinn, timing his bombshell to maximum effect, asked:

"How do you know Emlyn Parry?"

Emlyn?

Garton and Parry were, as far as Shaun knew, unconnected. Why bring up Parry? What was he to them, or to Peter Garton?

"Emlyn? I met him at a boxing club. Down the road from me. I went five or six times a couple of years ago."

"And when was the last time you saw him?" enquired Daley.

"Summer maybe? In the street. We said hello for thirty seconds."

"So why are you looking for him now?"

It was an unexpected line of questioning, and Shaun couldn't fathom it. His disorientation at it did, for a moment, prompt him to think about asking for a Solicitor to be present before saying anything further. But he checked that impulse. That was what criminals did, and he was by no means that.

"Because he's missing. Why are we talking about Emlyn?" he asked.

There then unfurled a stunning set of facts. Chinn and Daley revealed that Emlyn Parry had, for the past eleven years, been Garton's captain in Wythenshawe. He was responsible for controlling the sales of around four hundred grand's worth of drugs a year. He was the only one of the six captains not accounted for since Garton's arrest and, not unreasonably, the Greater Manchester Force was interested in where he'd gone.

Shaun hoped that his surprise at this news appeared genuine. Emlyn was clearly not a choir boy, he had always suspected as much, but Manchester was crammed with rascal sorts, and relatively few of them were serious criminals. The nature of Emlyn's day job had rocked him.

There was a possibility that Daley, Chinn and Pitt were trying to work a potential connection between Shaun and the Garton gang – Shaun had after all been openly enquiring after Parry across the city, and had visited the missing man's boss in prison. Simple mischance, of course. But it didn't necessarily look that way, he could see that.

This was how justice ended up in the weeds. A coincidence misread as design, a critical shift in probability in the minds of those who mattered, and suddenly the authorities were trying to lasso the wrong horse.

Graham Daley had no significant suspicions of him, however. No credible indication of wrongdoing. He knew Chinn in particular would have loved to make something stick to Billy-big-bollocks, anything whatsoever, but it was unlikely.

Mullin was probably clean.

Probably.

7

There was no facet of his job at The Manchester Herald Shaun enjoyed more than the morning stand-up. The meeting was designed to ensure everyone knew what they were doing that day (and what everyone else was doing too). But the practicalities were a mere sideshow.

Most days the meeting was a raucous bunfight of put-downs and gags and asides, with smart and competitive people trying outdo one another. In-jokes ran for months on end in these meetings, variations on a seemingly inexhaustible series of themes. Missing the day's stand-up meant your references could become obsolete very quickly.

As today's meeting came to a close, Shaun Mullin stood three kilometres away at a tram-stop, with Greater Manchester Police Headquarters a few hundred yards behind him. His morning had been a good deal less comfortable than he'd anticipated, as evidenced by the ringing in his ears and a slight dampness in the hollow of his back – both clear signals of an emerging anxiety that was all too familiar. But he knew how to keep panic in check, these days. He was a veteran now.

He checked his phone for messages – his niece Claire had sent him yet another unfathomable meme, this one involving a badger running over the top of a parked car. Ben had texted to ask where Shaun had got to that morning, then followed up swiftly with 'Sorry, forgot, see you 11ish'.

In the early days of mobiles, Shaun had regarded texting as a Godsend. It meant he didn't have to speak to people with anything like the frequency of the old days, and that was a boon to any introvert. But now, texts were just another stack of tiny burdens that had to be worked through one by one, day after day. Modern life was the fulfilment of endless minuscule obligations.

Shaun got onto the 10.22 tram and sat in his favourite spot – the end of the carriage, with his back to the direction of travel. The tram slid off towards Piccadilly Gardens.

Emlyn fucking Parry. Bloody hell.

Explains the Audi and the Paul Smith shirts, I suppose.

≈

The office of *The Herald* was fully populated by the time Shaun arrived. It was a sight he relished - industry and bustle and the noise of creation. A collective focus on making something exist that currently didn't.

There was the familiar gauntlet to run between the front door and his desk at the far end. Nearest the door, as always, was Gary, the senior sports reporter on the paper. A blazingly proud Australian, 'Gaz' insisted on bleaching the tips of his hair as if he'd spent the last six months atop a surfboard.

While the Antipodean drawl was still very much in evidence, the bronze tone to his skin had faded over the three years he'd been in Manchester, as one would expect. Shaun had joked that if he got any paler, Passport Control in Sydney wouldn't let him back in the country.

Shaun loathed sports while being perfectly tolerant of Gary, who could certainly write in Shaun's opinion, but was wasting what talent he had reporting on the most irrelevant and stupid set of activities indulged in by twenty-first-century humans.

Rugby, as Shaun had explained to Gary on more than one occasion, was innately homo-erotic, involving as it did men wrestling in mud and sporadically shoving their heads up one another's arses. Cricket was even simpler to dismiss – men threw chunks of rock at each other until it got dark or everyone got too bored to carry on any longer and went home. Gary took all of this in good heart, banter being woven into every Aussie's DNA.

Gary referred to Shaun as Arnold. In an attempt to get a rise from Shaun by positioning him as a 'serious' and pretentious writer, he had once referred to him muddle-headedly as 'Arnold Hemingway'. When asked by a sniggering Shaun to name a few of the works of this previously unknown novelist, Gary recognised his error and doubled down on it. Shaun would be Arnold, now and forever.

So, for Shaun, most mornings in the office began – as today - with a "morning Arnold". He returned the greeting with a thumbs-up and proceeded towards his desk.

A recessed nook to the east side of the office housed Jamie and his two slack-jawed Ad Sales interns.

Morning, mouth-breathers.

The central block of desks was populated by the journos, a dozen or so of them. Sandra Billings was the only one of them Shaun had real respect for.

First and foremost, she was a stellar writer who could have adapted her enormous skills to any written medium. It was well within her means to have been a highly successful screenwriter or novelist; instead she had stuck to regional journalism out of the strong sense that it was where she belonged. She could do most good here. It mattered to her, because she mattered to it, and she had produced page after page of insightful, challenging journalism on important issues over ten years at *The Herald*.

Shaun tended not to acknowledge her on the morning walk across the office, as she would invariably be deep into her work by the time he arrived, and he knew plenty about the frustrations of being interrupted.

There was Rebecca Felix, something of a lightweight writer who had, it must be admitted, an uncannily sharp nose for the kinds of stories her readers cared about. Shaun was astonished by the success of her work. Even the most mundane pieces seemed to catch some sort of local zeitgeist.

Rebecca was an inveterate chewer of pen lids, going through a couple of dozen a month. This had led to the creation of her official work nickname, Chew-Becca (another nice piece of work from Gary).

Ferdy and Janet were very much part of the furniture, and were in Shaun's view ten-a-penny journos. Their longevity was testament to the power of simply being there. Shaun had long known that the world was run by those who bothered to turn up. So these two were reliable and generally amenable, but they had never exhibited any particular flair or energy for their work. They were the very definition of hacks, which was the only unforgivable trait in a writer, and would be first against the wall if Shaun had anything to do with it.

The Herald had taken a gamble a year previously and employed a trio of graduate journalists en bloc. It had, with a few qualifiers, been a successful initiative. Imelda, Farook, and Will all made rookie errors on a daily basis, but each was displaying plenty of 'the right stuff' after twelve months in post. They were dedicated enough (for a younger generation prone to obsessions with 'work-life balance' and 'mental health') and were officially regarded as promising.

The terminally vapid Perdita was a dead loss and was on borrowed time, despite her well-connected mother having pulled every string she could to get her daughter through the door in the first place. She simply wasn't a journalist other than by name, in the same way a rocking horse isn't an actual horse.

Then there was a work experience lad called Fabian, who had been there a week and so couldn't yet be fully evaluated - although it had been established quickly that he was, to some degree at least, French. This boded badly in Shaun's opinion, not on any grounds of national prejudice, but because Manchester was such a *particular* place, and one had to have lived in it to understand it.

On the west flank of the room were the non-journalist staff who dealt with the accounts, Web publication, legal queries and matters to do with the purchase of paper and ink. Pleasant enough, in Shaun's experience, but an irrelevance to his daily work. They socialised separately from everyone else for the most part, which suited all parties.

Eleanor Brake, the paper's Editor, sat in a glass cube at the far end of the floor near Shaun. Beside her office was a large meeting room.

Shaun marched towards Ben. The two made eye contact, and Ben sat up slightly straighter in his chair. Shaun had forgotten more about the newspaper business than Ben had ever known. Since falling under Shaun's wing, Ben found it uplifting to spend his working hours with an elder statesman.

"Morning" said Ben, "how's the Old Bill?"

"Ben" said Shaun, ignoring the question. "Seen the online edition?"

He hadn't. Shaun's phone was out of his pocket in a flash.

"If that twat, Digital fucking Dave or whatever his name is – "

"Jolyon."

"Jolyon" sneered Shaun.

Of course he's called fucking Jolyon.

Shaun was now holding up his phone for Ben to see. The screen showed a page from *The Herald*'s online version.

"If Jolyon ever puts an advert in the middle of one of my paragraphs again, I will ram his twinkling modem up his arse."

"I'd be careful, mate", said Ben, laughing. "This will all be online only one day, and he'll be Lord of the Manor."

Tragically, Ben was right of course, and this smart bullseye wrong-footed Shaun for a second. Shaun thought of the beloved smell of newsprint, the rough tactility of a newspaper against the fingertips, and promised himself he'd retire the day they became obsolete.

The moment Shaun's backside landed on his seat, Eleanor Brake turned to look at him through the glass of her office, as if operating on a sixth sense as to his whereabouts. Shaun glanced back at her. The look Shaun picked up was at once troublesome to him. He'd seen it before.

Shaun knew Eleanor to be a highly effective editor. She was proof of the old maxim that the best editors aren't always exceptional journalists – they serve to corral, and restrain. She had a natural capacity for it, and could on rare occasions balance it up with a decent sense of humour.

In relation to Shaun Mullin and his eccentricities, Eleanor had a common-sense policy. She allowed him enough leeway to keep him happy, but not enough to jeopardize the paper's standing in any way. There would, she knew, be problematic episodes during the course of his employment here, given his prickly nature and propensity for displacing noses. But her policy was not to ask for too many details, or criticise too readily.

She beckoned him into her office from across the open plan floor. He nodded his compliance.

It always surprised Shaun how weighty Eleanor's office door was. Opening it and walking through felt like the crossing of a significant threshold. The fun and games of the office floor didn't extend this far. Here, at the edge of the rattle and hum, lived rationality.

"Alright Brakey?" opened Shaun.

"Afternoon. Have a sit down if you want."

Shaun did so. Clearly, this wasn't going to be quick. He eased into an angular leather armchair, which left him a couple of feet lower down than Eleanor, who had perched on the edge of her desk.

Trying to maintain a level of neutral disinterest in her voice for now at least, Eleanor said "I've had a phone call this morning from Graham Daley at Greater Manchester Police."

Shaun nodded.

Shame on you Daley, you grass.

"You've been to see Peter Garton in Strangeways, I gather."

Shaun kept nodding.

"To get some background for an article. First I've heard of it."

"That's because it's not true" said Shaun. "I have been to Strangeways. But there's no article" he said, keen to explain that the visit had been nothing to do with *The Herald*, and by extension nothing to do with Eleanor.

"I went to see Garton because I'm writing a book on him."

This statement thudded almost audibly onto the carpet between them.

Eleanor's head tilted just slightly, and her mouth fell open.

"You're writing a book?

"That's the plan."

"On Peter Garton?"

61

"Indeed."

"And Garton knows about this?"

"Yup".

"Are you mentally ill?"

Shaun had prepared his riposte to Eleanor's disapproval, which he knew was inevitable. He'd seen her operate at close quarters for a couple of years now, and was aware of her aversion to risk. She wasn't one of life's swashbucklers, and that wasn't her fault.

Garton's comment about having a long reach had set Shaun back a little. But the risk/reward axis was still pretty favourable. Garton would now die in prison, Shaun was confident of that. Even if the initial 'handling and proceeds' charges proved optimistic, the Police would surely get him on trafficking soon enough, given he was off the streets and his men were patently showing zero loyalty.

Twenty years ago, this assessment may have been a bit of a reach. DNA was flawed in its early years, and there were no cameras on the streets. But Policing was now a sophisticated business, Shaun knew, and almost no-one slipped through the net. This was a shit era in which to be a criminal.

If Shaun was careful, Garton would likely be no threat from the confines of his cell. Neither did his captains now that the boss was neutered. None of those men were stupid enough to risk their own liberty on behalf of a hand that could no longer feed them, so they would surely testify against him.

Peter Garton was yesterday's bogeyman. The king was, figuratively speaking at least, dead.

But that didn't mean his profile had entirely diminished with the citizens of Manchester. A new biography on the shelves by the time of Garton's trial was surely in the public interest (as well as Shaun's, it went without saying).

Shaun Mullin and Eleanor Brake went to and fro on the matter for a while, both knowing the other would give no quarter. Eleanor remained dumbfounded at Shaun's recklessness, and Shaun confidently dismissed the risks she outlined. Stalemate.

Ben glanced over to see what shape the conversation was taking on the other side of the glass divide. Shaun and Eleanor were clearly working out a fundamental disagreement in philosophy. They looked to Ben like a pair of newlyweds who had just uncovered some dreadful incompatibility and were discussing in purely practical terms if anything of the marriage could be salvaged. Connected, but apart.

≈

Ben da Silva powered down his laptop. It was Monday, which meant a prompt finish, always.

There was a weekly activity Ben indulged in that he kept hidden from everyone. He didn't really know why – it was a bland, un-scandalous pastime. The secrecy was about controlling his experience. Keeping it covert prevented it from becoming adulterated by the opinions of others.

Every Monday night for going on three years, Ben da Silva had played six frames of snooker, alone, at a subterranean members' club in Hale. He interacted with nobody, and simply tried to build break after break to the best of his modest ability for two hours. Mildly odd to outside eyes, perhaps, but perfectly sane and respectable as a hobby.

On the way home to grab his custom-made cue, Ben evaluated his current piece of work. It had been tricky, this particular article (on the possible misspending of Council funds in the building of a new shopping centre in Bolton). But Ben felt it was tonally on-the-money now. From there it was simply about the narrative. As Shaun would say, "I knew it would be good. And when it is…" He would burnish his prose in the morning.

Having grabbed his cue and his bike, Ben left his flat in Gatley and cycled merrily in the direction of the Altrincham and Hale Social Club.

8

Shaun opened his front door at number 44 North Road, Clayton, and reached down to retrieve the post that lay behind it. There was a free newspaper (unreadable shit in his considered opinion, but useful for lighting fires) and a couple of envelopes with his name and address on the front. He placed these on the shelf that ran along his hallway.

Opening his mail was, for Shaun, an optional activity. If he didn't like the look of an envelope, it went in the bin. There had been surprisingly few ramifications from this behaviour over the years.

Tonight would be one of those evenings accessible only to single people living alone. Total silence (aside from the television), the rest of Saturday's lasagne and a smooth, unhindered descent into sleep. Unimprovable.

Long stretches of time that contained nothing of note were a commodity of great value to him, these days. It hadn't always been that way – he was a part of many overlapping social circles when younger, until he realised how exhausting he found it all. People, at this stage of adulthood, were best in small doses.

Shaun found an old episode of *Morse* on ITV4. He had always wished that Morse's sidekick Lewis wasn't such a damp flannel. It gave the great man nothing to push back on. But he enjoyed the cosy feel of TV shows he'd already seen, in the same way people love hearing a favourite record.

In this episode, the misanthropic detective found himself at an illegal rave, and became immediately appalled by its uncontrolled Bacchanalia. A man at odds with the times in which he found himself.

As he lay on the settee, Shaun was aware of a familiar unease - a light fluttering in his chest and a pressure at the top of his skull. It had been there all day, but stillness and solitude brought it more sharply into focus. His brain felt, at times like this, as if it were a series of unexplored crevices connected by frayed synapses that struggled to get their messages through coherently. Perhaps a relapse was due. Another visit to the underworld.

Please. No.

Once the lasagne had been dispatched, Shaun stretched out on the sofa for the second half of *Morse*. When it began to swell, the fear didn't frighten him like it used to. Sertraline and the occasional beta blocker had neutered it years ago. It was simply a state, a way of being, and was manageable.

As Morse concluded his investigation and his limp-minded assistant expressed his admiration yet again for the man's investigative skills, Shaun's eyelids began to wilt. His mind was easing.

Shaun had embarked, a couple of years ago, on a programme of 'self-improvement', as it was apparently called. There had at that time been frequent occasions on which Shaun's patience had expired in response to one minor incident or other. He felt as if he were lurching from one frustration to the next, several times and day.

It had definitely been getting worse since his forties. But he tended to internalise rather than expel this anger, which was apparently very unhealthy.

Although he spurned psychotherapy (he viewed it as a middle-class indulgence – compared to 90% of the world's population, he didn't really have any problems), he was walking more frequently and eating better. He'd started boxing training at a local club, which was fine until the first time he was properly punched in the face.

And he had taken to listening to an app in bed. This app contained a library of soothing recitations by a Californian called Dave, who was a colourful throwback to the seventies.

Judging by the various serene photos of him that appeared on the app, Dave could have been anywhere between sixty years old and a hundred and ten. There were beads around his neck, and he wore what appeared to be a beige dishcloth. Invariably, he was situated in bright sunshine in these pictures – easier to be happy in California, Shaun had thought.

Ridiculous though Dave was, Shaun found that he helped. This feller was obviously 'at one' with something or other – it was never clear precisely what – and it rubbed off if you listened to him often enough.

Shaun had at last discovered a way to relax.

As Shaun began to drift off, there came three taps at the front door. Not a knock, but something far more tentative. His eyelids parted.

Silence for a second, then another three taps.

Fuck is that?

Shaun rose reluctantly, walked into the hallway and saw the blurred outline of a figure at his front door, indistinct through the frosted glass but obviously male. Whoever this was, they were unwelcome tonight.

He pulled the door open.

In the lifetime pantheon of uninvited guests, this was a prize-winning entry. On his doorstep, shrouded in black from head to toe, his face obscured by the drooping hood of his anorak, stood Emlyn Parry.

"Emlyn. Where the fuck have you been?"

"Can I come in?" asked Parry.

Shaun almost said no. His instinct made him recoil at the prospect, given Emlyn's status as a fugitive and associate of Peter Garton.

Then Emlyn stepped onto the lip between the porch and the doorway, assuming the consent of his old acquaintance, and it was too late.

"Was that you watching my house the other night?" asked Shaun, as the two men went into the living room.

"Sorry, yeah. I was thinking about coming to see you, but you saw me first and I panicked."

"Why would you come and see me?"

"I need you to do something for me, buddy."

Without elaborating further, Emlyn went to the furthest end of the room and pulled the curtains closer together. He paced the carpet anxiously as he unburdened himself of the details of his current predicament.

As far as Shaun could make out (the story didn't seem to have any chronological coherence as it emerged from Emlyn's memory), the trouble began at the end of the previous summer. According to the fugitive, Peter Garton's captains began, on certain evenings, to huddle together in quiet public houses and talk. Sometimes in pairs or threes, and at other times in larger groups, all without the knowledge of their boss.

They were, it had become clear to Emlyn, discussing the merits of a kind of coup d'etat. This idea had been prompted by a previously unknown gang who promised them a larger cut of the proceeds if they were to take over the trade in Manchester.

"And who are they, these blokes?" enquired Shaun.

"Don't know."

"Any names?"

"Run by a bloke called Arjan, that's it."

"Arjan. Have you met this man?"

"Twice. Foreign accent."

Shaun's money was already on Arjan being an Albanian name. It would fit the trend happening in many towns and cities of the UK, as explained by his mate Ken Cooper a few weeks ago in the Half Moon.

According to Ken, Albanian gangs had altered the criminal landscape of the UK profoundly in just a few short years due to their readiness to perform quite breathtakingly violent acts. They were already the stuff of terrible legend. The stories of death, torture and disfigurement were legion.

The vacuum created by Peter Garton had already been filled.

Emlyn, loyal to the point of his own personal endangerment, was the sole refusenik among the group of captains. Garton had looked after him, made him reasonably affluent, and that deserved fealty in return. He would always treat Peter with respect. This decision had placed him at odds with some unreasonable people, so Emlyn had taken it upon himself to disappear.

"Where've you been staying then?" asked Shaun.

"Not telling nobody that" came the reply.

Next came the crux of Garton's current circumstance. Emlyn explained that the planting of narcotics and cash at *The Angel* was a fit-up designed to frame Garton, remove him from the equation and make way for a new regime.

It was a pretty shabby effort, as these things went, implemented cack-handedly by chancers. There was none of Garton's DNA on the packages, no evidence he'd been anywhere near *The Angel* in days previous, and no witness testimony placing him in the pub's cellar.

But, of course, it had worked. Garton was inside, and his gang was not.

It did strike Shaun that every single captain would soon be in the crosshairs of a trafficking investigation. They would each, in that instance, be reliant on Garton keeping his trap shut once he'd been charged, and seeing that the knife was firmly buried deep in his back, that felt unlikely.

So Emlyn Parry was in hiding from a gang of Albanians, five drug dealers, and – soon – Greater Manchester Police. Shaun was impressed he was still at liberty, and wondered why he was still in Manchester.

"I won't be. Not for long."

"Where are you off?" asked Shaun, aware that secrecy was in Emlyn's best interests but wanting an answer all the same.

"I'm trying to get to Spain."

Of course you are. All money says the Costa del Sol.

"Not the Costa?"

"Yeah."

"I wouldn't."

"Why not?"

Shaun sighed. It would be simple from here to patronise Emlyn, who for all his misdeeds and self-inflicted penury, was clearly out of his depth.

"There are dozens of British coppers roaming the streets permanently in the Costa, you know that? It's the first place they'll look for you. Honestly, you're safer walking round the Arndale on a Saturday afternoon."

Emlyn's shoulders dropped. This was obviously his one and only idea thus far. The Costa del Sol was the bog-standard hideout for a British criminal and he knew people there.

"Go further north. A city. Valencia's nice" said Shaun.

Apprehension flashed across Emlyn's face.

"What would I eat?" he asked.

Shaun began expounding on the cuisine of metropolitan Spain, but realised this probably wouldn't fly. There was a hunted man in his living room who couldn't give a flying fuck what an empanada was at this point.

Shaun suggested somewhere closer as a destination. It would be a lot simpler. After positing the idea of a temporary re-location to Wales, or Newcastle, or Norwich, Shaun ascertained that the only people Emlyn knew outside of Manchester were a few fellow crims in Spain. He had no appetite for being friendless in a new city, and had set his mind on the Costa del Sol, where he had been promised a job and all the sangria he could get down his neck.

He asked what plans Emlyn had for fleeing the country.

"I can't leave. I need help, Shaun."

"What sort of help?"

Emlyn Parry looked over at Shaun, who suddenly knew this was why the man had come here.

"I need a passport."

≈

On the other side of the City in the windowless oblong of the Altrincham and Hale Social Club, Ben da Silva lined up a simple black to the right corner pocket. He drew back his cue and then slammed it forward again through the bridge made by his hand.

He knew at once the contact with the white ball wasn't what he had wanted, and the black rattled in the jaws of the pocket before rolling free across the baize. Another break had come to an end. Five consecutive pots totalling twenty-six this time. Perfectly decent, by his standards.

Ben had played well in patches but hadn't quite settled into his normal rhythm. He'd been distracted on a few occasions this evening by a boisterous group of five men at another table.

Three of the men, whom Ben had correctly diagnosed as being in their mid-thirties, had familiar faces. A couple of others bantered with them in heavily accented English and dropped occasionally into another language when they wanted to converse privately. It sounded like a Slavic tongue, but one Ben couldn't place.

But he knew those three faces, he was certain.

≈

It wasn't until a few minutes before one o'clock the next morning the faces finally acquired their rightful owners in his mind. Ben sat upright in bed, hauled up from semi-sleep by a thunderclap of realisation. And, he noted momentarily, a sudden thrill.

9

Shaun Mullin solved most of his problems by fixing every ounce of his consciousness on them until a resolution was found. Nothing else that might happen to be going on around him – raging fires, keening sirens, multi-vehicle pile-ups - would register when he was in this fixated state of mind. It was a characteristic he had developed in his teenage years, and felt now like a sort of super-power.

As he stepped off the tram at Piccadilly Gardens, he had no memory of the journey he had just taken, such was the totality of his preoccupation. It was as if he had shut his front door in Clayton and emerged three kilometres away a split second later.

It was Emlyn Parry – and the audacious request he had made – that was exercising him so completely.

Shaun was, apparently, the only person Emlyn knew that wasn't to some extent familiar to the Police (although this itself wasn't strictly true, Shaun knew). Emlyn also expressed the view that Shaun was a stand-up sort of guy who wouldn't grass, or renege, or fuck things up in any of a thousand other ways. He was intelligent and of good character, which was faint praise indeed coming from Emlyn Parry.

Emlyn had brought with him a plastic bag containing three thousand pounds in twenties and a strip of passport photos, as well as the phone number of a man who could be relied upon to procure the illicit document. Two grand was for the passport, and the other thousand was for Shaun.

Shaun had said no. Unambiguously not.

He wished Emlyn well and hoped he remained safe, but wouldn't invite the wrath of the law – and God knows who else – by involving himself in the matter.

Emlyn pleaded. Shaun said no again. The money would be poor recompense for the potential consequences. This wasn't his world – he was a professional observer of it, of course, but there was a vast difference between watching a boxing match and climbing into the ring, he had said.

Twenty minutes later – Emlyn was a persistent bastard – a compromise was reached, of sorts.

Emlyn had asked Shaun for a roll of masking tape, which he duly procured from a drawer in the kitchen. Emlyn rolled the plastic bag up tight and wound the tape around it several times.

"There" he said, "You've got no idea what's in it. I've just asked you to drop a parcel off to a mate. End of."

Rationally, Shaun felt there was a plausible deniability in this should the episode ever come to light. He told Emlyn he'd think about it, largely as a way of escaping further discussion and ridding himself of the fugitive.

≈

Now, as he walked through Piccadilly Gardens towards the office, the taped-up plastic bag weighing heavily in his satchel, he pored over the respective merits of 'do' and 'don't'.

Obviously, rejecting the proposal meant the avoidance of an awful lot of potential trouble. Life-changing trouble. There were numerous officers at Greater Manchester Police who were itching to pounce and teach him whatever perverse lesson they assumed he needed, should he ever set a toe out of line. They'd love this.

But there was also something to be said for helping Emlyn expatriate himself for a while. Who knew how many late-night knocks on the door there would be now, how many predicaments Emlyn would ask for help with. He was a desperate man who had the ear and the address of a sympathizer.

Shaun didn't have the heart – or frankly, the balls – to tell Emlyn to fuck off and leave him alone. A passport would mean he was out of Shaun's hair until the current situation had settled.

He strode into the office just before eight – a touch earlier than was usual – and found Ben da Silva already at his desk. This was a rare circumstance.

"Morning Ben. Not been home?" he asked.

Ignoring the invitation to one of their regular slanging matches, Ben responded conspiratorially "I need to talk to you."

God's sake, not you as well.

At Ben's insistence, the pair dove into the large meeting room at one end of the office floor.

Why am I flypaper for other peoples' shit?

This is my lot in life now, isn't it?

There was an eager edge to Ben's voice.

"Ok, I was at a snooker club in Hale last night."

"A what club?"

"Snooker" Ben said, defensively.

Shaun pulled the precise face Ben would have expected him to pull – equal parts mockery and distaste. He continued in defiance of this.

"Garton's men were in there."

Shaun sat upright, engaging at once.

"Which?"

"Stuart Barber, that mental case Craig Phillipson, and Michael Rossi."

"Are you sure?"

"Googled them this morning. Hundred per cent."

Shaun ruminated on these names for a moment. He'd been led to the belief that the Captains were very much out of sight and out of mind. A sudden desire on their part for a few frames of snooker seemed bizarre.

These three men had formidable reputations, Phillipson especially. He had been known around Manchester for the past few years as The Butcher of Baguley – a rather sensationalist nickname attributed to him only slightly in jest. According to urban lore, his only friend was a highly alarming machete that surfaced every now and again in the furtherment of his – and

Peter Garton's – best interests. His best-known legend involved a publican on the take, a dozen kebab skewers, and a blowtorch.

Craig Phillipson, the captain of the Cheetham Hill district, was a man you'd pay good money to avoid. Barber and Rossi were hardly amenable characters either, but they weren't in the same league as their associate Craig for pure mendacity.

"They were talking to two foreigners. Slavs, I reckon."

Shaun nodded. He was putting this together quickly, and what Ben had already described bore out his recent conversation with Emlyn Parry.

"Albanians" he said.

Ben realised that, as usual, his boss was a mile ahead of him. Shaun seemed to be a conduit through which every ear-to-the-ground morsel for a hundred miles flowed. He was a magnet for intrigue to a degree that was bordering on miraculous.

Shaun shared with Ben some of what he knew. The vacuum problem described by Ken Cooper, the steady march of Albanian dominance in the UK's drug trade, and the framing of Peter Garton to facilitate an easy takeover with no blood spilt.

Ben absorbed it all, and considered carefully his next words. Straight down the line was usually best with Shaun, Eleanor had told him on day one. It was an approach that hadn't failed him yet.

"I want to go back. Tonight."

Ben's eyes flicked up to meet Shaun's.

"Why?" came the reply.

"Dunno. There might be something in it. Something we can work with."

Shaun leant forward across the table.

"Ben, listen to me. With people like this, if you're not clear on why you're doing something, you don't do it."

"Yeah I know –"

"And let me make it crystal clear that we are not about to take on the Albanian mafia via the pages of *The Herald*. Life's too short."

In this case, possibly very fucking short.

Ben's tone rose in intensity. He was set on his course of action. There was something significant in motion at the snooker club. There was mileage there. He knew it and he wanted in.

"Just come and see if they're there again tonight."

"Oh, I'm coming too now, am I?"

Shaun took this as an indicator of Ben's uncertainty. He didn't want to go alone, and with good reason. These sorts of recces were all shits and giggles until the moment they weren't, and that moment could arrive swiftly and without warning.

"If we do go – and that 'if' is doing some heavy lifting here – there's no fucking around. No attempt at contact with any of these people unless it comes from me. And when I say we leave, we fucking leave, sharpish."

"Is that a yes?"

Of course it's a yes.

"It's a maybe."

Shaun's heart was beating a little faster already.

10

*N*eil Burrows was a simple lad, both in terms of his mental capacity and his threshold for satisfaction. His recent incarceration in Strangeways had hardly disrupted his equilibrium. He didn't want much from life, which was fortunate as life was disinclined to offer him anything.

Weeks back, after attending a raucous wedding reception, Neil had been drawn into a brawl that had inexplicably burst into life on a bowling green in Trafford at four in the morning. Misjudging his own vigour, Neil had applied half a dozen hard blows to a young groomsman from Bradford a little too enthusiastically, and killed him.

This grey cell had been his home for the past two months, while on remand for his crime. A single bed, a tiny window, a sink, and a steel toilet.

Neil lay on his bed, bolstered by the fleeting realisation that it was Monday, which meant sausages for dinner. Decent. He was absorbed in a tattered copy of *Bravo Two Zero*. He had read three books in his life – this one, three times. He liked to convince himself he didn't know what was coming next and give himself over to the unfolding narrative as if afresh.

As he reached a particularly tense episode involving a tank berm and an Iraqi goat herder, Neil's focus was drawn by a face at the window of his cell door. On registering who the face belonged to, he flinched.

Peter Garton pushed the door open. His bulk blotted out the light from the walkway behind him. Instinctively, as if he had received a pulse of electricity through his bedframe, Neil stood up.

"Sit down Neil" said Garton.

Neil sat down.

After a short stroll up and down the eight-foot-long sarcophagus that passed for Neil's living quarters, Garton leant against one wall.

"Nice place you've got. Love what you've done with it."

This clearly didn't make any sense to Neil Burrows. Garton recognised that the gag – an old prison chestnut – was beyond the wit of this lad.

With a nod to the book in Neil's hand, Garton asked "Any good, that?"

"Oh aye, Pete. Cracking book."

Garton took the book from him and flipped it over to read the blurb on the back cover. He then dropped it back on the bed, seemingly unimpressed.

"I need you to do something for me, Neil."

"R-right. Yep."

"Your cousin. Emlyn Parry."

"Oh aye."

"I need to find out where he's got to, Neil."

Already on the defensive, Neil jumped in a little too quickly with "Nobody knows where he is."

"Now you've hit the nail on the head there Neil. Emlyn has something of mine, and I need it. So first of all I need him. Making sense so far?"

Neil nodded.

"Speak to your family, your mates, his mates, whoever the fuck you need to. And let me know where he's got to, alright?"

There was silence in the cell, as a pained Neil worked through the significant obstacles to achieving this task.

Eventually Garton spoke.

"Problem?"

"No" replied Neil. "It's just hard in here, isn't it? I only get one phone call a day."

Garton stepped closer, looming over the youngster all of a sudden.

"I can't really get into the practicalities with you, Neil. I'm a busy man. I'll let you handle all that. OK?"

Peter Garton picked up Neil's beloved copy of *Bravo Two Zero* and strolled nonchalantly out of the cell with it. He expected no reward from his conversation with the dolt Burrows. He wondered how such men survived, with so few mental resources to work with and so much trouble to navigate.

≈

Arriving home after work, Shaun took his satchel home and locked it in a cupboard in his hallway. Its contents had caused him a growing discomfort as the day had worn on.

He knew that Emlyn Parry would be walking the path along the River Medlock at Clayton Vale every night at eleven-thirty. It was the only information Emlyn had been willing to share about his daily whereabouts, and would allow the two of them to make contact should that be needed.

Shaun had promised himself numerous times, as if it were a mantra, that he'd walk over there later that night, give Emlyn his cash back, and tell him the passport suggestion was beyond the pale. He didn't need the grief. The risk was too great for a confirmed civilian such as himself.

He was, however, prepared to stake out some Albanian mobsters with Ben for an hour or so – that felt like work. Legitimate.

Ben had alluded a number of times since he joined *The Herald* to Shaun being 'soft'. It was a joke, of course, but Shaun wasn't convinced he was entirely wrong. He missed his personal golden era, when he would follow his nose wherever it led him in search of something illicit or salacious.

The demands on him were of a different ilk these days. There was more structure and stricture in his work. Or perhaps he'd simply lost his sense of adventure and succumbed to middle-aged comfort just like the rest.

Either way, opportunities like this were few and far between now. Best to take them when they came, and pray they didn't vanish forever. For Shaun, life would be two-dimensional without the occasional thrill of this sort. It was the stuff of life. It was his calling.

He thought through the lecture he would give Ben about modern criminals, and how it had all changed. In the old days – which for Shaun meant the '90s – a journo could keep a respectful distance and be tolerated, as long as lies weren't printed. If they were, and 'liberties' had been taken, a

78

quiet but forceful word would be had. Criminals understood that the likes of Shaun were simply earning a crust, and would give them a second chance if they strayed out of line and published something unacceptable.

These days, this wasn't the case.

Modern criminals made savage and emphatic exhibitions of authority. They worked quickly and mercilessly.

One of Shaun's acquaintances at a tabloid in London had recently made a particular insinuation in print about the wife of a suspected people trafficker. Nothing too scurrilous, in all honesty. But it resulted in the beheading of his family's dog, in front of the man's kids. He swiftly changed lanes and now writes about caravans.

That was the landscape now. Savagery.

Shaun would impress upon Ben the need for great care tonight.

He wolfed down a refrigerated Cornish pasty before going upstairs to change his shirt, get out of the door, and cab it over to Hale.

PART TWO

This Thing of Darkness

11

*B*en da Silva stood outside the Altrincham and Hale Social Club, its fringed plastic awning spanning the doorway onto the street. It was nice around here. He might move over this way if he ever earned enough.

He was waiting for Shaun Mullin to arrive. This Shaun duly did, only seven minutes later than promised, in a taxicab. As he clambered out onto the pavement, he nodded to the cue case Ben had brought with him.

Ha! He's only got his own bloody stick!

"Oh go on" said Shaun, "play us a tune on your flute."

Ben smirked, but only just. He was nervous, and not because of whoever may be on the other side of the door. He wanted to be validated tonight, for Shaun to concede that their visit had some worth, that Ben had displayed the necessary journalistic 'nose'. Perhaps they would eventually be the ones to break the news to a concerned city that its drugs trade had taken a dark turn.

Ben opened the door and led the way, familiar with the slim corridor that led to a stairway. The two men descended the twelve steps that opened out into the A&HSC Snooker and Bar Room. This contained four full-sized snooker tables, some banquette-style seating along the walls, and a small bar area accommodating three high stools. The air down here was stale and still. There were the odours of brass polish and microwaved gravy.

In truth, the word 'social' in the club's name was a cruel exaggeration. Ben had rarely seen more than four or five souls inside at any one time, and tonight there was nobody else here whatsoever.

Ben marched over to his favourite table, which was furthest from the door. Shaun followed him and removed his coat.

Ben stood and stared.

Shaun stared back, all innocence. "What?"

He was wearing a starched white dress shirt with the sleeves rolled up to his elbows.

"What have you got that on for? We're not at The Crucible."

"Well I don't know what the deal is in these places, do I?"

Ben knew he was taking the piss.

Shaun continued "Hey, if you're going to do something, do it right. I'm all in. Bring the fucking snooker, big boy."

As Ben racked up the balls onto the table, Shaun walked over to the ramshackle bar, likely constructed in the seventies and neglected since. There was no-one to be seen behind it. After a second, Shaun hollered a "hello".

A man of around sixty-five ambled into view from somewhere deep in the bowels of the building. He wore a Primark sweater and polyester trousers. Not tons of money in the Social Club game, Shaun surmised.

"Hello mate. Can I have a couple of drinks and two hours on table four please?" asked Shaun.

"Yes my friend. What you like?"

The accent was Slavic.

"Pint of IPA and a lime and soda."

"Yes yes, I get for you."

The man reached overhead and took a pair of pint glasses from a high shelf. Shaun perched himself on one of the stools. The man caught his eye with a playful glance.

"He bring a friend today" said the man with a smirk, nodding towards Ben.

"Yeah. Is he normally on his own then?"

"Always."

"Tragic individual" said Shaun, with a glint of mischief.

The glint was returned.

"Little bit."

Shaun's pint was placed on the bar with an unsteady hand, and the barman turned to fetch a bottle of lime cordial from the shelf behind him.

"You've got an interesting accent" said Shaun.

The man looked at him. Shaun wasn't certain he'd understood.

"Your accent. The way you speak. It's very interesting."

The man smiled and appeared a little apologetic.

"I am European" he said, as if it were some minor infringement of society's norms, like doing thirty-five in a thirty, or putting the wrong item in the recycling.

Shaun nodded.

In fact, the man - whose name was Dardan - came from a grimy strip of sand on the Albanian coast called Saranda. This impoverished town faced the Greek island of Corfu across a narrow strip of the Ionian Sea. There was a large Roman ruin up in the hills nearby which had significant pulling power for tourists, so Sarandans were exposed regularly to the trappings of first-world success via a steady flow of day trippers.

As a boy, the Brits and Germans and French had seemed to Dardan impossibly stylish. The clothes and watches and cameras were all way out of reach of the average Albanian. From his early teens, Dardan knew he'd leave.

He had aspired to - ached for - the good life overseas. He wanted the trappings of prosperity afforded to citizens elsewhere on the continent. Their ease with the world, their lack of preoccupation, and their charisma.

Finally making the move to England twenty years ago, he had discovered how hard these luxuries were to come by. He had learned the hard way an indisputable fact of twenty-first-century life: there is an underclass anywhere you care to go, and a move upwards is a lot harder to achieve than a move sideways.

Shaun went back to the table with the drinks and set them down on a ledge attached to the wall for just that purpose.

"What's his deal?" asked Shaun, with a nod back towards the bar.

"He runs the place" replied Ben.

Ben thrust a snooker cue into Shaun's hand.

"Right" said Shaun, "a side wager for the evening. If I win a frame –"

"Yeah, you won't."

Bit presumptuous.

"Just managing your expectations" Ben said, with a wide grin.

"OK then, you cocky bastard. If you don't get double my points in any one frame, there's a forfeit."

"Which is what?"

"You have to have a proper drink with me. I can't be doing with this soda pop nonsense."

Shaun saw Ben disengage from the conversation. A flash of distaste crossed Ben's face, and Shaun knew at once he had touched upon something significant.

"Not going to happen" said Ben, controlled and quiet.

There was one possibility Shaun hadn't previously considered, and now that it did occur to him he suddenly felt crass. He may be sharp-tongued in his judgmental moments, but he was never knowingly cruel.

Ben leant over the table and struck the white ball towards the pyramid of reds. A couple broke away and touched the far cushion, and the white came back to the D.

Shaun eyed up his options which, for someone with no skill whatsoever at the snooker table, were limited.

"Shaun" said Ben.

Shaun looked at him.

"I don't drink because I used to" said Ben, in a tone that was loaded with regret. He was for the moment in possession of the voice of grim experience, and it made him seem older suddenly. It took Shaun aback.

"Sorry man" said Shaun, shifting his stance uncomfortably. "Shouldn't have brought it up."

"No reason you'd know."

Ben had brightened a little. "I don't tell many people on the whole, and apparently I don't look the type, so…"

That much was undoubtedly true. Ben da Silva was a darker horse than appearances suggested.

"Tell you what" said Shaun, "if I get less than half your points, I'll have a lime and soda instead of a beer."

This rescued things to an extent. Both parties found the wager agreeable, and Shaun's noble sacrifice dispelled any lingering awkwardness. They began to play.

≈

As it turned out, snooker was insanely difficult.

Shaun had trouble potting anything whatsoever, and at times missed his connection with the white ball completely. Ben quickly decided to treat this like a normal solo session, and simply play for his own breaks. Shaun was soon quaffing from a tall pint of lime and soda, bemoaning his own total incompetence with cue in hand.

Shaun started glancing at the clock above the door barely thirty minutes into the session. The two of them were still alone in this joyless crypt, so the function of his evening was now to get home as soon as was polite.

People tend to enjoy what they're good at and are good at what they enjoy. Shaun was a horrible snooker player and, ergo, he hated it. How was this irritating activity preferable to a good book, or Scrabble, or a film? Sport would remain an undiscovered country forever, he realised.

Just as they were into their second hour, Shaun potted two consecutive balls for a break of five, which lifted his spirits a little. He then ruined it by accidentally potting a red out of sequence and his frustration at the pointlessness of it all returned in full.

Ben potted a tough blue and screwed the white perfectly in line for the next red. The shot of the night so far. Shaun bumped his cue end on the floor in appreciation. He'd picked that bit up successfully, at least.

Seventy minutes after their arrival, it became clear the two men were done. It had been a flat experience, their snooker experiment. Inevitable really, given the lack of vim coming from fifty per-cent of the participants.

Shaun suggested, quietly, that they make an attempt to engage to proprietor for a while before calling it a night. They had drawn a blank on the characters Ben had seen the night before, but they may be able to get something illuminating out of the old man at the bar.

Dardan served another round to his only two customers of the evening.

"Quiet tonight" noted Shaun.

Dardan threw his response over his shoulder as he poured lime cordial into a glass.

"Yes. Not busy."

He turned and began filling up Ben's pint glass with soda water from a nozzle attached to a thin pipe. It seemed to Shaun something of a default for Dardan to look a little lost. Almost penitent.

"Weekends OK, but Monday and Tuesday, no. Some days I close eight, nine o'clock. I am old man. I need beauty sleep."

Shaun looked at Dardan's weathered face. It was prematurely lined and aged, an outward symptom of thousands of hard days.

Six months in a coma wouldn't sort that out, mate.

Ben took his drink and sipped. He had developed a fondness for this character over the course of his many visits. He was unfailingly genial, if a little slow on the uptake. He did have a jumpiness in him, a propensity to look agitated at nothing much. Ben wondered if that was founded on the need to be alert to the world around him.

Shaun leaned onto the bar as Dardan pulled his pint. He spoke lightly, as if without consequence. Mere chit-chat.

"You're Albanian, yes?"

One of the first things Shaun had learned as an investigative journalist was when to shut up. When no immediate response came, he let this statement hang in the air, hoping Ben would resist the urge to fill the gap.

After a moment's consideration, the man nodded.

"Not easy to be Albanian here. But better than home."

"Do you have any friends here, from Albania? Family?"

Dardan's face twisted itself into an uncomfortable smile. He shrugged.

"Not really."

Shaun nodded, giving every signal of being fully engaged.

"There were a couple of blokes in last night from your part of the world, weren't there?"

This was a misstep. Too much too soon. And Dardan was no hick. He now sensed the agenda beneath this innocent conversation. But he persisted, polite as ever.

"Some men, yes. They come often. But not friends. Customer."

"Good to hear your own language now and again though, I bet?"

Dardan seemed to deflate a little, and Shaun saw in him a deep sadness.

"It reminds me of many things. Some good, some no."

The door opened abruptly, having been thrown wide with some force. Shaun and Ben now saw a figure marching into the room.

The man was Michael Rossi, until recently Peter Garton's representative in Stockport. He made his way across the room and through a door in the wall at the far end. Through the door Shaun glimpsed a desk with an old computer on it, and an office chair, before it slammed shut again.

Three other men now followed, descending the stairs until they stood backlit in the doorway. Near-facsimiles of one another, each of them had the same buzz cut and angular cheekbones. The tallest wore an extremely stylish and well-fitting tan suit.

After registering Shaun and Ben's unexpected presence, this man barked an order at Dardan, who complied by taking a whisky glass from the shelf and producing an untouched bottle of single malt.

The new arrivals ambled towards the bar, glaring at Shaun and Ben as they approached. One of them asked a question of Dardan with an aggressive chuck of the head, and Dardan responded in the same language.

Ben touched Shaun on the elbow, prompting him to make a move for the door. Shaun shot Ben a resolute look. He didn't want to leave without investigating the new arrivals. These men were the entire point of tonight's exercise. Why leave now?

The man in the tan suit looked directly at Shaun, tilting his head slightly as he did so as if looking at an unfamiliar species for the first time.

The intelligence Shaun had detected when looking Peter Garton in the eye four days ago was not in evidence here. Rather, there was a shark-like absence of anything. In this man, the eyes performed their basic ocular function and that was all. They gave no hint of his character.

He had, however, the loose, controlled relaxation that comes from natural high status. It was a collection of micro-gestures. A rhythm. In his preferred endeavour, whatever that might be, this man was successful.

In response to Dardan, he switched back to English.

"If they want to stay, they can stay" he said, and smiled directly at the two English strangers, in a way that suggested the precise opposite of what he had just said.

Ben didn't want to stay. Not now. But leaving on his own terms suddenly felt like a conundrum that would take a bit of solving. The moment to simply walk out of the door with no further complications had probably passed.

Shaun was in his element, defiant but relaxed.

Ben. On the other hand, piped up at a half-octave above normal.

"We were just leaving actually."

The suited man nodded. He let the ensuing silence hang for a moment, before responding with deliberate quietness.

"As you wish."

The way this sounded brought to mind a Bond villain. Shaun wondered if these men watched movies like that for inspiration, or whether this melodramatic edge was inherent to villains like this. There was no doubt by now that a villain was what they were looking at. Did they know how they sounded, these characters? That this was a false note, an over-egging that undermined their power?

Stillness in the room.

Ben glanced at Shaun, and with nothing to explicitly prevent him, stood up to leave. Shaun stayed precisely where he was.

"You are from newspaper" said the suited man.

Shaun felt his fingernails press against his palms.

Oh fuck.

Being clocked as a journalist in public was never, ever good news.

Ben now noticed that the elderly man behind the bar was nowhere to be seen, and the two subsidiary characters that had just entered had somehow floated back towards to entrance. He and Shaun may not be leaving here without at least a little further interrogation.

"I see your picture" said the man in the suit, indicating Shaun.

Shaun had become too well-known up north, he had long suspected, and this was proof. Nobody could really operate as an investigative journalist without anonymity, and the genie had waved goodbye to that particular bottle some years ago.

Shaun replied in the most offhand way he could.

"Just two fellers playing snooker" he said.

"Of course" replied the man, and smiled again.

The suited man moved closer to Shaun. Ben's chest tightened.

"I think you know a man called Emlyn Parry."

There was then an uncomfortable pause, which was mercifully short.

"Only a bit. Not really."

"Have you seen him?"

"Not for a long time."

The man nodded thoughtfully, then echoed these last words.

"Not for a long time."

Shaun felt it would be prudent to play along.

"If I do see him, I'll tell him you asked after him."

The man knew this was pure artifice, a faked innocence, and nodded along silently once more.

"What name shall I give him?" asked Shaun.

The man fixed Shaun in his sights for a second.

"Anything you like. He knows who I am."

The man made the merest of gestures to his two compatriots. They moved away from the door. Shaun Mullin and Ben da Silva needed no further invitation, and exited the Altrincham and Hale Social Club as casually as they could manage.

≈

Shaun strode north along Hale Road, resolved to walk the four miles home to Clayton. This would give him a necessary hiatus - time to re-order himself and straighten his mind. Ben wheeled his bike along the pavement beside him, scuttling occasionally to keep pace.

He felt chastened by the events of the evening, having been given a sharp lesson – bogeymen were fun to speculate on, but they were, occasionally, real. Shaun's warnings could so easily have been vindicated this evening, and Ben felt naïve.

This was an affluent suburb, with ornate red-brick mansions and high-spec apartments. Nobody seemed to notice these two imposters from the real city just up the road as they trotted busily along, putting welcome distance between themselves and the Altrincham and Hale Social Club.

Together but apart, solitary in their partnership, they spoke only occasionally. It was as if they were unwilling to risk an opinion until they were nearer to home turf, where there would be no consequences to expressing themselves.

Shaun and Ben rounded a hedgerow at the corner of a residential lane and made for the A56. This necessitated traversing the railway line, which they would do by means of a poorly lit underpass, scarred with graffiti.

They strode down a slight incline towards its entrance, walked silently into the mouth of the concrete chasm, and were enveloped by the dark.

12

Shaun closed his front door behind him, breathing hard. He had completed most of the journey back from Hale alone, Ben having turned east at Shaftesbury Avenue and ridden off towards Gatley. He'd set himself a testing pace. A brisk walk aided thinking.

In the hour he had spent getting home, Shaun had gained some clarity on tonight's encounter. It had reminded him of the old days, when he was far more inclined to take risks in the search for a valuable lead, or simply to coast on the surge of adrenalin it gave him.

"You're getting soft in your old age..."

Probably am.

He had once lied his way into a pub in a Kilburn backstreet to witness the wake of an Irish Republican Army soldier. There were a hundred or so in attendance, mourning their way through an ocean of Guinness and Jameson's. The doors had been locked, the old songs had started up, and Shaun was the only man there without a broad Irish brogue.

While tonight had been nothing like as intimidating as that, he and Ben had definitely transgressed into unwelcome territory. They had, mercifully, found their way back with no harm done.

But it might have been different had the dead-eyed man in the tan suit decreed it so. Rossi's face, suffused with anger, had surely suggested an unrest between the men. The mood had not been one of harmony.

Shaun would make it clear to Ben at the earliest opportunity that there would be no further involvement with the plight of Emlyn Parry or the activities of anyone associated with him. These matters were the domain of Greater Manchester Police, who had the clout to deal with the situation.

If ever Shaun needed evidence that he was now less reckless than he once was, this was it. There would be circumspection with regard to Arjan Marku. If Parry was caught by either faction, so be it. If the local drugs trade became a more brutal one, it was not the responsibility of Shaun, of Ben or of *The Herald*. What would be would be.

How much of his breathlessness was down to the march from Hale? How much worse might the light spinning in his head become? Shaun felt as if he were balanced on a high ledge, with a bustling city going about its business beneath him. It was a familiar feeling, and one he needed to dispel. He knew what lay ahead if his mind wasn't soothed.

Shaun went to the cupboard in the hallway and retrieved his satchel. It was now almost ten. Within the hour his hands would be washed of the matter for good. Emlyn would have his money back, and Shaun would free himself from further entreaties. He couldn't believe he'd entertained the idea of procuring a fake passport in the first place. Madness.

He perched on the edge of his armchair and focused on creating a regular pattern of breathing.

≈

Five years ago, not long after relocating to Manchester and starting work at *The Herald*, Shaun's conscious mind had capsized. He had psychologically come apart at the seams.

He referred to it now as his 'episode', which had the benefit of being euphemistically undescriptive. A clinician had categorised 'the episode' as being a psychotic one, a detail Shaun generally left out in the re-telling, but was secretly proud of. He had been, for a few days at least, certifiable.

It was Christmastime. Shaun had been out drinking for three consecutive nights – which felt like a mighty feat of endurance at his age – and on the morning of December 19th he had woken with a catastrophic hangover. He felt dizzy and discombobulated, and noticed a shallowness of breath as the morning wore on.

Over the next few hours he became increasingly light-headed and breathless. A ringing developed stealthily in his ears over the course of the day, along with an undercurrent of restlessness that had become familiar to him since. It could be best described as a foreboding, as if something dark and hulking were getting nearer, unseen and slow, but dauntless A great, dark hound approaching through the darkness. The strength of this feeling had begun to unsettle him.

The next day, Shaun fell over as he got out of bed. An extreme dizziness meant his balance had abandoned him, and he toppled sideways into a chest of drawers. He crawled to the sofa in the next room, and faced the unavoidable truth that something was very wrong.

He hoped it was a virus, or some other temporary glitch in his equilibrium. But he already suspected it was something more fundamental than that. Whatever this was, it felt ingrained, a component part of his body's ailing machinery. Shaun began to fear he had a significant problem.

The voices came that same day.

At first, a whisper from the direction of his kitchen:

Shaun.

He dismissed it. Perhaps, as he sat in the armchair, he was closer to sleep than he'd realised, and the voice had belonged to that other realm. It had been a glitch in the separation between unconsciousness and waking.

Then, louder, a few minutes later:

Hiya Shaun.

Auditory hallucination can be disappointingly mundane.

Frozen for a full minute, Shaun had weighed this up. He knew at once that the voice was not connected to a body. There was no-one actually there. Whose voice was it? His? Perhaps. And why now? What dysfunction was occurring in his brain that had brought a phantom into existence?

The voice became more frequent over the next few hours. Banquo getting his feet under the table. Shaun spent the evening tortured by affirmations that came from outside his own head.

It's alright, Shaun.

You'll be fine, Shaun.

Don't worry, Shaun.

It's all good.

By nightfall, his mind had begun to fragment. He could feel it uncoupling from the rest of him, seemingly determined to exist on its own terms in the manner it had always craved. It required physical effort to keep himself together as a single, coherent entity.

Shaun decided he would sleep if he could, and absorb whatever the truth may be when he woke. He was mad, or dying, or both, and he was certain tomorrow would be the beginning of the end of Shaun Mullin.

That night was the darkest of his life by a considerable distance. Perspective is easily lost in the dark. Fear expands when not held in check by sunlight.

Before leaving his home for the hospital the next day, with the voice and the fear vibrating in him more powerfully than ever, Shaun made the decision to have a haircut.

It was lunacy in retrospect, but this made sense to him at the time in a clear and fundamental way – Catholic notions of humility in the face of a higher power, of penance, of shame, and of rebirth, collided in his brain. It seemed obvious. Before the doctors disclosed his fate, he needed a trim.

He teetered down the street towards the barber's shop, staying close to the walls of the houses and shops in case he needed to steady himself. The buildings in the middle distance seemed to be warping before his eyes. He could hear every breath in and out, and looked at each face that passed with a strange new perspective. It was as if he were exploring a new planet populated by creatures reminiscent of homo sapiens, but not quite the same.

Shaun's regular barber, a flamboyant Egyptian by the name of Hamid, was one of the world's more contented creatures. He was born to cut hair, and as such rejoiced in his good fortune to be taking up the scissors every day.

Shaun always imagined Hamid to belong to a family of barbers with a lineage stretching back centuries, so powerful was the existential fit. It was as if his forbears had been hairdressers to the Pharaohs.

As he sat in one of Hamid's leather chairs, Shaun caught sight of himself in the tall mirror opposite. Haunted. Ruined. Out of time. He was shocked at the sight of himself, and for a moment couldn't discern whether he was the man in the chair or the man looking back. They were not one and the same.

The usual inconsequential chat bounced between Shaun and Hamid, with one of them oblivious to the whirlpool occurring inside the brain of the other. Hamid's words seemed to be emanating from the walls, the floor, the ceiling. Shaun could hardly make them out, so alien had they seemed. Language was slipping away from him.

He was out of his mind. He was played out. Whatever this was, it was final.

Hamid click-clacked expertly at the back of Shaun's head. Shaun began to feel a visceral panic rising in him now, pushing his heart down into his guts, perhaps as a consequence of his own distressed visage staring back at him – a face he barely recognised as his own. His chest heaved with every thudding heartbeat, and he could feel the racing within his blood vessels.

As Hamid trimmed, the voice returned. Its tone had changed to something colder.

This fucker's going to kill you, Shaun.

He thinks you're a prick.

He's going to put those scissors through your neck.

He wasn't. Shaun knew that. The suggestion was insane. But Hamid's face was now not Hamid's face – it was a precise replica worn by an imposter.

Do him first.

Go on.

He knew he was being goaded into something unwarranted and outrageous. He would not succumb. There was still just enough logic left in his mind to resist this exhortation to madness.

For an instant, Shaun caught Hamid's eye in the mirror. Hamid saw the fear in him, and stopped.

"Are you alright, Mister Shaun?"

"Sorry" mumbled Shaun, as he rose from the chair and began rooting in his wallet for a banknote. Sanity still prevailed.

"Sorry, Hamid. Got to go."

Shaun dropped a twenty-pound note in the chair he had just vacated, and darted from the premises.

Twelve minutes later, Shaun got out of a cab outside Withington Hospital and went into the Accident and Emergency department complete with half a haircut. His vision now swimming and his heart attempting an audacious escape from his chest, he threw himself on the mercy of medical science.

Here today, gone tomorrow.

Dust to dust.

The full tranche of tests took most of the day. Shaun went from ECG to MRI to CAT, from heart to brain to lungs, in a procession of clinical probings. There were prods and attachments and devices, and a dozen of the miniature humiliations involved in a trip to hospital.

At the end of which, in the late afternoon, his name was announced to a waiting area by a male doctor holding a clipboard. Shaun followed the man into an anteroom and sat.

Doctor Purtell took a few moments to appraise the results of Shaun's marathon diagnostic visit, then looked up at him and said:

"There's nothing wrong with you." Off Shaun's obvious disbelief, Purtell continued. "Nothing wrong physiologically, at least."

He seemed to take pity on Shaun in this moment. The doctorly façade slipped a little, and his manner softened.

"I'm going to ask you three questions. I already know the answers, but I want to hear them come from you. OK?"

Shaun nodded in total obedience. He had abandoned himself completely to these people now. He had found it calming to wash his hands of all responsibility for himself.

"One. Do you live alone?" asked Purtell.

"Yes."

"Two. Are you invested in what you do for work to an extreme degree?"

"Yes."

"Three. Do you find normal social interactions stressful or draining?"

"Yes."

Bingo. The Holy Trinity. A workaholic introvert with nobody at home.

Doctor Purtell advised Shaun to slow down. Go for a massage. Rest more. Swim occasionally. Eat better food and take the air once in a while.

His life had become compressed, frenetic, unmanageably full of obligation, and people cannot operate that way indefinitely without the edges beginning to fray. Especially not people like Shaun, for whom relaxation in the company of others was a constant challenge.

So the diagnosis, ultimately, was that a punishing routine – perpetuated month upon month and year upon year - had sent Shaun Mullin a little bit mad for a while. And what could be a more appropriate response to modern life than that?

≈

Shaun often recalled the 'episode', and now reminded himself that he was very much still here despite his expectations at that time. He still functioned. He wasn't insane.

As he sat on the edge of his armchair, ruminating on his encounter in the basement of the Altrincham and Hale Social Club, his phone rang. The display told him it was Ben. Shaun may normally have ignored the call, but he felt a responsibility for the welfare of his protégé after the strangeness of the evening. He answered the call.

"What's up?"

"Shaun, mate" said Ben. "You're not going to believe this..."

13

*D*I Graham Daley hated these sudden, unexpected excursions, and cursed himself for his lack of foresight once again. No matter how many times he'd fallen for it, he was always unprepared. Yet another pair of shoes were now ruined by mud and filthy water. Why had he not put his Wellingtons in the car this morning in anticipation of something like this?

He squelched his way towards the yellow tape that created a cordon between the banks of Gorton Reservoir and the adjacent Denton golf club.

Daley was currently on the edge of the sixteenth fairway and through the gloom could just about see the college buildings that rose above the bank on the far side of the water.

Arc lights were already being erected by his diligent officers. Half a dozen Greater Manchester Police vehicles were at the scene, and their headlights were having to do the job of illumination until a better method was up and running. Daley could see the site of the incident from fifty yards away due to the tight knot of Officers forming a half-circle on the bank.

On seeing him approach, a PC broke away from the group to intercept him. This was Kylie Charles, who wouldn't have even made it onto the force in the old days, standing as she did a hair over five feet one.

The removal of a minimum height from recruitment rules had been yet another sop to the lunatic fringe, in Daley's opinion. Coppers had obligations in the course of their duties, some of them physical, and they needed to be equipped to meet them. But opening the door to all and sundry had become the vogue - at the expense of Officers being able to actually do their jobs.

They'd be recruiting bank robbers next, in the interest of fairness, he thought to himself.

As Kylie Charles spoke to her superior, he noticed she looked unsettled. Her hands were shaking, and he assumed it wasn't down to the cold. Perhaps this was her first dead body. She briefed him on what was known.

At just before 9pm, a teenager had called the emergency services to report a corpse on Denton golf course. A nearby car was dispatched to the scene, and two Officers were in attendance by 9.15.

Three trembling youths had been spoken to. The earthy-sweet fug coming from the group made it clear they were skunked out of their minds, and therefore had a rather lurid recollection of finding what they'd found. Their details were taken and they were driven home.

There was a discernible change in mood among the group of Officers - a definite tightening of the sinews - as Daley arrived at the scene of the crime.

There lay, on the very fringe of the fairway as it sloped down towards to water, the body of a man in his twenties. His throat had been cut, very thoroughly on further examination – he was almost totally exsanguinated, most of his blood saturating the grass around him. He had been killed no more than two hours previously.

On first looking at the body and the scene around it, two things occurred to Graham Daley immediately.

Firstly, the likely nature of the murder was clear to him. There is a particularly barbarous mindset required, a pathological detachment from human distress, to hold a man down and saw through his windpipe this thoroughly. A crime of passion or an amateur's momentary loss of control was usually manifested as a blow to the back of the head or a couple of jabs of a blade to the ribs.

This was sustained, thorough, and sadistic. The poor man's head was more off than on, such was the severity of the knife wound.

The second observation he made that would be meat and drink to any detective concerned the positioning of the body. There hadn't been any. In other words, the victim now lay where he fell. No attempt had been made to hide him, as if his discovery were of no consequence to whoever had butchered him in this way.

Both of these features pointed to a definitive conclusion. This had not been a drug deal gone sour, nor a desperate act of self-preservation. It had been a calculated hit. And probably not the killer's first.

Forensic work was in progress and the temporary lights had been erected. It was going to be a long night.

≈

"Please don't be Emlyn" begged Shaun from the passenger seat of Ben's car. He was the keen favourite in Shaun's mind, the prime candidate for an execution-style killing on this night, at this time. He thought of the Albanian Arjan – the man Emlyn had mentioned a couple of evenings ago. Arjan was likely to have been the character in the tan suit at the snooker club.

Where had Arjan marched in from before his sudden appearance tonight? Here? What had unsettled Michael Rossi so clearly? This?

Ben steered his car into the car park of Denton Golf Club, where he was met by a well-organised cordon and three Officers. Each of them was doing their best to protect themselves from a chill wind that was now blowing – gloves on and collars up.

As Ben brought the car to a halt, one of the Officers approached. Ben wound the driver's side window down, and PC Mark McGill peered in.

"Press" Shaun said.

"Yeah, I know your face. *Herald*, right?" responded McGill.

Bloody hell, I might as well rent a billboard.

"A murder, I gather?" asked Ben.

"Oh aye. Nasty one an' all."

With this, the Officer drew his finger across his throat in a slitting motion. This might have been expressed in a more professional manner, it struck Shaun.

Inexperienced coppers tended to get a buzz out of working higher-profile incidents, and McGill seemed a little too excited given that a man was newly dead just across the fairway.

"Any idea who he is?"

McGill paused. Shaun surmised that McGill knew the victim's name but was hesitant to divulge it.

"It's Emlyn Parry, isn't it?" Shaun asked.

"No" said PC McGill. "But you're not far off."

He leaned in a little further before offering a name.

"Craig Phillipson."

The Butcher of Baguley, slaughtered on a golf course in a howling gale. An inevitable end, it felt to Shaun, given the extent to which Phillipson had lived by the sword. Violent men rarely died peacefully, and those as reckless with their violence as this man were almost guaranteed a brutal finale.

There was little else they were able to glean from McGill. There wasn't much else they would get until more was known by the Police. But they had a headline, and some facts around which to shape a narrative.

And, to the best of Shaun's knowledge. Emlyn Parry was still alive.

≈

It transpired, of course, that Craig Phillipson's awful murder had indeed been carried out at the hands of the Albanian Arjan Marku - the man in the tan suit that Shaun and Ben had met earlier that night.

Phillipson's offence was a minor one to everybody but Marku. He had attracted the attention of Cheetham Hill Police by way of a pub brawl. A woman's arm was broken and her husband sustained a bloody nose, and the landlord wanted his smashed barstool and broken toilet door paid for.

So a Police report was filed naming the offending party.

Arjan Marku deemed this 'conduct unbecoming' of a key member of his new regime, and Phillipson was disposed of as a liability. A loose cannon. Such would be the way of things under the new management.

All of this was a pretext, of course. Killing the nastiest of the Captains was pre-ordained, and sent the strongest possible message to the others. A message that could be described as "Fuck around and find out".

Craig Phillipson was sacrificed in the pursuit of obedience.

His death gave Shaun a profoundly difficult decision. In pragmatic, self-preservation terms, it changed nothing. In fact, it should probably have bolstered his resolve to knock back Emlyn Parry and stay out of this business altogether. But morally, it thickened the plot considerably.

Parry was of interest to this new kingpin – Marku had told Shaun as much at the Altrincham and Hale Social Club. Parry's continued allegiance to Garton had been made clear, and so the lines were now drawn.

Shaun debated abandoning Emlyn to the possibility of a similar encounter with Marku. How would he feel knowing the poor man was skulking around Clayton at night, his face obscured beneath a hood for fear of this sort of brutality? He would be scared, there was no doubt. And if he were badly beaten, tortured, killed even? How much responsibility would Shaun bear by not helping him flee when he could have done it so easily?

Perhaps, after all, procuring the passport wasn't a big deal. All he had to do was make a call and drop off a package - the contents of which he could convincingly deny any knowledge of. It struck him now that seeing Emlyn's plan through might make his own life simpler, and Emlyn's safer.

Ben dropped him off at home that night at around a quarter past eleven. On entering the house, the first thing he saw in the corridor was the satchel in which he'd stowed Emlyn's package.

He glanced at his watch, which showed he had seventeen minutes to intercept Emlyn tonight at Clayton Vale and return his cash to him. That was surely the right course of action.

But Shaun had a murky history when it came to doing the right thing.

Perhaps Emlyn reminded him of the unfortunate bullied kids at school, or Shaun himself as a put-upon cub reporter, the butt of every joke. But after wrestling with the issue for as long as it took to boil the kettle, Shaun didn't venture out to Clayton Vale, didn't rendezvous with Emlyn Parry, and didn't return his money.

He couldn't have explained himself if he'd wanted to.

14

For the past thirty years the shops, bars and amenities of Manchester city centre have been perpetually primped and scrubbed up.

Ever since the IRA sent glass and masonry skittering across forty streets here in nineteen-ninety-six, the cosmetic renovation has been unceasing. And the more of it that occurs, the more there seems left to do - the commitment to beautify every exterior expands with time, like an octogenarian actress spending longer and longer in front of the make-up mirror each morning.

There remain, however, a few sorely neglected corners - alleys and cut-throughs with pre-war grime still caked onto their facades.

One of these unloved backwaters was Appleby Lane, where there stood a scruffy row of antique shops. Each of the half-dozen businesses sitting cheek-by-jowl here looked on its last legs; it was only a matter of time, surely, before their proprietors would lock the door for one last time and look for another way to eke out a living.

Under various moss-spattered rooves you could find second-hand nick-knacks garnered from the houses of the recently deceased, Victorian fireplaces ripped from re-developed properties, and all manner of artefacts culled from other lives. Other times and places. Tin baths and rocking chairs and silver picture frames. In the back door they came, and out of the front they went to their next owners, until they were returned to Appleby Lane a generation on.

The largest premises, squeezed into the middle of the row, was The O'Hare Timepiece Company. This was the place Shaun Mullin was looking for.

Its exterior was filthy, covered in a film of exhaust soot accumulated over the course of a century. It had tiny, curved panes of glass in its windows, and faded signage. Charles Dickens would have moved in here at once and had his belongings shipped up from Kent, in full confidence he had at last found his quintessential backdrop.

On crossing the threshold of the shop, Shaun half expected to encounter a chimney sweep, or a busty woman selling meat pies. Neither was in evidence, much to his disappointment.

Instead, there sat a man in his mid-forties behind a dark mahogany counter. He was hunched over the entrails of a pocket watch and was performing a delicate operation with the cogs therein. As a result of his bent posture, Shaun got full visibility of the man's combover, which was clearly well-tended but was fooling no-one.

As Shaun closed the shop door behind him, the man looked up. A monocular eyepiece was wedged into his left eye socket. He removed it to get a look at his visitor in full stereo.

"Mister O'Hare? said Shaun.

The man, annoyed by this erroneous assumption, seemed to signal a no, and pushed a button beneath the counter. He replaced the eyepiece and continued his delicate work.

This gave Shaun a moment to look around. Antique clocks and watches were piled up on every surface, each of them in need of some form of repair. There were miniature plastic buckets containing springs and cogs of various shapes and sizes. A shelf high up on one wall housed what looked like a dozen grandfather clock pendulums. This wasn't really a shop - it was a field hospital.

Mister O'Hare emerged from a room at the rear. He was of a similar age and build to the character with the combover. And no less shabbily dressed.

"That there man has a whiff of Mister Fleetwood" said O'Hare.

And odd greeting, but Shaun went with it. Fleetwood was the name Shaun had given him on the telephone. It was his first pseudonym for almost a decade and his fourth Lancashire seaside town, having previously operated for brief periods as Mister Morecambe, Mister Blackpool, and Mister Fylde.

Shaun nodded his confirmation, and O'Hare beckoned him to the rear of the premises. As they passed the counter, O'Hare indicated his colleague with the eyepiece and said:

"You'll have to pardon him, Mister Fleetwood. Working with the enemy, as usual."

Shaun didn't understand. There was the tone of a riddle in the way the statement had been delivered, but its meaning was beyond him.

"Sorry?"

"Time. Time is the enemy. It is against us."

This visit was getting more eccentric by the second. Emlyn Parry had some odd associates.

"Follow me, if you would" requested O'Hare.

Get it done and get out of here, for fuck's sake.

In the backroom of O'Hare's shop, the proprietor explained the process he undertook in procuring illicit passports. Its simplicity made it very clever in Shaun's opinion, and he wondered why everyone didn't do it this way.

First of all, a stooge must be found. Someone in on the scam who had no desire to travel abroad. At least, not for a few years. In exchange for a couple of grand, they were asked to apply for a passport. Their details would be submitted honestly and accurately, but with someone else's photographs instead of their own.

The outmoded safeguard of having the rear of the photograph signed by a doctor or a teacher could be easily faked. The passport was posted back to the applicant's address, collected from there, and given to the intended recipient. That was it.

So, within ten days, courtesy of a higher fee for emergency processing, Emlyn Parry would be Ben Wainwright, a car mechanic from Huddersfield. And from there, it was viva Espana.

By the time O'Hare brought this explanation to an end, Shaun was convinced the man was deranged. When he spoke, some of his sentences sounded as if their words were in reverse order – you got the sense, but its formulation was miles off. Was there some chemical involved in watch-fixing that eroded the brain, like in hat-making?

That was when Shaun saw the photograph.

A passport-sized snap sat on the desk behind O'Hare, partially obscured by papers. The subject was a girl, Mediterranean in complexion and raven-haired, who would have been fourteen or so. There was no trace of innocence in her face, or childhood joy. She had the expression of desolation Shaun had seen in many a photograph – it usually belonged to the victim of a particularly unpleasant crime. There was a distressing hinterland suggested by this image.

That kid's foreign.

Shaun made an immediate connection, for better or for worse, between the child and this man's illicit profession.

Trafficking, pound to a penny.

"Sorry" said Shaun, "who's that?" He nodded to the picture.

O'Hare turned his shoulders stiffly, and glanced at the photo.

"Don't know" came the matter-of-fact reply.

"Why would someone want a forged passport for a child?" Shaun's words were clearly accusatory.

O'Hare picked up this train of thought at once, and met Shaun's challenging stare with one of his own.

"Circumstances…." O'Hare was unable to complete the thought. "I've no idea."

"And you didn't feel you needed to ask questions?"

"In matters pertaining to clients, circumspection, Mister Fleetwood, I prefer. That way I don't know what I don't know."

Filthy coward.

This was what it came to for souls like this, who operated in the no-man's land of black commerce. Scraping a living, inch by inch, by whatever means. And losing all their humanity in the process of doing it. How does this happen? By increments, or in a single, long leap towards damnation?

O'Hare may have been eccentric, but he was also a scumbag. Shaun hoped there would be a reckoning for this vile character down the line, somehow. O'Hare would get what was coming, one day. The world wouldn't miss what he had to offer it.

Shaun now had a strong urge to bring an end to what had been a surreal and distasteful encounter. It had been a strong contender for the strangest twenty minutes of his life, and that was a crowded field.

He opened his satchel, took from it the taped bag given to him by Emlyn Parry, and placed it on a pock-marked work surface by his right hand-side. O'Hare registered it with a business-like nod.

"I'll give you a bell when it's ready, Mister Fleetwood, for collection" he said coldly.

Shaun realised he'd been grinding his teeth for some while in the company of O'Hare and had to make a conscious effort now to relax his jaw. Violence had never been part of his character, but he could cheerfully have slapped this appalling fucker all over his grubby little premises and some distance beyond.

Without acknowledging the man further, he stood and returned to the front of the shop before exiting briskly to rejoin the twenty-first century a street away.

≈

That night, at precisely eleven twenty-eight, Shaun stepped onto the slim pathway that led through Clayton Vale.

The Vale was a nature reserve created by the Council in the eighties. Formerly the site of a smallpox hospital and before that a dye works, it was now a marshy haven for the wildlife (nothing spectacular – squirrels, mice, blackbirds) that thrived on the banks of the River Medlock. It smelled peaty. High rushes and unkempt shrubbery flanked a winding path through it. One could walk here and not be seen from the fields beyond.

It wasn't long before Shaun detected some movement on the path up ahead. A figure hooded in black was coming his way. He was soon able to make out the very distinctive silhouette of Emlyn Parry.

Shaun offered good news - the passport was on its way. But this was utterly negated by his report of Craig Phillipson's execution. Emlyn paled as Shaun described what had happened at Denton Golf Club.

Shaun and Emlyn agreed that the man in the suit he'd met at the snooker club was certainly Arjan Marku, and that Marku was the most likely culprit in the death of Emlyn's former colleague Phillipson.

Spain must have seemed more inviting than ever, and was a little closer tonight. The two men agreed that, on security grounds, this nightly walk should be put on hold for a week – wherever Emlyn was hiding out, he should stay there. The earliest they could expect delivery of the passport was seven days. Shaun would bring it to him as soon as he could after that.

Emlyn clapped Shaun on the shoulder in recognition of a meaningful act of selflessness, and evaporated once again into the night.

On the walk back home, Shaun reflected that Emlyn had looked beaten. Ready to capitulate. Whichever dark hole he was existing in from hour to hour was taking its toll on his features, and the news about Phillipson had surely worsened his mental state. If Emlyn did escape his fate in the UK, he surely couldn't return for a very long time, and perhaps that realisation was presenting itself as a very real prognosis at last.

This wasn't going to be six weeks in the sun for Emlyn Parry. It would have to be a new life.

≈

The next morning, across the city in far less appealing surroundings, Peter Garton lay beneath a rough twill blanket. The fabric of these blankets was an irritant against any exposed piece of skin, but was the only protection he had against the chill of the morning. A rash was the lesser of two uncomfortable evils.

He was entering the final chapter of *Bravo Two Zero* when there was a timid tap-tap-tap at his cell door. As was his preference when visitors knocked, Garton rose from his bed and made his way to the door. On opening it a few inches, he saw Neil Burrows, the owner of the book he was currently reading.

Burrows announced that he had news concerning Emlyn Parry. Naturally, this secured him an invitation into Garton's domain.

Neil was secretly thrilled to have discovered something of value to offer Garton. Perhaps this would secure him some measure of protection going forward, a status as someone who couldn't be violated or exploited in this shithole without there being consequences.

"I've spoke to a mate of mine. On the phone. He says he's seen Emlyn. With that feller who came in here to see you a few weeks ago."

"What feller?

"The writer. Emlyn went into his house."

"Shaun Mullin?" asked Garton, incredulous.

"Yeah."

"And your mate saw this himself? This isn't someone-who-knows-someone-bullshit-bullshit?"

"No, he lives round there. Clayton. He saw Emlyn go in."

Neil felt the entire cell darken at this revelation, as Peter Garton began joining dots – real or imagined – in his mind.

Garton sensed at once an unwelcome collusion between the oddball Parry and the smart-arse Mullin.

Garton's experience told him that his most promising line of thought was to start at the end. The outcome so often brought to light the method. How were the two of them attempting to con him?

He believed that Parry held something of great value that belonged to him, and may well now be looking to exploit it for his own benefit if he could. Recruiting his friend Shaun Mullin to this end was logical. Mullin was clever, well-connected in his own way, and anonymous as far as criminal circles went – unless they were devoted readers of *The Herald*, of course.

Garton came to some quick conclusions. There was no book planned, no empathetic connection between him and Mullin. The entire visit had, in fact, been subterfuge. So why had Shaun come to see him? What was he scouting for, during their conversation?

The simple reality of a coincidence – that one man he happened to know had reached out to another in a moment of desperation – never occurred to him. Such was the mind of a lifelong miscreant, wedded to connivance and deceit, thoughts blackened by a lifetime of amorality, with no room left for an innocent truth.

No, these two – Mullin and Parry – were in cahoots. There was a plan in place, and it had to be brought to an immediate halt.

Garton made Burrows sit, and handed him a pencil and a piece of notepaper.

"You're going to write something for me" he said.

Burrows's expression changed. There was a sudden look of sadness on his face. Of sympathy.

"Pete… I had no idea" he said.

"No idea about what?"

"There's literacy classes. You've just got the speak to the Duty Offic – "

Garton interrupted Burrows, thunderously.

"I can fucking write, you prick. I just can't have my DNA on the notepaper."

Without questioning the dangers of his own DNA being present instead, Burrows withered and took up the pencil.

Garton paused. Then:

"Shaun."

Burrows scribbled.

Garton continued.

"You absolute fucking maggot."

15

Shaun sat in Eleanor's office in a chastened state. Meeting the likely murderer of Craig Phillipson had unsettled him. And the encounter with the egregious O'Hare had thrown his equilibrium off even further.

There was a residual tightness in his gut, and an ache behind his eyes. As Shaun was these days particularly sensitive to the dangers of existing 'off centre' for any length of time, he needed to restore some balance.

"I need a few days off, Eleanor. A week."

"Right" she replied. Shaun wasn't prone to ad-hoc holiday requests. Or, in fact, any type of holiday requests.

"Everything OK?"

"Oh yeah. God yeah, no, everything's fine."

"Starting work on the book?"

Shaun paused, and sighed. He had no answer ready – it was formulated in the moment.

"I don't think there's going to be a book, mate" he said. "Not right now, anyway."

Shaun of course knew the commercial value of capturing the zeitgeist, and had spent most of his career tapping into the issues of the day as effectively as he could. But books demanded a different perspective to newspapers. An alternative rhythm. They were designed for longevity rather than immediacy, so there was surely something to be said for letting the dust settle on Peter Garton's arrest, and employing the considerable benefits of hindsight in a couple of years' time. That was the rationale he gave himself, anyway.

In truth, he wasn't sure he could stomach it. Writing a book on a situation that was essentially 'live' could only bring a psychological volatility he didn't think he could handle.

The last couple of weeks had been a taster of what might lie ahead if he inserted himself into Peter Garton's narrative, and it had done him harm. Best let it be until such time as he could embark on the book without such difficulties.

Shaun was avoiding trouble. Seeking calmer waters. Older and wiser.

Today was Tuesday, and he and Eleanor came to an easy agreement that he would be back in the office on Wednesday week. Seven days clear.

≈

Claire Louisa Mullin-Townsend found it healthful to escape from the company of her mother every few weeks. Like most people, she regarded Shaun's sister Susan as a rather dry companion, and when her mother's uprightness became oppressive Claire fabricated an excuse to disappear for a while.

This often meant a couple of days staying with her uncle Shaun, who was the perfect antidote and always redressed the balance in the required manner. Stupid jokes, too much booze, and vibrant conversations. She considered her uncle Shaun to be the smartest man she had ever met, and the world's biggest idiot at the same time.

Shaun liked his nineteen-year-old niece a great deal - a garrulous young woman with a blunt turn of phrase. She let nothing pass without thorough investigation and had a strong opinion on anything that moved.

Claire had in fact been a world-class little shit from about the age of ten and was now, in the parlance of the city, a fucking chippy cow. Her mother had given up trying to constrain her through the teenage years, and had by now retreated into a selective deafness with regard to the argumentative, expletive-laden exchanges that were Claire's chosen method of interaction.

Shaun, on the other hand, regularly egged her on, offering an avuncular credence to her considerable facetiousness.

Claire shared many traits with Shaun. Most prominent among these was a disinclination to leaving any argument unfinished. The two shared a dog-with-a-bone tenacity when it came to disagreement, and in the snug of the *Penny Whistle* her combative energies were in full force.

The current subject was the continued gaping hole in her uncle's romantic life. He hadn't been 'involved' with anyone, she recalled, since she was in nappies. Shaun was attempting to defend himself against a charge of emotional constipation – that his feelings were so buried by paranoia and cynicism that he could no longer recognize the natural pull of affection.

This was not what he wanted to be doing with the time he had taken off work, but Claire could be incorrigible, so here they were.

There had been a few women over the years who had gained a significant status in Shaun's life. He sometimes thought of them, and usually fondly, but knew that memories were inclined to re-emerge with an added gloss that probably wasn't justified by the time they'd spent together.

Shaun's curmudgeonly manner wasn't something that had evolved in early middle age – he'd been this way since his twenties. Women in particular took his irascible nature personally, and that made him difficult to love. As one of his longer-lasting partners had put it years ago, "I think you're just too angry for me, Shaun."

In summary, his romantic liaisons had been misfires.

Apart from Madeleine.

≈

Shaun Mullin met Madeleine March at the age of nineteen, at the start of his second year of University. It was always Madeleine, never Maddy.

She was a year older, and was studying Philosophy at Birkbeck. Tall, mousy-haired, freckled, and very clever. They both happened to be at the same gig – *The Wedding Present* at The University of London Student Union – and after a few furtive glances one way then the other, Shaun bowled over to where she was stood and simply handed her his beer. She sipped from it and gave it back, as they both pretended to be more interested in what was happening on stage than they were in each other.

They introduced themselves in the gap between *Give My Love To Kevin* and *Everyone Thinks He Looks Daft.*

And that was that.

They kissed at five o'clock the next morning in Regent's Park, until a watery sunrise broke the spell.

The two of them agreed at some point in the next fortnight that their being together felt pre-ordained, and as such should never be questioned. They were, by mutual consent, the real deal.

Her long silences didn't bother him, and his contorted, expletive-filled outbursts didn't bother her. They laughed together a fair bit, and were generally regarded as a good influence on one another.

They never lived together on paper, but split their time between each other's accommodation from day one. They were almost never apart. He started drinking a bit less, and sleeping at more sensible hours, and she became a bit more sociable, less introspective.

But the deeper Shaun's feelings became over their first six months together, the more keenly he could sense a reticence in Madeleine. She was easy company, always, but something drew her back from him in the most passionate or romantic of moments. It was if she couldn't quite fulfil her obligation to him as a mate for life. Perhaps theirs was not a meeting of souls after all. Maybe they were destined only to be accomplices.

This caused no tension between them. They were honest with one another and made sure they talked about the real world as well as the one in which they were cocooned together, away from all outside influence. But Shaun began to suspect that their bond was less permanent than he'd assumed it to be.

And so it turned out.

One Tuesday afternoon outside the *Scala* cinema in King's Cross, Madeleine announced she would be undertaking a post-graduate qualification in Montreal for two years upon graduation from Birkbeck.

Shaun was surprised, and yet not. This was the source of her caution. She'd had this in the back of her mind since they met, and hadn't wanted to share it until her fate was clear.

He didn't feel betrayed. He knew her too well by now to assume the worst of her. She had just wanted things to work, and had avoided throwing this particular spanner into the works for as long as she could get away with it.

A plan was laid out. She had constructed a scenario in which Shaun went with her and got a job in Montreal, and had even investigated Canadian visas on his behalf. There were no fewer than six newspapers in the Metropolitan area, and only two of them were published in French. He'd find something to do with himself.

She wanted him to follow her, but in her heart she knew he wouldn't. He was still wrestling with London, the toughest foe on the planet, and she knew he needed to get the better of it. This was the only arena in which he felt he could prove himself. He would have to stay here.

They both assumed she would be back in two years' time, and knew a resumption of their relationship would be very likely if that came to pass. The move to Canada didn't feel terminal.

Then, part-way through her secondment, Madeleine was offered a position at Montreal University. A grown-up job that came with a large house. She accepted, and stayed in Montreal.

Three more years passed. Then four.

She loved Canada, and found her career exceptionally rewarding. Despite this, her unspoken arrangement with Shaun remained in place. She would be back. Not quite yet, but not before long.

By now, she and Shaun were communicating perhaps twice a month – by text message now, mobile phones having become ubiquitous by the mid-2000s. There was the usual jokey status check – "You not married yet?" or "Go on then, what's his name?".

Neither of them developed a relationship that might be considered serious enough to inform the other of. This was their holding pattern.

Then, on the cusp of his thirties, he received a phone call one Sunday morning from a man called Simon Spencer. He'd shared a flat with

Madeleine in Holloway Road many years back. He'd been an agreeable housemate, according to her, and Shaun always found him pleasant enough.

Simon's voiced faltered as he told Shaun that Madeleine March had gone. An obscure and aggressive lymphoma had been diagnosed four months previously.

She was thirty years of age, and she was dead, and she hadn't told Shaun it was going to happen. Finding out from Simon Spencer felt crass and inadequate. For the first and only time, Madeleine had made Shaun angry.

Shaun was convinced by the age of sixteen that God did not exist, and never had. But if he were wrong, if indeed there was a supreme being overseeing the day-to-day mechanics of the universe, in Shaun's opinion he was a nasty bastard. What else could explain the torture and anguish inflicted on one as blemishless as Madeleine March?

Madeleine left him her favourite earrings in her will – they were his favourite too - along with a hand-written poem that, in truth, wasn't very coherent. Probably a drug-addled effort in her last days, Shaun has always supposed. He stowed these things in a drawer beside his bed.

Of course, in the years since her passing, Shaun imagined Madeleine to be ever more golden and splendid. She could never be old, perfectly preserved as she was in Shaun's mind. There she now lived, untouchable. She became wiser and more accomplished with each passing year.

≈

Thoughts of Madeleine were less frequent than they once had been. But they made the topic of relationships an uncomfortable one for Shaun. In The *Penny Whistle*, Claire was still pressing the issue.

"It's like your radar's broken" she said. "You need to fix it. Stay in the game. These things need work, and you've let it all wither."

"Well I have to tell you Claire, that isn't the only thing that withers at my age."

Shaun hoped that might be a revolting enough change of lane to cap the discussion, but after a disgusted "euw" Claire persisted. She asked him which of the women in his office he found attractive. Who might he be inclined towards, romantically, if he absolutely had to pick somebody?

But, thank God, he didn't absolutely have to pick anybody. He needed a change of subject, and quickly.

As luck would have it, a distraction presented itself in the form of a loud American voice from the bar.

"Oh my Gaaaaaad, you guys are Hillierryis" bellowed a besuited figure holding half a pint of Guinness. He was with three other men who were apparently British, and (Shaun assumed) colleagues. Insurance, or Consulting, or IT, by the look of their boilerplate suits.

The trio were joshing in an overblown manner about English place names, as if they were unusually quirky (which they were not, in comparison to, say, Ding Dong in Utah or Accident, Maryland). Claire clocked the accent first, rolling her eyes at Shaun as Brits tend to do when a boorish Transatlantic presence is detected.

Shaun had a carefully formulated opinion about America and Americans, developed over dozens of encounters with the species, and this was the perfect moment to share it with his niece. It allowed him to wriggle out of the conversation about women, for a start.

He found Americans tolerable individually, but less so in groups. As a nation they were characterised generally by a sort of doltish sincerity.

Most Americans, according to Shaun, were one-dimensional people, the two missing dimensions being nuance and self-awareness. This made them predictable in conversation, and largely indistinguishable from one another intellectually. They were alarmingly homogenous.

Their attempt to emulate punk rock was a good indicator of their deficiencies– even as a child, it had been obvious to Shaun how utterly inauthentic *The Ramones* were in comparison to *The Sex Pistols*. The former were a low-grade facsimile of rebelliousness that reeked of art departments and corporate brainstorming. Americans didn't have ideas, they had focus groups.

There was one redeeming feature to meeting one of our cousins from across the pond, however. Shaun liked to play a game with American names – specifically those of men, which fell into three categories in his experience.

"Right Clairey" he said. "I've got a game we can play. Five quid to the winner. Here's the rules."

Shaun outlined the three main categories.

The first were the ethnic names – probably the most common of the groupings. In respect of pronunciation, O'Leary and Garcia were of course straightforward, but occasionally a Kripziczowicz or a van Greuzmeier had to be negotiated. The Great Melting Pot threw up monikers from all over the planet, many of which seemed to have more letters than were expedient. One simply had to default to the manageable, Anglicised pronunciation and hope nobody took offence.

Shaun had titled the second category 'Golfers'. These were the Chets, Chads and Chucks– names that gave away the owner's nationality wherever they may happen to find themselves in the world. Solid, good-ol'-boy names that suggested front stoops and barbecue rub.

Often with golfers, there would be a number appended to their surname. Shaun had once met, for example, a Chip Frankham III. The number indicated how many removes the descendent was from the original Chip Frankham, who had clearly been so star-spangled-awesome that his family felt the need to memorialise him down the generations.

The final grouping was peculiar to the middle classes and was most prevalent on the East coast. These men tended to wear polo shirts and slacks, and had almost always been to a University Shaun had heard of. They were usually mundane individuals with modest share portfolios and an uncle who had a Directorship in Something Big.

They had a curious trait. Their forenames and surnames were the wrong way round. Over the years Shaun had found himself in the company of Americans named Baxter John, Merriott Adam, and Riley Patrick.

Perhaps, in the absence of any individuality among the populace, a certain section of society had decided to try and switch things up in this manner to suggest something – anything – out of the ordinary was going on with these people. 'God I'm boring. Let's try the ol' name-flip.'

"So which is he?" asked Shaun. "Immigrant, golfer, or wrong-way-round?"

Claire, treating the challenge with the utmost seriousness, took her time to think. Eventually, she opted for the first category.

"I reckon he's a Paddy. He's on the Guinness and his head's quite big."

"Nope. He's got a golfer's name, I guarantee it."

Clair's mouth creased. She was unconvinced.

"Only one way to find out." said Shaun. "Come on."

Shaun strolled over to the bar, with Claire lingering a little way behind. The American was listening to a colleague spouting off about the relative scarcity of guns in the United Kingdom. Shaun knew that firearms weren't quite as rare as people thought over here - there would be a couple of hundred in Moss Side, for example, hidden on the top of wardrobes and in garden sheds - but he would let that slide.

"Excuse me" he asked as he leant on the bar. "Where are you from?"

The American's face lit up.

"Phoenix, Arizona" he said.

"Wow. Right." said Shaun, offering his hand. "My name's Shaun. Welcome to Manchester."

The man shook Shaun's hand enthusiastically. These people were so malleable, so easily flattered.

"Thank you, Shaun. I'm Brett."

Yes. Golfer. I win.

He couldn't resist a triumphant glance to Claire, and with this, Shaun was perfectly happy to draw a veil on the conversation and set about trying to catch the eye of Shirley behind the bar. But Brett had other ideas.

"You been to the States?" he asked Shaun, full of puppyish enthusiasm for his homeland.

"Um, no. Never."

"Oh, you gotta. It's a great country."

"Is it?" Shaun smirked.

He realised at once he had said this rather too cynically. He had imbued his reply with a distinctly sceptical resonance he hadn't necessarily intended. The American raised a solitary eyebrow.

"You bet your ass it is, buddy" Brett said.

"Just asking" said Shaun. "Like I said, I wouldn't know."

He issued a wan smile in an attempt to drag things back to cordiality. The American had been affronted at Shaun's challenge to his national pride, and the mood had soured.

At that moment, Claire stepped into the breach. She had Brett sized up already. He was a flag-shagger. Men like this were both larger-than-life, and somehow smaller.

After moving herself to the edge of the group, she proceeded to deliver one of the great pub put-downs in Shaun's long memory. She elevated herself to the summit of Shaun's estimation with the following thesis.

"Sorry. Hiya. Bearing in mind I've not been to the States either, so what do I know, it seems from the outside that America is in fact fifty tiny countries, forty-six of them borderline first-world shitholes, and the only thing making them collectively 'great' is the insane amount of money they can raise together to play soldiers with. So maybe you lot should wind your necks in a bit, d'you know what I mean?"

Brett struggled to decipher all of it thanks to Claire's dyed-in-the-wool Manc scally act. But he got enough of it to be sickened by its sentiment.

"Hey, watch your mouth" he barked, as a colleague rested a placatory hand on his arm in a 'leave-it-Brett-she's-not-worth-it' sort of way. A tragic childishness had revealed itself, and the classy move was to leave things there. Apart from anything else, a hasty withdrawal would avoid the inevitable 'if-it-wasn't-for-us-you'd-be-speaking-German' claptrap.

Claire smiled and walked back to the table. Shaun could not have been prouder of anyone, for anything, in any circumstance.

There seemed little point in staying any longer, given the clinical nature of the execution that had just taken place, so the two of them drained their glasses and left the *Penny Whistle* on a white cloud of their own triumph, and giggled all the way back to Clayton.

≈

The remainder of Shaun's week off passed agreeably enough. He ate and slept, and walked a lot. And didn't do much else.

Fate had smiled upon him, kindly allowing him the maximum rest and recuperation possible before its next intervention. There were no interruptions by either the criminal or journalistic fraternities, and was now spending his Tuesday night poking chilli seeds into small pots on his kitchen windowsill. Growing things was therapeutic, as was (in Shaun's experience) battling a plateful of ragingly hot spiced food.

As his return to work loomed the next morning, Shaun felt distinctly and definitively stable. He had slept well the past few nights. His breathing was even and his thoughts clear, and there was even a case for suggesting he was bordering on contentment. His week off had righted the ship, and it was full steam ahead from here.

Then - fate having changed its mind - his phone rang.

He hadn't been able to bring himself to save O'Hare's number to his device the previous week, such was his loathing of the man he had encountered in the grubby shop in Appleby Lane. But he had written it on a scrap of paper and remembered that it ended with a double three.

And now, there the number was, on his phone screen. This would be the start of the final act of Shaun's dalliance with the dark side.

He accepted the call, and made the necessary arrangements for the collection of a parcel the next day from O'Hare's premises. It would all be over by sunrise on Thursday, thank God. Never again.

Shaun Mullin slept soundly that night, with relatively few murmurs from the troubled parts of his mind.

≈

Appleby Lane was no prettier by the light of the morning than it had been during the day. If anything, the shadows cast from the buildings gave it a sepulchral appearance, as if things once living and breathing had been buried beneath it. In this light, at this time of day, the shopfront of The O'Hare Timepiece Company resembled a tombstone.

Shaun didn't linger once inside, and O'Hare didn't mind that one bit. There was an obvious antipathy between them during this second meeting, brief though it may have been. Best they leave one another well alone from now on, thought both men.

There was a hurried and curt exchange, and the business was done.

On re-emerging into Appleby Lane, Shaun evaluated the parcel he had collected. It was a thin Manilla envelope addressed to a Mr. Wainwright in Huddersfield. This man was now the lucky recipient of a couple of thousand pounds, but not the passport he'd had ordered for him.

Surely there would be ramifications for Wainwright, thought Shaun. He'd need a passport at some point in his life. And they kept records of these things, didn't they? They were bound to check a new photo against the old, and see at a glance the discrepancy between the two faces.

Shaun supposed one could just play dumb and plead complete ignorance of the bogus application. That could get you a long way when dealing with Civil Service types, actually.

From O'Hare's shop to *The Herald*'s office was a ten-minute walk.

Once he'd reached The Arndale, Shaun realised what a pleasant day it was. Cold, of course, it being Manchester in May. But bright and holding something fecund on the air. He was beginning to feel oddly normal.

He'd be later to work than he'd promised, but that suddenly felt immaterial as he strode through the weak spring sunshine. Nothing mattered, really, apart from right now.

Life was, it occurred to him, in its right proportions this morning. He was able to fix it in his sights for once, and see it all for what it was. An unusual sensation accompanied this thought, and it was one he found complex. If he could bottle this feeling, he would.

Shaun started making plans. He would visit his mum in the next week.

Not under duress, but because it was what sons should do. And he'd check in on his sister while he was at it. He could manage these things, he told himself. They were navigable in his current mood.

Was this a new leaf? A peeling back of some psychic carapace?

On arriving at *The Forge*, Shaun went through the standard returnee's rigmarole of acquainting himself with his desk again, and with those who sat around it.

People seemed surprised by someone returning from a break, as if there'd been wild rumours of an absconding or elopement. And everyone had something to say in relation to the time spent away. They couldn't help but comment, it seemed, as if they were issuing a reassurance to the returning colleague that their absence had been noticed. Maternity leaves were the worst, so at least it wasn't that, thought Shaun.

Gaz congratulated Shaun on getting his venereal disease sorted at last (he was such a wag, Shaun had assured him) and Ad Sales Jamie alluded to his Costa Del Lancashire tan (i.e. no tan at all).

Ben brought Shaun up to speed with a few of the stories that were being worked up, which didn't take long, and told him all about a minor scandal involving some missing printer ink. It was a perfunctory morning.

Soon the pair had decamped to the *Penny Whistle* for lunch. They did this together about once a month. It was a Line Management activity suggested by Eleanor moons ago, and they had embraced it.

Any talk of work itself was deemed out-of-scope at these lunches. Instead, Shaun introduced a theme for each occasion, and would engage Ben in argument and counter-argument purely as a Devil's advocate.

They'd had an absolute humdinger a few weeks back on the topic of gender identity, one of the few times in his adult life Shaun had felt out of his intellectual depth. Neophyte concepts and language had flung themselves at him, and he had struggled to stay on top of the logic of Ben's (rigorous and sound) arguments.

On this occasion, Shaun sought to redress the balance by staying firmly on home ground. Today's topic was Catholicism - its place in the pantheon of religions, and status as the primary European belief system.

Ben made a few interesting observations while picking at his cheese sandwich. He proposed that Catholicism, because it regarded humans as intrinsically flawed, was the truest representation of mankind's relationship to God.

While the much milkier Church of England cheerily suggested we were all small miracles, wonders of God's creation and so forth, Catholicism took the basic view that people were a waste of space from birth. It then suggested we spent our lives trying to clamber up from that rather low bar. There was a reason Catholics never sang *All Things Bright and Beautiful.*

According to Ben, that echoed Biblical teachings most accurately. God did not, he maintained, love us very much at all.

Shaun's role in the discussion was to take the opposing view. Those were the rules. He attempted to counter by muddying the waters of the original thesis, diving into doctrinal detail that Ben couldn't possibly have any grasp of, given his comparatively secular upbringing.

To no avail. Ben introduced a trump card – science. He alerted Shaun to the following fact of biology: in human beings, the first part of an embryo to become fully formed and functional was always the anus. Meaning, literally, that every person on earth was, at some point in their development, one hundred per cent arsehole, thus proving Papist doctrine.

Catholicism had nailed it, and so had Ben. Shaun conceded the point and, once his laughter at this intellectual somersault had subsided, accompanied his fellow debater back to the office.

≈

Arriving home that night, Shaun kicked aside the envelopes that had landed behind his front door. He glanced down at them as he did so. One was clearly a demand for Council Tax (he could smell those a mile off without opening the envelope) and there was a fundraising letter from the Red Cross on top of it.

A third envelope stopped him in his tracks. A small, cheap, brown one.

It bore no watermark or stamp, and had nothing on it except the name Shaun Mullin, scrawled in pencil.

He picked it up, slid his finger beneath the lip, and took from it a single sheet of A6 notepaper. On it was scrawled a note in the same pencil and the same handwriting:

> *Shaun. You absolute fucking maggot. I've rumbled*
> *your scheme with the other maggot Parry. As I*
> *said to you before, I have a very long reach my*
> *friend. You can test that theory if you like, or you*
> *can change your mind about what you're doing. I*
> *won't hold a grudge as long as what's mine stays*
> *mine. It's up to you from here. You've been warned.*

There was no name and no signature beneath the message. Neither was necessary.

Shaun stood in his hallway, clutching the note and absorbing its message. There would be trouble here, if he were not very careful indeed. This was a fire that needed putting out with some urgency.

16

As was Manchester's most obdurate habit, darkness fell and the rain fell with it. Many bright days ended in this manner, as ill-intentioned rainclouds looked on enviously from over The Irish Sea and decided to repatriate. The city's high concentration of Irish emigrants was perfectly logical, given that Ireland was literally in the water here.

The walk from Shaun's front door to Clayton Vale took no more than five minutes or so, but like most single men Shaun would no more have considered buying an umbrella than he would a lipstick. His coat was inadequate as protection from the torrent plummeting from the skies. Shaun had decided not to tell Emlyn about the letter from Peter Garton. He was still processing it himself, for one thing. And to pile more fear onto the poor man at this stage was plain cruelty. If all went to plan, Parry would be out of the country by the end of the week, none the wiser and none the worse off.

But what of Shaun? What did the letter mean for him? He would have to convince Garton, somehow, that he and Emlyn had no plan. They were not concocting anything more complex together than a trip overseas.

He needed to get home and think. Re-read the note for nuance. Come up with a feasible course of action to rid Garton of his suspicions.

By the time he'd reached the Vale, Shaun was drenched. Emlyn had better not be late.

He was, by almost ten minutes. Shaun was staving off unpalatable thoughts almost as soon as his watch ticked past the half-hour mark – Emlyn had been killed, abducted, or scared into permanent hiding.

Shaun's concerns were unfounded. A familiar, rotund frame emerged through the gloom along the footpath by the river. Emlyn approached with head bowed, scuttling a little. Shaun lifted the envelope from his coat pocket, ready to offer it up, hand it over, and walk away for good.

Emlyn saw the envelope. His eyes widened. A particular kind of relief coursed across his face, and he let out a whimper of gratitude as he spoke.

"Thanks man. Thank you so much."

He had now reached Shaun, and grabbed him by the shoulders, shaking them as an expression of his passionate appreciation.

"How are you?"

"Fuckinell man. I'm losing my fuckin' mind."

From the half-crazed look of him, this was no exaggeration.

"I've got to get away, man."

Shaun nodded to the parcel he had brought with him, which was now in Emlyn's hand.

"Well. You can now."

Emlyn took it, and exhaled a celebratory "Yesss…", relief etched across his face.

He ripped open the top of the envelope, eager to view its contents.

But instead of the expected dark blue document, he pulled from the envelope a dozen or so blank, rectangular index cards. When held together, they were roughly the size and thickness of a passport.

Emlyn's face fell, as did Shaun's.

O'Hare, you thieving bastard.

Emlyn looked at Shaun accusingly, mouth agape. A moment of frozen consternation passed between them as Emlyn waited for an explanation. But there was none forthcoming - it would take Shaun a few moments to formulate a response to this grievous betrayal.

It was time he wasn't afforded.

A muscular figure emerged from the reeds that flanked the path, face obscured by a scarf, and descended upon Emlyn. In a second, the ill-fated fugitive had been dragged to the floor and the first of a dozen or more heavy blows had been struck.

The punches were calculated and controlled, as if well-practised. They were not the wild, rangy swings of, say, a panicked mugging or drunken scuffle outside a late-night takeaway.

Seconds after Emlyn was set upon, Shaun felt a weight drop onto his back and a forearm brace itself against his windpipe – a second masked figure. There were immediately a third man and a fourth, perhaps a greater number than that. Shaun couldn't tell - his face was ground into the dirt beside the path, and he was assailed by a blur of boots and fists.

Shaun strove hard to keep some clarity in these first moments as he was repeatedly struck; practical information would be important later – numbers, heights, colours. He felt no physical discomfort, not yet. That was still a few moments away, he knew. So in this small pain-free window, he came to the quick conclusion this was likely the doing of the Albanian in the tan suit. And that meant he was not the primary target but mere collateral damage.

That was positive. Not for Emlyn, of course, who Shaun could now hear squealing as the punches and kicks rained in on him.

Would these men regard Shaun as an associate of Emlyn's? Did they view him as an adversary in whatever matter they were looking to resolve, or simply a nobody they needed to scare away?

Shaun needed to separate himself from Emlyn in his attackers' minds, and portray himself as an innocent. A clueless bystander. Whatever this battle was about, Shaun was a civilian, and he had to make them see it.

Shaun and Emlyn – who was by now bleeding from the nose and the side of his head and crying out in panic – were then hauled up the bank of reeds towards the narrow road north of the Vale.

The rough undergrowth lashed at Shaun's arms as he was pulled through it, and whipped him across the face repeatedly. With every effort he made to gain a footing up the ridge, to be able to take a step or two under his own steam, the hands on him yanked him off balance again.

On the journey up the bank, a black hood was pulled over Shaun's head. Emlyn's too, he assumed. The hood was musty and thick.

As the reeds thinned and Shaun felt concrete beneath his feet again, a blunt object struck his skull in a single, heavy blow. It neutered all of his senses at once. He swore he felt his teeth rattle, and fell to the floor with the force of the strike. Its power had been exaggerated by it being unexpected – a blow you don't see coming is particularly disabling.

Shaun felt his wallet and mobile phone being wrenched from his pockets. He was lifted to his feet and thrown back against something metallic. A vehicle. A second impact next to him – Emlyn, surely.

There was then the sound of a door being slid open across casters, and the two men were thrown into the back of a van. The stench of burnt oil.

They were being taken somewhere, which was a minor positive. If a life-threatening beating were the only aim, why not do it in situ at Clayton Vale? An abduction suggested to Shaun that perhaps they might already have had the worst of it.

An engine coughed into life and, no more than sixty seconds after standing together on the pathway by the water, agog at the envelope's bogus contents, Shaun Mullin and Emlyn Parry had been extricated from Clayton Vale with clinical efficiency.

As the vehicle moved away, a knee drove itself into Shaun's back, between the shoulder blades, pinning him to the van floor. He tested the waters with an attempt to communicate.

"You alright Emlyn?"

Before any response could come, a punch landed on the left side of Shaun's jawbone. He winced at the impact.

"No talk" came a heavily accented voice.

Albanians.

Emlyn was sobbing. Shaun could only imagine the torments he'd been through in the past few weeks, his mind constructing this very circumstance over and over, then rejecting it by sheer willpower for a few minutes at a time, only for it to resurface like an unslayable demon. His mind would have plunged in and out of the horrors awaiting him, in an endless loop.

The battle for composure, for sanity, was now lost. This was the nightmare Emlyn had been running from, and his terror was palpable.

The accented voice in the van was very bad news, Shaun knew. It was confirmation that they were in the company of notoriously merciless men, whose reputations for barbarism had been well-earned.

Was this how it ended? Would he and Emlyn be dead by morning?

Stop that. There is no 'me and Emlyn'.

His mind now flitted through a picture book of similar crises he'd been through – running from neo-Nazis through Soho after a demo. Relocating to Cornwall for a week after the security services had picked up his name on Irish Republican 'chatter'. The malevolent glares of Millwall supporters in a pub in Deptford, as his cover story fell apart around him.

Was he in more danger now than he had been on any of those occasions? It was likely. But as rationally as he could, Shaun came to the conclusion that he probably wouldn't be treated too harshly. Marku knew who he was. His civilian status would surely count in his favour.

Emlyn, however, was not in remotely the same boat.

Time becomes impossible to measure when one is in a traumatic situation. It bends under duress. So Shaun didn't know if they'd been on the road for ten minutes or twenty by the time the van stopped. Emlyn was removed first, giving a low moan as he was hauled onto a gravel path.

As Shaun disembarked, four large hands clutching at his clothing, he knew they had left the city behind. The breeze was stronger across open ground, and the air fresher.

Saddleworth Moor would make the most sense. Shaun hoped he was wrong. This place had an ugly resonance to any Mancunian, and it gave Shaun the creeps. It was the burial site of murdered children, at least one of them as yet unlocated, dumped here by Hindley and Brady in the second half of the last century.

It was not a place that promised anything but the bleakest of outcomes. Shaun's mother lived on the edge of the moor. How close was she to him, right at this moment? She would be leafing through a historical romance borrowed from Oldham library about now, oblivious to her son's ordeal.

A shove in the back, and Shaun stumbled forward. Every part of him now hurt – the body's painkilling reaction to the beating he had taken was wearing off.

Within ten paces, there was an amber light seeping through the material that covered his face, and the breeze had disappeared abruptly. The acoustics of his footfall had changed, too. He was evidently now indoors.

≈

The silence had lasted five minutes or so. Shaun and Emlyn had been placed, sat down, side by side. There was the vague odour of mildew and earth. Neither captive risked a word, or even a movement.

This was valuable thinking time. Shaun had by now convinced himself he had the resources to survive this. He could save himself. There would be an effective ploy somewhere in his brain, and he needed to locate it and bring it into the open as quickly as he could.

How had he got here? O'Hare was involved, he thought. Men like that could be bought cheaply, egged on by threats and promises. He had likely been the informant. Shaun could easily have been followed to work after the pick-up this morning, and then to 44 North Road, and from there to meeting Emlyn at the Vale. He never even considered it a possibility he might be tailed.

Shaun now recalled an hour he spent years ago with a captive from the Iraq war, an almost absurdly dashing RAF pilot who'd been shot down near Basra and captured. He had said to Shaun, with a quivering voice, that he wished he'd known how to respond properly to being taken hostage.

The man knew now what he hadn't known then. There was only one chance you had to avoid severe punishment in an abduction scenario. Don't fight. Be a victim. Playing the hard man does not end well.

Shaun and Emlyn's assailants had spent themselves relatively quickly at Clayton Vale, having given fierce treatment to their two targets. Resistance by the pair would only have guaranteed a harsher punishment.

Shaun had done the right thing by adopting a passive response. And it made sense now for he and Emlyn to act as if they were already defeated.

Shaun now risked a muttered word of advice to his co-hostage.

"Don't fight, Emlyn."

Someone nearby moved closer. He expected another blow and screwed up his eyes in anticipation. But to Shaun's surprise, the hood was now removed from his head.

They were in a basement. A single bare bulb hung from the ceiling, and aside from the two creaking wooden dining chairs he and Emlyn had been positioned into, the room was empty of furniture. Stone walls and mildewed wooden beams.

Leaning against the far wall was Arjan Marku. That was no surprise. Shaun recognized the two Albanians from the snooker club, too, and another man whose face was new to him. This third man bore a reasonable resemblance to Benito Mussolini, thought Shaun, with his doughy neck and jutting chin.

Marku had a dark swathe of stubble across his jawline that hadn't been there the week before. His buzz cut had grown out a little, making his appearance less severe. The tan suit was replaced by a sweater and jeans.

He had a hint of military correctness about him now, and Shaun could envisage him in fatigues, assembling a rifle or driving a Jeep. Was that his provenance? Albanian Forces?

Do they even have Forces in Albania?

Shaun glanced across at Emlyn, whose head was bowed. Shaun hoped he was in better shape than Emlyn was, given what he saw of the poor man's face. It was bruised and swollen almost beyond recognition, with wide, purple welts on his cheekbones. Shaun's own injuries felt less severe.

Marku took a couple of paces forward and seemed to be sizing up his captives. Eventually, he addressed Shaun.

"I am sorry for the violence, Shaun. I know it is not... your way."

Shaun shrugged, as if he had understood the necessity for it all along. Arjan smiled.

"I can make sure there is no more for you. If I get what I need."

132

Drawing exactly the wrong sort of attention at exactly the wrong time, Emlyn whimpered at this. He drew Arjan's gaze.

"Emlyn. Your friends have been looking all over for you."

"Fuck off, spic" came the reply, barked furiously through blood and saliva and swollen tissue.

One of Marku's cronies took a half-step in Emlyn's direction, but was halted by a gesture from the boss. There seemed little point subjecting him to any further punishment – the condition of his face couldn't possibly be made any worse.

Don't fight. Play dead.

"We can still get along, Emlyn. Your friends all come to work for me. But if you don't want, that's fine. You can go back to your life. But you need to tell me where it is. If you let me know where, I can take you home."

Where what is?

Emlyn began to sob again. Shaun's mind was clearing after the last half-hour's adrenalin storm. Whatever Arjan wanted, Shaun could honestly deny all knowledge of it. He had no idea what the man was asking for.

Arjan continued, bending his knees a little to take himself down to Emlyn's slumped position.

"No? You have no information for me?"

He looked on Emlyn with, it seemed to Shaun, an expression of pity. He then looked to both of his men for a suggestion as to what should happen next.

Shaun had to do whatever he could to stop what was coming. Emlyn was already in a dreadful condition, and to abuse him further might prove irrevocable. Shaun intervened, with the first thing that came into his head.

"Did you put Peter Garton in jail?"

Marku looked back to Shaun.

"Why you ask me this? Garton is your friend also?"

"No" said Shaun. "He claims he was framed. I just want to know if he's told me the truth."

Arjan nodded, and paused. Then he moved closer, and leant in.

133

"Do you know where it is?"

"Where what is?" replied Shaun.

The interrogator considered this response for a moment.

"OK. I am sorry gentlemen."

A table was brought into the room by one of the men. It was the kind that might be set out at a jumble sale - folding A-frame legs and a Formica top. This was set in front of the captives with each of them at opposite ends.

Mussolini, who it now seemed had the most unpleasant face of all of them, brought in a roll of masking tape. The wide, heavy sort, used by tradesmen.

The fuck is this now?

"Dora" uttered the man in Shaun's direction.

Shaun stared back at him blankly.

How am I supposed to know what -

"Dora" he said, once again.

Arjan intervened.

"Give him your hand."

Oh Christ.

Shaun looked up at Arjan. Why would he offer this man a body part? What for? As he ruminated on the instruction, a fist connected with the side of his head, at the temple, and his brain fizzed momentarily. Someone in the room possessed a serious right hook.

Emlyn intervened: "He's nowt to do with it. He knows nowt."

This didn't seem to change anything at all.

By the time Shaun had regained his equilibrium and his head had stopped swirling, his left hand was taped to the table from the wrist upwards, and was immobilised. Only the tips of his fingers were visible.

To Shaun's left, Emlyn was attempting to repel the two guards as they pinned down his right hand in the same manner as Shaun's. It took them several more blows than Shaun had needed in order to ensure compliance.

Don't fight.

Soon, both men had one hand taped to the table.

Arjan spoke.

"One of you knows where it is. Or maybe both of you. All you have to do is tell me, and we can stop. Shake hands like English gentlemen and go home."

Shaun now noticed, in the left hand of Mussolini, a pair of steel pincers – the sort that might be used by a carpenter. They had sharp blades that curved round to meet one another when closed.

This disturbing development created unpalatable pictures in Shaun's imagination. His friend on the Force, Ken Cooper, had related some of the horrors these men were willing to carry out. Shaun could feel his pulse coursing through his body. Sweat was now moistening his forehead.

This was of a different order to the everyday kind of anxiety he felt so regularly, and the rising panic he had learned to quell. It was real fear, which grips at the guts and blinds the mind. This was the fear of death, rather than of mere madness.

Stay calm. Think clearly.

He looked across to Emlyn again, and noted a determination on the face of his fellow captive. He clearly still had some energy left to resist with. They hadn't quite broken him yet.

Shaun's mind was foraging eagerly for a way out of this, before events became gruesome. And that might only be minutes away.

Arjan Marku wanted something – Shaun didn't know what, but his strong hunch was that Emlyn had it. Whether or not he would talk he couldn't guess, but Shaun couldn't allow the poor man to be mutilated or tortured. Whatever Shaun needed to do or say to prevent any further escalation, he would do it and say it.

The pincers closed in around the end of Emlyn's little finger. He moaned, low to start with but rising in intensity as the blades parted and were placed against his fingernail.

No no no no no.

"Stop" yelled Shaun. "Stop it. Wait."

135

The room froze for a second. Then Mussolini's proud chin tilted upwards and left, towards Shaun. All eyes were on him.

"I've got it. I know where it is."

The pincers were withdrawn.

Arjan moved closer.

"What is it you've got, Shaun?"

Good question. Shaun had no idea. The panicked gambit would be scuppered almost before it had begun.

Fuck.

Anyone looking at Emlyn Parry right now could not have reasonably expected anything coherent to come from him. What he'd endured for the last thirty minutes would, surely, have rendered his logical mind immobile.

Not quite.

"He's got the key" slurred Emlyn.

"The key. I've got it" added Shaun.

Arjan Marku looked doubtful. A smirk had formed at the corners of his mouth, indicative of his scepticism.

"Why?" he asked. "Why do you have it, and not him?"

Again, this was incisive. Rationalising this was going to be difficult.

Shaun now employed a well-worn tactic of his: when lying, include as many true details as you can. Only change what you absolutely have to.

There is a particular tactility to the truth, a tangibility, which is hard to manufacture. Real events 'feel' authentic, somehow. There was, at this point, no other option worth considering than the following.

"I went to see Garton in prison. The key was down his sock. The guard left the room for a minute and he gave it me." Shaun gave this story a downcast tone, as if the game was up, framing it as a defeat.

"The prison guard left? Why did he do that?" enquired Arjan.

"Peter told him to" came the truthful reply.

Arjan laughed out loud. He could clearly envisage the exact exchange Shaun had described, and it seemed to make sense to him. People usually did precisely what Peter Garton told them to do, he knew that much.

"Garton said he didn't trust any of his people with the key. He thought they might bring it to you" continued Shaun.

This amused the Albanian further. The idea that Emlyn Parry, a man who had displayed such fortitude in rebuffing the advances of the new regime in town, would have ever been this amenable, was wide of the mark. The others, yes. They had switched their allegiance with no more thought than a man would give to changing his socks.

"Well, that would have been easier for everybody" said Arjan.

As Shaun was reminding himself not to overreach, not to elaborate further without good reason, Emlyn interrupted.

"I might as well have given it to him, now you've fucking rolled over" he said to Shaun, with convincing venom.

This was good work. Through his ringing, blood-clogged ears, Emlyn had picked up the thread of Shaun's thinking and was playing along. This could get them both out of here if they played it right.

"Yes, Emlyn. This has all been very unnecessary. Your friend Shaun owes you an apology" said Marku.

Shaun hung his head in mock penitence. What a fucking charade, he thought. Sat bleeding and bruised in a cottage on Saddleworth Moor with one hand taped to a table, pretending to feel guilty for something that he hadn't done.

"But this is good" said Arjan. "Your friend is trying to save you."

Arjan now fixed Shaun with great focus.

"So. Where do we go to collect the key?" he asked.

"I'll take you" said Shaun.

The rejoinder to this was a forceful one.

"No. You and Emlyn, you will stay here. Tell me where to go, and I will send someone. Then once I have the key we can take you home."

Neither of us are going home. Pull the other one.

Shaun replied emphatically.

"Absolutely not. We're not staying here any longer. We need to be out in the open when I hand you the key. So I know you'll let me go."

"You don't trust me, Shaun?"

"Of course I fucking don't."

A frown from Arjan Marku.

"Shaun. Your tone is not pleasant."

"It's the only one you're getting. We all go together to get the key. That's it. Take it or leave it."

Where Shaun had found such boldness from, he had no idea. Perhaps the righteous outrage at the treatment he and Emlyn had received was beginning to surface.

There was something about the gang dynamic Shaun objected to. One man was paying money to others to do the unpalatable on his behalf. Marku hadn't lifted a finger himself in the assault, the coward. Garton was the same, he realised – hands clean amidst the carnage he provoked. All the benefits, none of the risk. Nice work if you could get it.

With a look of distaste, Arjan scanned the room, catching the eye of each of his men in turn. The last of these was the man who held the pincers. Arjan shrugged slightly in his direction, as if he were bowing to an inevitable outcome.

The man moved in quickly. He placed the pincers over Shaun's little finger. Instinctively, Shaun suspected this was going to be an episode in brinkmanship. A last chance to comply. Arjan would be expecting him to fold. Perhaps he would have to admit the lie and take whatever punishment was deemed to fit.

These assumptions meant he was unprepared for what happened next.

The man with the pincers brought the flat of his hand down on their levers with force. The blades, trying to meet one another, sliced clean through the tip of Shaun's finger, about halfway down the nail.

The first Shaun knew of what had happened was the two-centimetre piece of him that snapped into the air and performed a perfect parabola before landing on the floor five feet away.

Shaun screamed in shock, then again in the profound horror at what other treatment might now be forthcoming, and third time in searing pain. White hot pain.

"I'll stay" yelled Emlyn. "He can go with you, and I'll stay here. Just fucking stop, you bastards."

Emlyn Parry had never been able to cope with the sight of blood. Having spoken out in Shaun's defence, he proceeded to vomit copiously, spattering Benito Mussolini's shoes as he did so.

≈

Contrary to the opinion of his captives, Arjan Marku was not an unreasonable man. Emlyn's idea seemed like a compromise he could live with. Especially as it would lead to the recovery of the item he so badly wanted.

It was agreed that Shaun could lead the way, but Emlyn would remain in the cellar until the key had been delivered to Albanian hands.

But Shaun could not deliver it. He knew nothing about a key, and could only extend the artifice until such time as he might escape from these men.

Maybe he could scream for help at a passer-by once they got somewhere populated. Or there might be a millisecond of inattention from Marku's heavies, allowing him to run. Emlyn had saved him, for perhaps another thirty minutes at least. And possibly at the expense of his own life, which might well end once Shaun's fiction could no longer be sustained.

Or would Emlyn talk? Did he know the whereabouts of this key that had been spoken of, and push this mob as far as he could before divulging its location? And once he had, would that save him? Or might it be decided that the situation would be tidier with the key pocketed and Emlyn gone anyway?

These possibilities swam around Shaun's jolted brain. He couldn't unpick them from one another, let alone decide which were most likely. But he knew Emlyn Parry had bought him time. It was a priceless window for Shaun, and one he intended to utilise.

The now-only-partially-complete finger was wrapped tightly in the masking tape that had been used to secure Shaun's hand. An inadequate dressing, of course, but it was marginally better than nothing. It had stemmed much of the bleeding but none of the pain.

His entire hand pulsed in time to his heartbeat, sending fibrous, urgent, electric surges to the point of maximum nerve exposure. He shivered and held back shell-shocked tears as three of the men discussed his imminent fate in their mother tongue.

As a conclusion was reached, the hood was produced once again. The tallest of the three men turned to Shaun and spoke matter-of-factly, as if he were addressing a fare he'd picked up in his taxi on a Sunday lunchtime.

"OK Shaun. Where we go?"

Shaun had to think. And fast.

"Salford" he replied, for the want of anywhere better.

17

*I*n the back of the van he had been abducted in an hour previously, Shaun lay prostrate with a hood over his head and a knee in his back, once again. This was becoming a very uncomfortable habit.

His entire left arm was aflame with pain. It sourced itself as a twinge in his elbow and intensified the closer it got to the site of his injury.

A blazingly obvious realisation had presented itself to him now. The kinds of things Shaun had written about for thirty years with such clarity and skill, the events that had earned him his living, were real. He was no longer at one remove from what he related in print - it was happening at the front and centre of his own existence.

And it felt far worse than he had ever guessed it could. The possibility of a pointless, violent death - now, today, or tomorrow - was utterly disabling, and horrifying beyond the sum of all his previous experience.

This was terror. Existential horror. He had described it often from his imaginings. But this was what it really meant.

There might still be a reprieve, he knew. For the rest of his days – and he hoped with all his thumping heart there would be some – he may yet be able to say blithely "I was tortured by the Albanian Mafia once" and hold up his trimmed digit as evidence. That would be a tremendous wheeze, a lifelong badge of his adventurer's spirit, and he prayed to be allowed to indulge in it by surviving whatever was to come.

The van trundled through the countryside. Shaun knew they were in a rural setting – there were no junctions to be stopped at or the sound of vehicles passing in the other direction. It had to be Saddleworth Moor.

On the basis he was right, he'd told his captors he needed to go to Salford Quays, on the far side of the city. It was a longer journey than to home or the office, and he had promised Arjan the key could be found there. If he wanted to avoid the severest consequence, he knew he couldn't afford to actually arrive in Salford. There, Shaun would run out of road.

Five minutes after being hustled out from the basement, into the cold air momentarily and then into the van again, Shaun had got his bearings with a little clarity.

There were three men in the vehicle with him – the driver, the man kneeling on his back, and another in the rear of the van. He had clocked by its sound as it closed the whereabouts of the latch to the rear door of the van – clean in the centre of the double doors. And he knew – he hoped - those doors were now eight inches or so away from his face.

Every hundred yards or so, the van would travel over a rise in the road and lift its cargo from the floor slightly on the way down again. Whenever this happened, the force applied by the knee at his back waned for a second, as gravity was counteracted momentarily.

Shaun now waited, breathing in shallow gasps, with every ounce of his consciousness funnelled into a single course of action.

You can't wait 'til Salford.

Do it now.

The moment came.

A bump in the road lifted the Albanian's knee a fraction, and Shaun reached forward, blindly, in the hope he was positioned in the expected spot. He folded his body into a foetal shape as he did so, sliding from under the weight of the man on top of him – a weight diminished for a brief moment.

He was where he had expected to be. His right hand felt metal. The latch on the rear van doors was pulled down and opened in a split second. The man on top of him responded instantly, grabbing for the door and taking his attention from his prisoner momentarily. Before Shaun could be restrained again he had squirmed free from his captor and rolled himself to the rear of the van.

Despite a desperate grab at the last second from his captor, Shaun successfully flung himself from the van and onto the tarmacked road.

One of the men in the van began immediately banging on the partition between himself and the cab.

"Ndalo! Ndalo!"

The driver, not fully understanding the urgency of the situation from his detached position at the front of the van, slowed the vehicle rather more gracefully than was appropriate, pulling into a lay-by before bringing it completely to a halt. The stop had taken six or seven seconds, which was enough to put more than a hundred yards between the van and Shaun.

Shaun came to rest on the road. There was, for a moment, silence.

The hood that had been placed over his head was long gone, coming off on his second or third bounce along the hard road. He knew his skin had been shredded from his extremities, and this would soon be the locus of yet another agony. He felt a dull but significant ache in his left thighbone.

As he dragged himself to his feet from the tarmac, he looked back at the white Ford Transit he had just thrown himself out of.

Three figures had now got out. The red lights at the rear meant he could make out their hulking forms, but he wasn't entirely sure they'd seen him yet, further down the road as he was, and in the black of the night.

Shaun looked leftwards towards open country – the moonrock of the moors – and then right. Trees, thirty yards away, murky and forbidding.

He picked himself up from the tarmac and ran towards the woods as fast as his beaten body would allow.

≈

In his first few minutes of freedom, Shaun made blundering progress through the closely packed trees. The moon was obscured by rainclouds, and there was no source of ambient light to assist his journey.

He made a conscious decision not to turn around to check if he was being chased. The density of the woods meant he couldn't have upped his speed even if the situation had warranted it, so the distance between him and his captors was an irrelevance.

To city-dwellers, it's hard to describe the true character of genuine darkness. Urbanites rarely experience it, so pervasive are their sources of artificial light. And they have to move through it at speed even more infrequently.

Shaun took a number of sizeable thwacks from unseen branches as he bullied his way into the depths of the wood. His own breathing became a sort of metronome, a rhythmic point of focus that gave him a strange kind of comfort. Not for the first time tonight, he could taste metal in his saliva. He recognised it as a symptom of panic.

Think Shaun. Think. What happens now?

But he couldn't organise his thoughts to follow one another. His mind had been spun in too many directions, too forcibly, for there to be any logic left in it. He ploughed on, his face and limbs taking the brunt of the punishment from the branches that lashed away at him.

When he was some way into the wood, Shaun's foot hooked itself around a root, or dead stump, or some other treacherous appendage. He tumbled forward, landing heavily on his hands – the left of which let him know in no uncertain terms how much it objected to further abuse.

Prone on the forest floor for a moment, he clutched the arm on his injured side. It throbbed in a terrible, relentless rhythm. The ground was fusty, and the smell of it reminded him of his mother's greenhouse.

He turned to look back for the first time, and through gaps in the undergrowth he could see a little of what he'd left behind him.

Pleasingly, he'd travelled a greater distance than he'd thought. The van was further off than he had expected. It had been manoeuvred across both lanes so that the headlamps shone into the trees. Thankfully, not in his immediate direction.

His tormentors had spaced themselves out along the road at intervals of maybe five or six van lengths. One of the men was speaking urgently into a mobile phone while the others peered into the dark, on the lookout for a sign of their escapee.

He resisted the feeling that he might have made a successful escape. It was too early for assumptions of that kind, and they were dangerous. But the further he moved into the trees, the harder he would be to find, given the head start he'd been afforded. Shaun felt a renewed energy, a fresh vigour that defied his physical state.

Keep moving.

He continued to put as much distance as he could between himself and the Albanians. There would be a village, or a farmhouse, or maybe even the outskirts of Oldham on the other side of this forest.

He hoped the men weren't intent enough to hang around until daybreak, when the job of finding him would become significantly easier for them. At first light, when he'd be able to see that the coast was clear, he would make a dash from the treeline to open ground and avail himself of whatever help he could persuade a stranger to give him.

It was both comforting and alarming to know that his mother was probably no more than three or four miles away, snoozing away in the hinterland between urban Oldham and the wilds of the moor.

But he would steer clear of her homestead, Bluebell Farm, on the off-chance he may lead others there unintentionally.

And Emer Mullin would surely never recover from the shock of seeing her only son in this condition. That trauma would have to fall to persons as yet unknown.

After five more minutes forging a difficult path through the tight foliage, Shaun could no longer see the road behind him. The forest had closed in on him suddenly, and what little light there had been was all but gone.

He was blanketed from the world by pure dark, and felt as completely alone as he ever had done. The forest felt tight now, breathing him in and enfolding him fully. He was grateful for it, and began to feel something akin to relief. Heavy foliage parted in front of him more easily than before, as he began to find some sort of 'feel' for the forest. It was less alien to him with every passing moment. His senses had adapted a little to its particular challenges, and it felt less treacherous now.

Don't stop. You can't stop.

Shaun began to consider his physical condition. The finger was an obvious and significant problem, but it wasn't going to hinder his progress in any meaningful way. It was just pain. Short-term, it could be overcome.

His thigh was likely only bruised. The blows he had taken to the head earlier on were old news by now, and their effects had stabilized.

A new source of discomfort had now presented itself. His ribs, on the left side. He wasn't sure how he'd injured them, but his exit from the van was the most likely culprit.

Overall, he judged himself to be just about in working order. He could function for a few hours yet. It would hurt – with every step, with every breath - but he could do it.

It could be worse.

Keep going.

As Shaun continued to navigate his path through the woods, something drew his eyes to the right. A flash of illumination, perhaps a mile away, through the trees. It flickered, zoetrope-like, and Shaun realised he was closer to the outer flank of the forest than he'd expected. He could see now that the trees began to thin out fifty yards or so from where he stood.

Headlights, travelling along what Shaun reckoned to be the Holmfirth Road. The speed this vehicle was travelling at suggested at once that it wasn't driven by a local pootling home, or students off out into Manchester.

Reinforcements.

Suddenly frantic again, Shaun needed a clearer sense of where he was. The proximity of the forest's edge had surprised him, and he felt less secure in the bosom of the woods now.

He looked at his immediate surroundings. All he could make out was the corpse of a fallen ash tree right in front of him. He stood on top of it, raising himself a couple of feet from the forest floor. Then, utilising the dense branches, he began to clamber upwards.

It was awkward, unstable work, made considerably more difficult by the aching in every part of his body. But he managed to shimmy and claw himself free of the forest floor.

At an elevation of perhaps fifteen feet, Shaun looked roadwards. The foliage was thinner at this height, and he could make out the Transit van – lights still blazing into the trees – maybe half a mile away.

The speeding vehicle approached the van and came to an abrupt halt beside it. Someone exited the driver's side and Shaun thought he could hear raised voices carried on the breeze.

The rear passenger side door to the saloon car – now visible to Shaun in the umbra of the van's headlights – was opened. Shaun couldn't make out what had emerged, but someone or something had come from within.

Then he heard it. It was unmistakable.

The deep, resonant barking of a dog.

≈

It would be a stretch call Arjan Marku's dog Emina a pet. He didn't treat her as one, keeping her outdoors and feeding her on the scraps from his table. There was no sleeping-at-the-foot-of-the-master's-bed for Emina.

Arjan regarded her instead as an asset to his business, just like the men he kept on his payroll. And in fact, Emina was a priceless employee, used by Arjan and his gang as an enforcer. There are very few men who do not blanche when confronted by a slavering Doberman of Emina's size – her function was to change minds, which she did on a regular basis.

Once Emina was released from the back seat of his car, Arjan wasted no time. He pulled a plastic bag from his pocket, opened it, and introduced to dog to its contents – the tip of Shaun Mullin's finger. He held the bag up to Emina's nose, and said "Sulmojnë, Emina. Sulmojnë."

An order to attack, which the animal recognised. She began to leap and snarl at the prospect of the chase.

Arjan's hand came off her collar, and Emina bolted towards the black woods. The men followed, Arjan with a torch in one hand leading the way.

≈

Shaun had made the assumption he would spend most of the night in

147

the woods, hunkered down somewhere impenetrable, until Marku's gang gave up hope of finding him.

As he saw Emina's muscular frame hurtling in his direction, the parameters of his escape plan changed in an instant. There'd be no hiding from this animal. It was as if it had eyeballed him immediately through the trees. She was half a mile away, but it felt like she had 'locked on'.

Christ, that thing is travelling.

He'd be chased down in two minutes flat if he simply ran. He had to formulate a plan, and right now. He stumbled over, eastwards, to where the trees began to thin.

Get out of the woods.

Urgent thoughts began to pile on top of one another. Shaun tried to give the practical ones his attention and banish the rest. Panic and fear were of no use to him. But banishing them from where they sat, deep in his chest, was impossible.

He knew he couldn't outrun the dog. He couldn't fight it successfully if it was even remotely in the mood for a scrap. And he couldn't hide from it, given the tracking power of a trained hunter like this.

He thought about a weapon. But what was there? He reckoned he had little more than two minutes before the beast caught him up.

Just keep moving.

Aiming for the open space he had seen to his right moments earlier, he burst clear of the treeline.

Suddenly there was night sky above him. And as Shaun hit the outer edge of the forest, he was forced to an abrupt stop.

Shaun found himself at the lip of a reservoir, a couple of hundred yards across. Still, black waters were retained by sheer concrete walls - another three steps and Shaun would have dropped thirty feet down and into the water. From within the woods there was no hint it was even there.

This sudden and beautiful vista contrasted completely with the tight forest he'd been navigating, and it made Shaun gasp momentarily.

If it came to it - if the animal was upon him and ready to attack - Shaun would have to jump. He hoped the dog's determination to complete its mission wouldn't quite be strong enough to follow him in.

There were maybe half a dozen bodies of water like this on the moor. Shaun frantically scanned his memory for any clue as to their construction – if he went in, how could he get out? The walls were sheer, and smooth, if he remembered correctly.

He was breathing hard. He could hear now the disturbance in the woods caused by his pursuer's progress through it. He looked back, but could see nothing.

Thirty seconds? Forty?

He turned to face the water again. The beam from Arjan Marku's distant torchlight played across it for a second.

Branches began to crackle behind him as they were trampled.

Twenty seconds.

His mind fought for a rational decision amid the wildness of his thoughts. What was the course of action that would give him the best odds?

Clothes.

Shaun wrestled his sweater over his head and dropped it at his feet. Then his shoes, jeans and shirt.

The creature in pursuit of him was moving at phenomenal speed, he had seen that. And it was working off of Shaun's scent, hunting down the source as it had obviously been trained to do. That scent now lay partly in a pile of clothes on the ground.

Shaun kicked the bundle of clothes right to the edge of the reservoir, in the process losing a shoe that toppled over into the water.

Naked aside from his boxer shorts and socks, Shaun sprinted back into the trees and hit the ground. It occurred to him that his pale Irish skin, now exposed to the night, made him easier to spot than he had been when wearing a navy sweater.

Bloody Mick complexion. I'm like a beacon out here.

But he'd be found anyway, he knew that, if this instinctive, last-minute plan didn't work. The dog would be on him before he knew much about it. And then what? Would it simply try to keep him there until its master caught up, toying with him like a sheepdog might do with an errant lamb? Or was it trained to unleash its full savagery on its target at once?

Maybe it could be strangled, if the opportunity to grip its throat came about. That was it. However appalling a prospect it was, Shaun would try – unsuccessfully, probably - to throttle the dog. It was an unlikely last resort.

Shaun held his breath and prayed to an entity he had always been sure didn't exist.

Emina was seconds away now from where Shaun lay. The smaller branches in her path snapped as she bolted through, and the thick foliage was brushed aside with every stride.

The dog came into view, springing from the undergrowth ten feet or so from Shaun. She was a big animal, and was moving in great, muscular bounds. Shaun heard her heavy breaths now.

The dog knew her fate at once. She knew from the moment she saw the water that she would overshoot, such was the velocity of her travel. She made a sudden and forlorn attempt to reverse away from the reservoir's edge but had simply picked up too much speed on the approach.

Emina overshot, and yelped in alarm. As she went over the edge of the reservoir, taking Shaun's shirt with her, she scrambled in desperation to find a foothold on the concrete walls. But of course there was none.

She plummeted out of Shaun's view.

Yes. Fuck off. Yes.

By the time he heard the dog's contact with the surface of the water, Shaun was already upright and on the move. His remaining clothes would stay abandoned at the reservoir's edge, a decoy as to his whereabouts. Arjan might assume the dog had followed him into the chasm.

Inexplicably, Shaun began to laugh. The dog's fraught scrambling had brought to mind the cartoons of his childhood - Wile Coyote treading air above the Grand Canyon, maybe - and he'd found Elmina's mimicking of this disproportionately funny. He heaved a dozen or more big, heavy exhalations as he ploughed his way back into the forest.

Marku's torchlight, which would flash across the sky every few seconds, was still some distance away. Shaun could make good ground before they got here.

With Emina's barking resounding against the walls of the reservoir, Shaun was enveloped by nature once again. One more hurdle overcome. One more step towards an escape. Back to the solace of the trees.

He soon had his hysteria back in check. The rush from his near miss with Elmina had subsided, and the pain was returning. It was keener this time than before, as if it had worked out the most dastardly route through his nervous system to the sites of greatest discomfort.

After a few minutes he heard the distant commotion made by the gang and their leader as they reached the site of his clothing. Elmina's barking had led them there.

Shaun had no idea as to the animal's fate – he hoped she would have been able to swim to part of the wall where there was an escape point, but from what he recalled about the construction of these pits, that was wishful thinking. His brief view of this one had suggested no way out.

He tracked the light from the torch for a while as he put more and more distance between himself and it. It looked as if the chasing group were moving in the opposite direction, towards the far side of the reservoir. Within ten minutes or so he could have howled at the top of his voice and they would not have heard him. His escape from Arjan Marku – at least for tonight – was almost complete.

≈

For the next hour, Shaun's biggest enemy was the cold. He tried to move at a brisk enough pace to keep his breathing quick and his core temperature up. But now the extreme discomfort from his injuries had begun to swell. His body was a wreck, and he felt less confident in its ability to carry him to the far side of the woods.

For the first time since he tumbled from the van, he realised that his mind was in an equally debilitated state.

He needed his medication. Or, come to think of it, something stronger that might normally only be prescribed to the chronically deranged. Anything that would remove the pressure that had formed inside his skull, pushing against the back of his eyes. His thoughts were becoming splintered in response to his panic, as they crashed into the immovable object of his subconscious mind.

Silence and darkness were not his mind's allies now. They seemed to allow greater space for it to wander into, fragmented and disordered. He needed to keep focused on a single aim. Deal only with whatever was next. Remind himself that this would pass.

Shaun began to mutter reassurances to himself as he wandered. Vague, morale-boosting platitudes that meant nothing and had no effect, other than providing a sort of rhythm his legs could keep time to. At least there was time. He could hold onto that.

Time heals all wounds.

He stumbled frequently, and felt now as if he might topple over with every step, such was his light-headedness. There was a draining of the vigour from his muscles, and he felt tremors in his thighs and torso.

I am exactly where I am meant to be.

I am exactly where I am meant to be.

His every heartbeat resounded in his ears. He felt drunk. Drugged.

The motivational phrases he whispered began to adopt a kind of musical cadence in time with his footsteps. Songs from the old country – the country where he'd never even lived – began to drift from his mouth as whispered incantations.

Come out ye Black and Tans, come and fight me like a man…

Who the fuck are Glasgow Rangers? Who the fuck are Glasgow Rangers?

These were soon joined by half-remembered snippets of the liturgy forced upon him as a child.

Through this holy anointing may the Lord in his love and mercy help you with the grace of the Holy Spirit.

Then snatches of jokes, truisms his father had utilised, and Anglo-Irish proverbs. Cartoon voices. Disembodied voices.

These were manifestations of childhood – expressions of an age he barely remembered; mantras handed down to him from a culture removed from its source and transplanted to England. Their resurgence in his brain represented a desperate desire for safety. A respite from fear.

Holy Mary, helper of the helpless...

After a while, the songs and the thoughts and the words and the feelings couldn't be kept apart from one another. The walls in his mind were crumbling, and this brought about a cacophonous medley in his head.

Things come and things go, only I am constant -

The famous Glasgow Rangers went to Rome to see the Pope, and this is what he said: FUCK OFF -

Soft the wind blew down the glade and shook the golden barley –

Two nuns in the bath one says to the other –

And I saw a pale horse with all of hell following on behind –

Rain down on me from a great height, from a great height –

Twenty minutes after his escape from Elmina, he had hit a wall. His physical capacity had plummeted alarmingly, and soon he could barely summon the energy required for each step. His legs were quivering and breathing now required effort. Every yard gained felt harder than the last.

He was in pain. Pain that had matured minute by minute, to bury itself deeper into him, more profoundly. It was burning him from the inside out.

He now heard the voice of Madeleine March, clear and pure, for the first time in decades. He snorted with laughter at the accuracy of his brain's impersonation of her.

She exhorted him to rest. To sink into it. To comply with nature.

Stop, Shaun.

Just fall where you are.

Wait for sleep.

That would be relief. There had been no sign of torchlight for a while. He was free of the monsters that had chased him here. He could be free of the panic and the pain, too.

Therefore, my brethren, you also were made to die...

But the cold had now penetrated to his very core. Through the fog in his head, he knew how dangerous that was. He had to keep moving.

Onwards.

Forwards.

But he couldn't.

God loves his children, yeah!

But he must.

Madeleine spoke again.

Lay down with me.

Lie here, Shaun.

No. He must keep on, until there was not an ounce of consciousness left in him.

That's all, folks!

Until the very end, whatever and whenever that may be.

It's not the size of the dog in the fight that counts, it's the size of the fight in the dog.

18

*K*eith Todd *was an uncomplicated man* with a simple, repetitive life. Since his wife died in the early 2000s, Keith had operated the Lonely Crow café on Holmfirth Road single-handedly. Almost every hour of every week was spent within its confines – at work downstairs serving up toasted sandwiches and coffees, then up the worn staircase to the two-bedroomed apartment above the café once the doors had been secured for the night.

His existence was undemanding and stress-free. A couple of dozen hikers, fishermen and delivery drivers would pass through each day, usually fairly cheerful sorts. Aside from a few run-of-the-mill difficulties – an emergency drive to the cash-and-carry for coffee beans, or the A-board in the yard outside blowing over - nothing ever really happened to Keith. He liked it that way, and had in fact engineered his life so that it presented him with as few challenges as possible.

So Keith was ill-prepared for a visitor calling in the middle of the night. This kind of adventure was exceptionally rare, and not at all welcome. A heavy thumping against the café's back door had woken him at 1.15am.

As he climbed out of bed and into his dressing gown, he wondered why it was the back door taking a hammering rather than the front. The rear of the café couldn't be seen from the road, and any visitor would need to travel through the garden at the side of the property to get to it. This meant it probably wasn't the Police. Perhaps it was a neighbour from one of the smattering of cottages on the wild hills behind.

Something had 'happened', he surmised.

He tiptoed down the stairs, wove his way past the silhouettes of chairs and tables, and pulled the door ajar to look into the property's rear porch.

At his back door was a man, almost completely naked, caked in blood and shivering with an alarming violence.

"Bloody hell" exclaimed Keith. This was most definitely not a run-of-the-mill Tuesday. His instinct was to blot it out, pretend it wasn't there, to close the door again and have nothing to do with any of it.

But then... would he have to answer for a dead body on his doorstep? Would the café be cordoned off while the Coroner investigated?

Perhaps he should help.

The bloodied man was swaying to and fro and side to side, as if under the influence of something he was long past being able to control.

He reached out an arm to steady himself and leant against the door. As he touched it he pushed it open further, then teetered forward, unable to maintain his balance any longer.

Shaun Mullin's last memory of this terrible night was the black-and-white checked flooring of the café's kitchen rising to meet him.

≈

Conference Room One at Manchester Central Police Station was rammed. This morning's meeting was compulsory for all Officers on duty.

At the behest of an increasingly grumpy Chief Commissioner Watts, the hunt for the evidence needed to put Peter Garton away for the longest stretch possible was being ramped up. DIs Pitt, Chinn and Daley were entrusted with briefing the rank and file.

To that end, a PowerPoint had been prepared (beat Officers knew that plain clothes were serious when that happened) and was now beamed onto a large screen at one end of the room. The two hundred coppers in attendance fell quiet as Graham Daley strode in front of the screen.

"Morning all. Thanks for coming in. As you can see..."

He gestured to the screen as DI Chinn brought up slide one.

"...we're here to discuss Peter Garton. Specifically, where his fucking money is. We need proceeds of crime in order to shore up his prosecution, and at the moment we've got nowt more than a bit of spending money."

The slide showed a diagram composed of silhouetted ClipArt heads-and-shoulders. A lone figure at the top was labelled 'Garton'. Six figures in a row beneath him – Phillipson, Rossi, Yardley, Parry, Barber and Kerimoglu – sat above a few dozen unnamed persons. Rather cruelly, Craig Phillipson's name had been scored through. Emlyn Parry's had a question mark beside it.

"We've found it useful to think of Garton's enterprise like a fast-food franchise. It's structured in exactly the same way."

Garton was the founder and owner of the business. The six named 'franchisees' each looked after a specific district (the City Centre, Salford, Cheetham Hill, Withington, Stockport and Oldham). These men each had responsibility for a brigade of half-a-dozen street dealers.

DI Pitt chipped in. "And by the way, we'll be nicking these known associates fairly imminently. Phillipson's no longer with us, obviously, and Parry is still AWOL, but we've got eyes on the other four."

Daley continued as if Pitt hadn't spoken at all.

"The interesting bit is this. The activities these people carry out do not overlap. Not at all, as far as we've been able to tell. So the smack-runners in Oldham have no knowledge of what the pill-peddlers in Cheetham Hill do. It's clever. It gives the impression of it not being joined up."

Daley went on to explain that, to external observers, the Garton 'empire' didn't exist. An operation of around forty individuals looked to the untrained eye like unconnected dots placed randomly on the map.

And atop the cake sat Peter Garton, largely uninvolved with anything that might look like criminality. Fully aware of how the authorities got Al Capone, he paid his taxes, his parking fines and his bills.

The straightforward process by which he had made his fortune was long-established by now.

"What this means for you" continued Daley, "is that your focus needs to be local. It's kebab shops, parks, community centres. Talk to anybody and everybody on your patch."

"Sorry DI Daley" said Pitt. "If I may."

Seeing as he'd asked so nicely, Daley deferred.

"Garton's pubs are important" Pitt said.

Garton's drinking establishments – resolutely spit-and-sawdust boozers - laundered some of the cash from narcotics by absorbing it into his lawful earnings. But they couldn't absorb all of it without some very suspicious profit levels emerging. There had to be some residue.

Financial Forensics had said that Garton was pocketing about three hundred grand a year from his drugs business. That was personal profit, after the cost of buying and selling and paying his dealers was deducted.

"If there's one of his boozers on your beat, find out as much as you can about it. Who goes in, who avoids it, late-night lock-ins, early morning deliveries. Anything."

PC Kylie Charles was the first to brave a raised hand. "What is it we're looking for?" she asked.

"Information. On Garton or any of the six captains. In particular Parry, who seems to have evaporated. He is of particular interest."

DI Chinn now joined the conversation.

"I'd like to throw another name into the ring" he said. "Shaun Mullin."

"Oh aye" said Daley. "Shaun Mullin works for *The Herald*. He's been to see Garton in prison, for reasons we've not been able to fathom. And we're getting plenty of gossip that he's thick with Parry. He may not have done anything wrong, but he's a bit too close for comfort in my view."

Daley was about to discover just how close.

As the three detectives reached the final slide of the presentation and began to wrap the meeting up, Sergeant Mohammed tiptoed in.

Pitt intercepted him as Daley addressed the assembly. Mohammed leant in and whispered earnestly into Pitt's ear for a few seconds.

DI Pitt shot a dark look to DI Chinn.

There had been a development.

19

Shaun didn't wake until lunchtime.

When he did, in a fog of morphine and exhaustion, it took him a full half-minute to recognise his surroundings as a hospital room. By the time he began to orientate himself and play back the events that led him here, nurse Eileen Duplock had already gone to fetch a doctor.

Keith Todd's Nissan Micra had transported a semi-naked man to the A and E at the Royal Oldham Hospital, semi-conscious and life-threateningly cold, at two o'clock in the morning.

Keith didn't hang around for long. This sort of incident was well above his emotional pay grade, and he wanted none of it once he'd helped the man to safety. He had a café to run, so had asked for his spare duvet back from the triage nurse and trundled off sharpish.

Hospital staff had rung the Police at shortly before seven o'clock, once Shaun's injuries had been fully assessed and the likelihood of them being accidental or self-inflicted became nil.

A broken nose, three cracked ribs, a dozen significant contusions and a broad gash on the top of the head that had required four stitches.

And then there was the finger. It was a clean-cut, at least. That made recovery quicker. And it would look neater once it had healed.

Doctor McGough brushed aside the blue curtain and approached Shaun's bed. He spoke with a casual cheerfulness Shaun found reassuring.

"Afternoon Mister Mullin."

Afternoon??

"Who's been in the wars then?"

Shaun became aware now of the bulbous mound of dressings and bandages covering his left hand, which seemed to him excessive. It was as if they had entombed his left mitt with a basketball for company.

He checked for pain. There was none. He was hooked up, via a cannula on top of his right hand, to a drip. Morphine. The bed he lay in was on a ward with others, but was ringed by a privacy curtain for now.

Doctor McGough informed Shaun that he had arrived without any identifying materials – no wallet and no phone – and it had been pure chance that the triage nurse recognised him from his writings in *The Manchester Herald*. A quick Google search had verified his identity.

"Always thought journalism must be a tremendous career" said McGough. "If I had my time again, Mister Mullin…"

He trailed off, lost briefly in what might have been, and then in the information on the chart at the foot of Shaun's bed.

The grass isn't always greener, my friend.

After checking a few numbers on the machine at Shaun's bedside, McGough continued.

"Your family's here. If you're up to it, we can ask them to pop in and see you briefly."

'Family' was a bit of an exaggeration. His blood relatives numbered three.

What was he going to say? How palatable would the facts of the matter be to his mother and sister? They could handle some of it, but not the whole truth.

"Before that, there's a Detective waiting to speak to you. Says he knows you. How do you feel about a quick chat with him? Get it out of the way, and then you can see your mum and your sister. Yes?"

Shaun nodded his assent.

Full transparency wasn't an option with the Police. He realised he could get away with saying nothing, such was his condition. Until an acceptable version of last night's events could be formulated he would remain mute. And even if he did speak out of turn, he could walk it back later under the excuse of his semi-delirium and the morphine fuzz.

Nurse Duplock led Graham Daley into the room. On his way over to the grey plastic chair beside Shaun's bed, he reached out a hand and patted Shaun reassuringly on the toe. It was an odd gesture that spoke of a familiarity Shaun wasn't aware the two of them had.

Daley sat. He wasn't going to push too hard for anything in particular right now – the man lying prone before him was a mess. But he could make a cautious approach for some of the basics and see how far he got.

"Now then Shaun. I know we've antagonised one another from time to time. But I just wanted to say, that is completely irrelevant at the moment. I'm concerned about what's happened to you and all I want to do is get to the bottom of it."

Shaun nodded in appreciation. He hadn't yet spoken since he'd come round, and wasn't confident his mouth could generate a coherent sound.

"I don't know what you've got involved with Shaun, but whatever it is, we can sort it out. Alright? Is there anything you can tell me about last night?"

Shaun now ventured a word. To his slight surprise, it emerged as intended, if a little more quietly.

"Marku."

Daley's eyebrows leapt skywards.

"Marku, did you say? Arjan Marku?"

Shaun nodded.

Graham Daley instantly began typing into his phone. That one word was enough. He knew plenty about Arjan Marku – his officers were looking at him closely for the Craig Phillipson murder, for a start.

Daley had no clue as to the nature of Shaun's involvement with the Albanian, but he immediately told the stricken man this much: there would be an officer present at the door to the ward twenty-four hours a day until Shaun had recovered. Then, there would be a car stationed outside his front door day and night. He would do whatever he needed to do to protect Shaun Mullin. Everyone on the Greater Manchester force would be aware of that responsibility.

Shaun was touched by Daley's concern. The DI had looked genuinely upset on his arrival, and spoke with a hitherto hidden sensitivity. This had the effect of encouraging Shaun to speak further. He would omit anything to do with the passport. And probably the key sought by Marku. For now.

"Emlyn" croaked Shaun.

Daley looked up from his phone screen.

"Emlyn Parry? Do you know where he is, Shaun?"

Shaun nodded.

≈

Within an hour of their boss interviewing Shaun Mullin in his hospital bed, Graham Daley's officers discovered the bloodstained basement of an abandoned cottage on Saddleworth Moor.

There was no Emlyn Parry, alive or dead.

But the blood spill was of a significant volume. If it had all come from the same man, he would at least be severely debilitated. In all likelihood, there had been a killing here.

A dead dog was found floating in the Westing Hew Reservoir, as was a blue corduroy shirt. The remainder of Shaun's clothing was discovered in the trees nearby. What Shaun had shared of his story checked out with no caveats, and Keith Todd had corroborated the final part of the narrative.

With this information in his possession, Leonard Watts brooded as darkly as he ever had behind his sturdy desk. He'd had the desk moved from his previous office in Darlington at some significant cost to the Force, as he had become fond of it. It screamed gravitas, he felt.

Graham Daley had been summoned, and Watts was keen to underline the seriousness of the emerging situation with a moody demeanour.

"I was informed by Scotland Yard not six weeks ago that Arjan Marku was not in the country" he said.

Daley shrugged, trying his best not to suggest that Watts' comment was a total irrelevance in the face of current facts.

"He wasn't. He is now."

"Why can we not keep bloody tabs on these people?" Watts continued. Home-grown villains were enough of a problem without half of the world jetting in to cause mischief.

"Brexit" replied Daley.

"Yes yes" said Watts, brushing the truth away with a wipe of his hand. He wasn't in the mood for a conversation about the operational ins and outs of leaving the EU. But Foreign Governments should be invoiced for the money we spent policing their citizens, he knew that much. It was a free-for-all these days.

"Do you have a plan, Detective Inspector?" he enquired of Daley. "Might I suggest you answer in the affirmative?"

"We do, Sir. Garton's old associates are now in the Albanian camp."

Watts shook his head ruefully. "Good God…"

There was no honour among rogues.

"Phillipson is dead and we haven't found Parry yet, but we can nick the other four tomorrow morning. We'll put the squeeze on them until they tell us where Marku is, and what he's up to."

Watts seemed satisfied with this. He assured Daley that any assistance he needed in catching the Albanians would be afforded to his Officers.

With a portentous nod from Leonard Watts, Greater Manchester Police began the hunt for Arjan Marku.

And across the city, so did Peter Garton.

20

*I*n any town or city you'd care to think of, the criminal fraternity is
small - a surprisingly low percentage of professional wrongdoers can
create an awful lot of noise. And fear. While secrecy is very much a good
habit to adopt for career villains, there is also invariably an efficient
grapevine in operation.

So by late afternoon on the day of Shaun's escape from the woods, Peter
Garton was aware that Emlyn had been taken by Marku's gang. While he
wasn't unsympathetic to Emlyn's personal plight, his main concern was for
his own property; namely a small brass key with a number engraved on the
hilt.

This key was his retirement. His escape. His triumph. A symbol of
victory.

It belonged to a strongbox situated at a secure facility in Brussels. In the
box was a collection of items curated over more than twenty years. Items
that were portable, valuable, and that held their value across decades.

In the early 2000s, Peter Garton had discovered a faultless money-
laundering routine, which he had adhered to ever since.

Belgium, it seemed, wasn't big on the regulation of high-value retail
transactions. Financial checks and balances were optional. In short, if you
were spending money over there in large enough amounts, nobody seemed
to give a toss where it had come from.

It was a far cry from London, where you could pull out two hundred
thousand in dirty tenners to pay for a Ferrari and be in handcuffs within
twenty minutes until you could prove the money's origins.

There were perhaps a dozen jewellers in Brussels that would accept no-questions-asked cash payments for very expensive watches. Once bought, they could be taken by an armoured van to a high-security safety deposit box in Rue Breydel, and locked away indefinitely.

Garton made the trip twice a year, on average. He usually went by boat, on a fake passport commissioned by his associate Mister O'Hare. The only point of risk was taking cash through the ferry ports – it would be a tough task to explain away a hidden suitcase compartment that contained a few hundred grand. But once he was through, it was a well-worn and fool-proof procedure.

He'd hand over British currency (they were very amenable like that, the Belgians) for two or three high-end Bremonts, Pateks or Vacherons on each visit. A couple of these timepieces could easily come to more than a hundred grand. He didn't have to identify himself to the seller, and they required no ID to match to the serial numbers. As soon as he was out of the door, he was untraceable and untouchable.

Over thirty-one trips to Brussels Peter Garton – carrying documents that identified him as a man named Howard Collins from Batley – had amassed a collection of eighty-four luxury timepieces. These had a combined value, he estimated, of roughly four-and-a-half million pounds.

There was a touch of vanity in Garton's choice of investment. These were James Bond, South of France, racing driver accoutrements, and hoarding them gave him a sense of sophistication. Of glamour.

Accessing the vault at the Sterkte Venootschap in Rue Breydel had become trickier in recent years, after the company had instigated the requirement for photographic identification to access the building. The faked passport he owned of course bore a pseudonym, but by necessity it showed Garton's face too. It had been photocopied for the bank's records. Not perfect, but not a deal-breaker either, given the paucity of laundering options in the UK.

Once inside, each keyholder was given a ten-minute slot alone in the vault viewing room. After that, the privacy door would open and another ten-minute slot would need to be booked.

Peter Garton never stayed that long. He would open the box, add a few small items to its contents, lock up again, and make his way up to the street for a coffee and waffles. He looked forward to his jaunts to Belgium, and had come to appreciate the qualities of Brussels over the years. It lacked the grit and energy of his home city, but it was elegant.

A far cry from a cell in Strangeways, where Peter Garton now sat with shoulders hunched, on his metal-framed single bed. The brass key was his freedom, and its whereabouts were still unknown.

It had been securely stowed for many years in a safe upstairs at *The Weaver's Tavern* in Blackley. On his arrest, Garton's first and only phone call was to Emlyn Parry, his most trusted and least devious lieutenant. A six-digit code to the door of the safe was shared. By the time Greater Manchester Police kicked in the door to his office at *The Weaver's*, the safe was empty and its door wide open in mockery of the chasing pack.

In Garton's estimation, Emlyn Parry would very likely have caved to the Albanian. He was weak, fundamentally. Not a hardened soldier like the madman Phillipson had been, but more like a regimental pet. He didn't have the nihilistic streak he would need to withstand Marku's methods. In all likelihood, Arjan Marku already possessed the key.

But in the absence of absolute proof, he had to assume the key could still be retrieved.

The bank had obvious safeguards against the loss of their keys, and for two hundred Euros would send account holders replacements on the provision of a twelve-digit PIN.

That number was on Peter Garton's phone and laptop, and a notebook in the safe at *The Weaver's* - none of which had been accessible to him since his arrest. These items were in the possession of either the Police or Emlyn Parry.

He had chided himself a dozen times since his arrest for not memorising the number. Twelve digits was not beyond the brain of anybody if they dedicated themselves to it for an hour or so. But complacency had prevailed.

He hadn't the first clue as to what the number was.

The bank would no doubt have some elaborate process for just this circumstance, but Garton was confident it would involve the rigorous examining and verifying of ID. That, quite simply, could never happen.

He'd attempted years ago to get a copy of the key made himself, but was told by someone who would know these things that it was a no-go. According to his contact, the key was 'Restricted'. This made it a criminal offence to reproduce it without the proper approvals from the issuer. And even if Garton had found a willing accomplice, the blanks required to create a second key were non-standard and not generally available.

These blanks – Dutch, by the look of the one Peter had shown his associate – were held in a secure facility by the manufacturer and released to a single approved cutter in the nearest major city. And this key-cutter would require a signed certificate from the manager of the bank before making the copy.

So there could be no duplicate. The single key in circulation was the only one there would ever be, now.

Garton had taken a measured stance on the smash-and-grab Arjan Marku had orchestrated on his livelihood. This was the sea he had chosen to swim in many years ago, and he knew sharks were rife. One of them had to bite him eventually. It wasn't personal.

Nothing would excuse the betrayal perpetrated by his own men, however. He had recompensed them more than fairly for their work over many years. Rossi, Kerimoglu, Barber, Yardley and Phillipson were treacherous, diabolical filth. No better than shit on his shoe.

But the Albanian, he understood. He knew the drive, the urge, the pull to dominate and conquer. To beat the bastards.

He had imagined Marku in childhood, a semi-feral urchin, deprived and beaten down, pre-programmed to steal, cheat and fight as if it were in his DNA. Although the streets and the weather and the buildings were different, he recognised that boy as a kindred spirit.

He'd kept it in proportion. It was business, and business only.

Garton was prepared to do his time, and recuse himself from the criminal world once his liberty had been restored in a decade or so, his throne having been purloined by a foreign power.

What had happened to him had felt, if he were honest, like the natural order of things. This kind of patricide among villains was a story as old as crime itself. It was a tolerable defeat.

But the loss of the strongbox key to his conqueror would not stand. His hidden fortune, so emblematic of his success over three decades, could not be allowed to change hands. A quick chat with O'Hare and a Eurostar ticket was all it would take for Marku to do the unthinkable.

Nobody would be robbing him of his legacy. There would be no trip to Brussels for Arjan Marku. Whatever it took, Peter Garton would ensure his safety deposit box in Brussels remained unmolested.

≈

Garton had kept himself to himself during his first few weeks in Strangeways. There was nothing to be gained by befriending any of the scumbags he was in with. Simply by dint of them being in here, there was nobody he could trust. He stayed in his cell for the most part, away from the maniacs and malevolents in the recreational areas of the wing.

But there were familiar faces at mealtimes. He was on nodding terms with a couple of men – drug barons whose careers had been curtailed years previously.

One of these men was the notorious Mick Stafford, who traded in some of the boroughs that flanked Garton's own territories. He was a Scouser by origin, which guaranteed an interesting reception on his entry to Strangeways. There is no love lost along the M62.

Peter regarded the members of criminal brotherhood in the UK, on the whole, as being thick as a whale omelette. They took stupid risks and made obvious mistakes through clod-headed arrogance. They self-mythologised and operated from ego. Mick Stafford was certainly in this category.

They'd known each other a little before Stafford's incarceration, but had been careful not to cross paths if they could help it. Both men were respectful of territorial boundaries, knowing that internecine conflicts over which streets belonged to whom was the quickest way to self-destruction. Few gangs came out of that kind of street war the better for it, so both men came to a tacit understanding that turf would be respected.

For half a decade or more, Stafford had made a million a year in Manchester, Sheffield and Leeds, until his arrest at the Burger King in a service station on the M1. He'd been inside for five or six years by now, and was looking at the same again, at least, before he was eligible for parole.

Garton and Stafford had gone about the business of selling narcotics in very different ways.

For the last twenty years, eighty per-cent of Europe's cocaine has arrived from South America to the port of Gioia Tauro, in Calabria, on the toe of Italy. The port was built, paid for, and is now run by the 'Ndrangheta, the most influential criminal group on Earth. Nobody had stopped them, somehow.

Their notoriety is nowhere near as widespread as their global dominance warrants. Everyone knows of the Cosa Nostra – there are books and movies and myths aplenty - but the name of the 'Ndrangheta would draw blank looks from the average man in the street.

They feel no compulsion to commit headline-grabbing acts for the sake of inflating their reputation. They quietly traffic billions of Euros a year in narcotics with as little fuss as they can. For this, they had Peter Garton's full respect. They did things properly.

To maximise his profits, Mick Stafford had dealt directly with the 'Ndrangheta for five years, arranging shipments of cocaine straight from the dockside in Calabria to his own transportation network in Greece and Turkey. To Peter Garton, this was indicative of Stafford's greed and extreme foolishness. He wouldn't want to share a pot of tea with the 'Ndrangheta, let alone negotiate wholesale prices for cocaine with them. It was fraught with risk. These men fed the corpses of their adversaries to pigs.

For Garton, there was some communication with traffickers overseas, mainly in central Europe, but these organisations had already done the dirty work of getting the drugs from source. He never saw, touched, or spoke overtly about drugs – others did those things on his behalf.

Mick Stafford had long ago accepted his fate as a prisoner, sharing Peter Garton's view that detention was an inevitable reckoning for any criminal. You made as much cash as you could and hid it, got caught, did your time, and then went back to your (very large) house to spend your illicit earnings. The circle of life.

So, for the two-hundred-and-eighty-ninth consecutive Tuesday, Stafford sat at his usual table in the Strangeways refectory, with the usual cronies, picking at the usual semi-gelatinous shit served up by HM Prison Service.

What made today unlike any of the previous Tuesdays was the presence of Peter Garton, who had ambled over insouciantly with his plastic tray and parked himself at the end of Mick's table. Odd behaviour, given the strict boundaries that established themselves in any prison refectory. Turf was important in here, too.

But there he was, ripping the corner off a bread roll and smiling benignly at Stafford and his gang.

"How's life, Mick?"

Was this a joke? Was Garton taking the piss? Stafford decided to give him the benefit of the doubt for now. After all, there was no chance this was a social visit. Garton wanted something.

"Think about the last two months of your life" said Mick, "and multiply it by about thirty."

Garton pulled a face. "Right. Not the best, then."

He dipped his bread into a puddle of translucent gravy that was masquerading as chilli con carne.

"And how's your lad doing? Kevin, is it?"

"Keiron."

"Keiron, that's it. How is he? Still back in Liverpool?"

Mick had never been chummy with Garton, who was too self-contained to be knowable, he found. His conversational gambit here felt passive-aggressive. Nobody did that to better effect than Mick, and he wasn't about to accept it from Peter. And aside from that, these ambiguous conversations were irritating. Garton needed to say what he'd come here to say.

"What the fuck's it got to do with you?"

Garton pursed his lips. He had been prepared for this kind of machismo. It was baked in with men like this. He could be patient. He was the bigger man, in every sense.

"Nowt, Mick. Just wondered if he'd like to make a bit of pocket money." Stafford frowned.

"Doing what?"

"A favour. For me."

Silence. The general sense at the table was that this might be a bit too audacious for Mick's tastes. He wouldn't want his lad working for another dealer. That would tarnish his image.

But Stafford took the bait.

"How much are we talking about?"

"Twenty grand."

The coterie of thugs around Mick seemed to approve. There were shared glances and raised eyebrows as the offer sunk in.

It certainly wasn't popcorn to a twenty-three-year-old scallywag with a father in prison and a mum who hadn't worked for a decade. Keiron would certainly have wanted to hear more had he been sat here at the table.

At this sort of price point, Mick was prepared to talk.

"Must be a fucking big favour" he said.

Garton smiled.

"Oh, it is. I need him for a week. It isn't going to be pretty. But, you know, it's a decent payday."

Mick looked to his left at a fat man with long hair and gave him a nod. The group stood in unison, picked up their trays, and moved away.

This left Mick Stafford and Peter Garton alone at the table. This unusual pairing drew a few looks from the screws monitoring the dining hall, but of course whom prisoners chose to converse with was ultimately none of the screws' business. It might be nothing more than old times, or hatchet-burying, or condolences for someone who'd recently passed.

"Is anybody going to be killed, Peter?" asked Mick.

"Absolutely not," said Garton, looking Mick Stafford in the eye.

Mick nodded.

"Continue," he said.

21

By Thursday afternoon, Shaun Mullin had pieced together the events of Monday night and the early hours of Tuesday.

The ribs were causing him the most discomfort, rather than the missing fingertip. Breathing was painful, even with generous amounts of Tramadol coursing through him. He'd avoided looking at his finger whenever the dressings were changed. He wasn't ready to confront his disfigurement. Even the memory of the incident made him feel sick.

Shaun felt sorry for the Officers assigned to the job of sitting on a plastic chair in a hospital hallway as countless staff and patients walked by hour after hour. It had to be the worst detail currently on offer – a tedious short straw. But he was thankful for them for sticking at it.

He was grateful to Graham Daley, too. It would have been easy for Daley to sneer. To have adopted a tone suggestive of Shaun getting his comeuppance. But there had been no trace of that. Just concern, and a determination to trace the guilty parties. That was dangerous of course – Shaun was in a bit further than he'd led Daley to believe, and a focused, thorough investigation would probably uncover the truth eventually.

Shaun knew by now that Emlyn hadn't been found. He tried to concoct a situation in his mind in which the poor, tormented man had escaped somehow and returned to his hideout to recuperate. But that made little sense. He surely had to be dead, even if he had ultimately caved in and handed over the key Marku wanted. Emlyn's survival would now be little short of a miracle.

Shaun felt this as a personal failure. Emlyn had been so obviously in need, so clearly unable to survive unaided. Shaun now realised how much he had invested in providing that aid to Emlyn. It hadn't been enough.

≈

Thursday night saw Shaun discharged from The Royal Oldham. Pain management was all they could now meaningfully offer him, and that could be done at home.

But he wasn't going home. Not for a while. It had been decided on his behalf that he would spend a few days with his mother at Bluebell Farm. He didn't have the energy or the inclination to challenge the decision. The pills would take the edge off her more grating eccentricities, he hoped.

≈

Brendan and Emer Mullin were regarded as 'good' Irish.

That meant they had arrived in England in the late '60s with a few qualifications and a profession apiece – Brendan was a draughtsman, Emer a midwife. As such, they were tolerated by their new neighbours, unlike the other kinds of immigrants from the bog over the water – the day labourers and itinerants who were shunned not only by the native population but by much of their own diaspora too.

These rough-necked Paddies were sweet-talkers to a man, of course, but that held little sway in Manchester, regardless of where you came from.

Shaun had once heard his mother express her dislike of 'them filthy Mick binmen'. This was somewhat rich, given that her own father had spent fifty years of his life shovelling shit around a field in Meath. This was the amnesia of the upwardly mobile.

Emer and her only son Shaun had little to do with one another these days. There was no hostility in the relationship, just an unspoken, mutual acceptance that their lives might be happier spent at a distance from one another. Neither harvested anything useful from the other's company.

That, and the fact that Shaun found his mother exasperating. He knew he didn't do enough to hide his irritation with her, and so she became discombobulated by him. It had become an awkward alliance.

Shaun had rationalised his antipathy towards Emer in the following way.

He reckoned that ninety-five per-cent of all the thoughts he had stayed inside his head, with only a small proportion escaping his mouth. The words he did choose to speak out loud had been sub-consciously triaged according to various criteria – whether or not they were fully formed, stupid, or obvious, or the likelihood of them being interesting to other people, and so forth.

With his mother, this ratio was in reverse. And the five per-cent of her thoughts she didn't actually verbalise stayed put only because she ran out of time to say them, Shaun believed. So, anyone in her immediate ambit was subject to an unceasing stream of disembodied queries, judgments, and exclamations. She produced, continuously, great formless dollops of chatter, unmoulded and of use to no-one.

You couldn't read a newspaper in her presence, or watch a film, or even daydream for a few meagre seconds without your focus being pulled by yet another pointless utterance. Emer's thoughts spilled from her unchecked in a kind of stunningly mundane Tourette's that demanded the constant attention of anyone else in the room.

Introverts and chatter do not mix. It was exhausting.

His objections to his mother were another facet of Shaun's general misanthropy, he knew. But they were too well developed and deeply embedded to shift now.

Emer's other child, Susan, exhibited far more tolerance towards her than Shaun could muster. Almost a half-decade younger than her brother, Susan was an industrial chemist, which bespoke both her academic excellence and a certain preternatural facility for logical, precise thinking.

She and Shaun got on tolerably well at arm's length, but she'd never quite understood the more creative aspects of his character, and the flights of conversational fancy he was prone to taking. She was a devotee of all things observable and quantifiable. Shaun gravitated to duality and nuance.

There were no men left in the family now aside from Shaun, Brendan having passed in the early Eighties and Susan's ex-husband now co-habiting with his Research Assistant in Stoke-on-Trent.

The familial foursome – Shaun, Emer, Susan and her daughter Claire - were now sat around the kitchen table in Emer's farmhouse. When sat together they were an ill-matched clan, like strangers in an Agatha Christie railway station waiting room.

But they had all, in their own way, aided Shaun's recuperation. And for that he was thankful.

He'd been here for three days since his release from the hospital, and in that time dressings had been changed, soups made, jigsaws completed and pillows plumped. Emer had fussed over him, Susan had done practical things, and Claire had played the jester.

Shaun had been prescribed double-strength Sertraline as well as beta-blockers, and was devouring Tramadol for the management of pain. All in all, he couldn't feel a great deal of anything, and probably wouldn't have minded too much even if he had been able to.

Graham Daley had suggested that Shaun come up with a cover story to explain his situation. Keeping any news on Arjan Marku under wraps was preferable from the Force's point of view. But the combination of his injuries had made this difficult.

He could have concocted a story about being mugged or beaten up by drunks, but that didn't account for his little finger being incomplete. That might have been explained away as a mishap with a waste disposal unit, but then where would the bruises and broken ribs have come from?

Shaun simply told his family that he'd become involved in a case of mistaken identity. Four ruffians had set about him at the tram station. One of them had brought pincers. Something about someone's wife and her extra-marital activities. And after five minutes or so the men ran away when they realised they had the wrong man. He was perfectly safe now, and the Police were investigating.

Emer looked frail, thought Shaun. He hadn't yet learned what older people knew: in human beings, decay began in the mind, at around fifty years of age. Familiar names became elusive and one's reasoning powers started to wane. Once underway, this decline was slow but constant and unerring.

The body, on the other hand, held up for longer, but when it did eventually fail it tended to capsize mightily, like a tower block brought down by gelignite.

The purchase of Bluebell Farm had been an ambitious, quixotic decision on Emer's part after the death of her husband. She'd grown up around animals in the old country, and wanted to return to her roots. Going backwards to move forwards was a peculiarly Irish philosophy.

Shaun was eleven when the move had happened, from a terrace in Fallowfield to here. Susan had been barely six years old.

For a good many years, Emer managed her three-dozen sheep and smattering of chickens pretty well on the small homestead, and never gave midwifery a second thought. Brendan's pension and the money she got for lambs each spring were just about enough. Now, in her old age, her stock had dwindled to a few scraggy beasts that were little more than pets.

Sunday lunch was all but gone. The light outside was fading over Saddleworth Moor, and gave its undulations their familiar lunar feel.

Shaun picked at the dreg-end of a roast chicken with as much facility as his bandaged hand would allow. Emer wittered on, something or other about Connie up the road and her enormous extended family – "Twenty-seven cousins! Lord almighty, where would you start!".

Susan and Claire were examining the component parts of a birthday gift for the older of the two of them, who had turned forty-eight the day before. Shaun had bought his sister a new blender, which contained a wide range of blades for different uses. It seemed to have gone over well.

"Connie's got a grandson over in the Middle East, in army logistics" said Emer. "Keeping sand out of everything all day, I should think. What is it, logistics, Susan?"

"It's organising. Moving stuff around so it gets where it's supposed to be on time."

Succinct, and correct. Classic Suze.

Emer continued "My older brother, your uncle Dermot, he was in the army. He got gassed in The Somme."

This breathtaking fallacy brought Shaun to a complete halt. He put down his fork just as it was about to deliver a scrag of chicken to his mouth.

"I'm sorry. He what?"

Susan looked over with an expression that begged Shaun to just leave it be. Just once. Emer was too old to be jostled about and bantered with.

"He did. He went to France and got gassed in the war."

"In the First World War, mum?" Shaun enquired.

"Well that was The Somme, wasn't it?"

"Mum, he was born in the nineteen-fifties. He was about minus forty when The Somme happened."

Emer immediately dissolved into her familiar flap. "Oh, not The Somme, you know what I mean."

"No, I don't" countered Shaun.

Susan interjected. "Shaun, let it alone."

"Well I would Suze, but I'm keen to hear about our time-travelling uncle."

Claire sniggered.

"See, this is the problem. She thinks you're funny" Susan said, before turning to her mother.

"I think you might mean your uncle, mum. Not ours" she said, hoping forlornly that it might draw a veil over the matter.

But Shaun had picked up the baton and was already at full speed.

"No, come on, tell us about Uncle Dermot and his masterly control over the space/time continuum. He must have had all sorts of adventures in his time machine. Fighting pirates on the high seas, sacking Jerusalem during the Crusades…"

With this, Emer stood up, grabbed a couple of plates from the table and said "Oh don't knit a blanket out of it Shaun for once, will you not?" and took the plates over to the kitchen sink.

She had a habit of expressing herself in this kind of fiddle-di-dee vernacular when annoyed. And the more irate she became, the more Irish she got. In her elderly confusion, more and more obvious with each passing month, anger came more quickly than it used to.

Shaun feigned being non-plussed. Susan looked as if she were about to chastise him, but instead rounded on Claire for finding the whole thing "fookin' hilarious".

Once Claire's mirth had subsided, the Mullins parked themselves in front of the television in the dim living room. Darkness descended, and with it more rain. Shaun found the hour or so after dinner the hardest to get through on these occasions. The pull of 'anywhere but here' was strong.

They watched a documentary about the bones of Richard the Third being discovered underneath a car park in Leicester. Mother speculated on the least glamorous locations famous people's bodies had ever been found, but couldn't quite top this one.

It occurred to Shaun that the chief archaeologist in the programme, an underfed creature called Professor Dolores Marchant, was a lot like Susan.

Susan would make a fantastic archaeologist, actually.

As Professor Marchant revealed the former monarch's remains in a pit four feet below the concreted surface, Emer's running commentary picked up pace: "Oh, there he is, King Richard! Bones are a durable thing, aren't they? Dead for centuries and still in one piece."

Shaun resisted the urge to point out that a skeleton was, obviously, many pieces rather than one.

Claire then asked "Do they know who actually killed him?"

Shaun, unable to resist, quipped "Uncle Dermot", which sent Claire sliding helplessly off the sofa and onto the floor in a cascade of laughter and wild hair.

Rather than suffer any further humiliations, Emer went off to fill the water troughs for the sheep. Susan began pottering in the kitchen.

The doorbell rang. The copper who sat at the top of the driveway in an unmarked car was under strict instructions not to approach the house. Only one of its occupants knew he was even there, and that's how it needed to stay. So was unlikely to be him. Neighbours rarely called.

Shaun opened the door to find Graham Daley on the step.

"Hello Shaun" said Daley. "How are you feeling?"

Shaun was pleased to see him. These two had come a long way in the space of a fortnight.

There followed a strange and brief interview between the two in Shaun's teenaged bedroom, where he'd slept for the previous three nights. There were still the vestiges of his youth in this room – a guitar with two missing strings, a few of the books that were a big deal in that era – *A Prayer for Owen Meany, The Secret History, The Bonfire of the Vanities* – and perhaps most telling of all, a *Silver Reed* word processor. Shaun remembered the sound its keys made, and had pined for the noise on seeing it again.

Daley chatted with surprising ease about his own relics from the '80s. He'd been a cricket obsessive from a young age, and had forty or so thick Wisden almanacs on his bookshelf. The conversation petered out quite quickly.

Daley kept it brief. He wanted to ask Shaun if Emlyn had ever mentioned a key that had belonged to Peter Garton.

Shaun feigned trawling back through his memory, then performed a slightly unconvincing shake of the head.

"Could you just go through again it for me? How you and Emlyn ended up in that farmhouse together?"

Shaun had previously claimed his meeting Emlyn at Clayton Vale was pure chance. He'd gone for a walk, and so had Emlyn, and there they'd found themselves. Shaun hoped the random meeting of two men didn't feel too outlandish for Daley's liking.

He had no idea of what Daley knew. Thanks to Daley's network of beat Officers, the City had eyes and ears - and mouths too. Shaun decided to say as little as possible.

"You said you were out for a walk, yes?"

Shaun set his mind on maintaining the fiction. Even if Daley knew he was lying, what could he prove without a confession? If Emlyn Parry was dead, then so was the truth.

≈

Back at the Station later that night, Graham Daley went through the photographs taken at the abandoned cottage one more time. He had it right, he knew he did. But he would check it again in case an alternative interpretation occurred to him.

He laid the clearest image on his desk and pulled the angle-poise into position above it.

The photograph showed a bloodstained trestle table. Shaun Mullin's blood, analysis had determined. What had Mullin done to rouse violence in Marku and his men? Why was he driven to the woods and let go from the back of a van to make his own way back home? What had the clandestine meeting at Clayton Vale really been about?

As he returned the pictures to their file and placed it with the others, he saw DI Chinn standing on the far side of the office. His colleague's face bore a look he'd seen far too many times. He braced himself.

Chinn came forward towards Daley's desk.

"We've found him, Graham."

"Parry?"

Chinn nodded.

"Bottom of a quarry near Crompton."

The location rang a solemn bell for the Detective Inspector.

"Yeah, I know it" sighed Daley. "Christ almighty."

He shook his head, lost suddenly in the pointlessness of all this.

"Found a woman down there about fifteen years ago. Husband did it, obviously."

Had there always been a surfeit of barbarians in this city, willing to bring the lives of others to an abrupt halt? Or had it got worse over the years? He could no longer tell. He'd been at it too long, seen it too many times, to get any sort of perspective on the past. But he knew there had been too much blood over the years he'd spent here. Too many grieving spouses and fucked up kids.

Phillipson and Parry within the space of ten days. Enough was enough. Arjan Marku and every one of his accomplices needed rounding up. And hours from now, rather than days.

22

In the master bedroom of his boxy new-build home in Blackfriars, Prison Officer Andy Wickens (MCR-34102) woke from his early evening snooze at just after nine, to find that his fiancée Dawn had made and packed a tremendous-looking batch of sandwiches.

He had a hunch they would be bacon and HP, but didn't ask so as not to ruin the surprise. Dawn was a bloody marvel, really. A proper good egg. He was a lucky lad all things considered, with a nice house and a decent job.

The long-established rota for Prison Officers at Strangeways was unsociable. Night shifts were a compulsory part of the job, and began at 11pm, an hour after lights out.

Given that the inmates were under lock and key by this time, nights were staffed at a quarter of the daytime numbers (meaning, thankfully, that they came around only one fortnight in every eight weeks for each Officer).

There was, in the normal run of things, absolutely nothing to do on nights, besides a bit of paperwork, an hourly round of the cell floors, and a hand or two of poker. There would sometimes be a lag with a sudden toothache that needed attention, or some other anomaly, but this was rare.

And Mondays were especially quiet. No deliveries from the Main Gate, no reports to be filed.

Andy Wickens pulled out of his driveway at 10.25pm. After twelve minutes on the road – the halfway point of his journey to work – his phone rang and was automatically picked up by the in-car speaker system. It was Dawn. What had he forgotten, he wondered?

He took the call.

"Eh-up chicken. Missing me already?"

A man's voice replied. Its cold intensity set Andy on edge at once.

"Pull over Andy. Do it now please."

"Who the fuck is that?"

"Pull over while I talk to you, or Dawn's getting her face smashed in."

≈

Larch, Barnes and Isted were already preparing the first brew of the night by the time Andy entered the mess room. He was late, which was unusual for him, but not late enough to invite comment.

Barnes noted that Wickens looked a little pale. As they dunked their biscuits into their mugs, he seemed distracted.

At one minute to eleven, these four men walked upstairs to the 'E' Wing Station, and sent the lucky bastards on second shift home for the night.

≈

At one fifteen in the morning, the second round of the night was due. It was Andy's turn to patrol the Wing in a twenty-minute circuit and check in on a few random cells as he went. This was the sound of the night shift – the occasional cell window cover being drawn back and the clang of a lone pair of boots on the metal walkways.

"You alright Andy? Quiet tonight" said Kelleher, and Andy busied himself in preparation for the round.

"Been sleeping like shit. Knackered" was the reply.

Andy opened the door to the Station and went out onto the Wing.

The relief at no longer having to hide his fear was immense. Andy's face creased at once, and a deep breath escaped him. It would be over soon. There was no chance of him being tempted towards something heroic. He simply wasn't the sort. In all honesty he cared little for the consequences of what he was about to do. His instructions had been simple and clear.

Seconds after completing his phone call in the car earlier that evening, the photo had come through to his phone – his beloved Dawn, hog-tied on the bed, and a man sat beside her in a balaclava, holding a club hammer. There was a dark patch around her thighs where she'd pissed herself. Thank

God he couldn't see her face in the picture. It would have slain him to see her that anguished.

Fuck this job. Dawn always said he was better than this, and she was right. He could be behind a desk within a few weeks, populating spreadsheets or cold calling. Anything would do. As long as Dawn was safe, he would take anything. Anything but this nightmare.

≈

Peter Garton sat on his bed, staring ahead at the peeling wall in front of him. He'd been here, motionless like this, for fifteen minutes. He was alert but perfectly still. It was silent, save for some disembodied snoring from one of the cells beneath him.

Eventually, he had heard the distant clang of boots on the iron walkway, and he knew another nightly round had begun.

Who was the poor bugger they'd targeted? Garton despised Isted, who was a bully, but tragically unimaginative with it. A risible individual, who wouldn't last five minutes outside of his uniform. Peter wouldn't give it a second thought if they'd chosen Isted.

Whoever it was had now arrived at the third tier of cells. Garton heard the key turn. His door was unlocked and pushed ajar. The sound of the boots receded as the Officer walked on.

Peter Garton stood and exited his cell onto the high walkway. He knew if he kept close to the wall he couldn't be seen by the Station, and that cameras F and G only swivelled to his part of the Wing once every four minutes. He looked up. They were pointing away. If they stayed where they were for the next thirty seconds he was in the clear.

Garton looked down the gangway that ran alongside the cell doors. A Prisoner Officer was about to descend the stairs thirty yards further on.

It was Wickens.

Shame. Decent kid. He hoped this didn't go pear-shaped, for his sake. Garton followed.

He descended the stairs as quietly as he could and followed Wickens towards the kitchen at the north end of the block.

The Officer unlocked the kitchen door and entered.

Garton went in after him.

As the two men faced each other for the first time, Peter saw that there were glistening tears on Andy Wickens' cheek. No need to be a dick about this, he thought. The lad was doing what he was told, and that was enough.

The rear door of the 'E' Wing kitchen led out to a small, concreted square beside the outer wall of the prison. Crucially, a door was situated in the wall, on the other side of which was Empire Street.

Freedom.

Garton knew he'd need a bit of luck. If Isted and his colleagues were paying proper attention to the camera feeds along the back wall of the Station, he'd be spotted crossing the small yard. But on nights, chances were they were reading books, playing cards, or dozing.

Andy unlocked the rear door of the kitchen, and a gust of cold Manchester air hit the two of them. He handed his bunch of keys to Peter Garton.

Garton moved in close and spoke softly, almost encouragingly.

"Well done mate. Sorry you've had to deal with this. It'll be OK now."

Wickens couldn't look at Garton, and didn't respond.

"But if you move from this spot in the next twenty minutes, I will know about it, Andy. Don't do it, son. Just play the game. Alright?"

Again, no response from the tearful Officer.

In sympathy for the young man's misfortune, Peter Garton offered his hand. No hard feelings, shake on it like grown-ups and move on.

Andy Wickens looked directly at Garton for the first time.

"Don't take the piss."

Which, even Peter Garton had to concede, was fair enough under the circumstances.

≈

Garton moved slowly along the exterior wall of the kitchen, plotting the most effective path through the shadows as he went. Every second without the rising scream of the prison klaxon was a second closer to escape.

He was a few feet from the door to Empire Street. One last look behind him, at the looming brick monstrosity that had held him for the last few weeks. He'd miss it even less than Andy Wickens would.

His time inside had reinforced a long-held notion for Garton; that society – whatever that was – had failed to move on from a Medieval attitude to law and order. There were better ways. There must be. But they cost money, he supposed.

Peter Garton turned the key in the lock. The door opened with an alarmingly loud creak. But there was nobody around to hear it.

≈

The grey Ford Focus was in precisely to the right spot, to the inch. The vehicle had a roof rack. The metal insignia on the front of the car was missing. This was definitely it.

Peter was impressed with the work of Mick Stafford's eldest lad. He didn't wish to tempt fate, but this had gone perfectly so far. A good plan, executed thoroughly. In fact, he was mildly disappointed it hadn't all felt a bit more audacious.

As he approached the vehicle, the rear passenger-side door opened to welcome him. Before getting in, he couldn't resist it – a shit-eating grin and the middle finger to the CCTV stationed on the wall of the prison.

He flung his large frame into the back seat, sat up, and said "Keiron fucking Stafford. You legend."

The driver laughed, and accelerated away.

≈

They had a four-minute drive to a part of the City not covered by CCTV cameras. Phase two of the operation would take place there. In the meantime, Peter Garton wrestled with the change of clothes that had been left for him on the back seat. As he pulled the final item – a pair of black Wrangler jeans – from a plastic bag, his hand brought out three small packages with it.

He looked down at the contents through the clear plastic wrapping.

187

"You're joking" he exclaimed.

"Up to you, Pete" came the voice from the driver's seat. "Can't hurt."

Garton laughed. This would be fun. Worth a try.

He tried the first two items on. They were well-made, in fairness, but immediately looked like just what they were – wigs. Definitely not.

The third wig was a terrible haircut. It gave him the look of a knackered old roadie for a soft rock band, he thought. Slightly mulletish. But at least it looked as if it belonged on top of a human being, unlike the others. He stuffed it in his pocket for now. He wasn't sure he could live with himself if he had that on his head, even in extremis.

Keiron had certainly gone the extra mile. He had clearly relished his mission.

≈

The Focus drew to a stop in a residential street by Mandley Park, about a mile-and-a-half from Strangeways. Unless Andy Wickens had panicked, there would still be close to fifteen minutes left before the alarm was raised.

The Victorian terraces around Mandley Park were not under the surveillance of CCTV. It was a proper community round here, housing as it did a clutch of Eritrean immigrants. Twenty families, perhaps, who had gravitated towards one other a decade or so ago. They were quiet people and had worked hard to keep their neighbourhood that way too. There was no necessity to surveil them on an ongoing basis, as a criminal thought scarcely passed through their heads from one year to the next.

Unmonitored, Peter and his rescuer got out of the Ford Focus. Keiron held out a key fob and pressed a button. Six cars down from where they had parked, a saloon car bipped as its headlights flashed. Garton walked over to it and got in.

There was an important bit of logistics left to do for Keiron, who was determined to leave nothing to chance at any stage of the operation.

He detached the roof rack from the Focus and stowed it in the rear of the vehicle. He then produced a Rochdale FC sticker from his inside jacket pocket, peeled away its backing, and attached it all the way along the base of the rear window – a large and striking strip of blue. He then grabbed a metallic Ford badge from the glove compartment, walked round to the front of the vehicle, and reattached it just beneath the bonnet.

This was all good misdirection, thought Garton. Very thorough indeed.

But the icing on the cake was yet to come. Keiron reached under the driver's seat and produced two number plates. After a quick double-check to see if any lights were on in the surrounding houses – they were not – he clipped the bogus plates over the originals by means of a couple of small clamps at either end.

The Police's much-vaunted number-plate recognition system was now useless. This was simply a different vehicle to the one that scooped up Peter Garton from outside Strangeways Prison. In the space of ten minutes, the grey Ford Focus the Police would be hunting for had disappeared.

The saloon the two men transferred to was a new, white Kia, spacious and comfy. The back windows had a dark tint, which was essential for the next forty-eight hours. This was to be Peter's home, until the business at hand was completed.

Keiron Stafford jumped in, and they pulled away. There was a route out of here, all the way to the Bury Old Road, that was unmonitored. By the time they got there and could be seen again by CCTV, they would simply be one vehicle among many traversing the City.

≈

Andy Wickens had done Peter Garton's bidding. Twenty minutes had now passed.

At 1.49am, those living within the orbit of Strangeways Prison were woken by the rising sound of a siren climbing towards its top note.

≈

Graham Daley poured yet more coffee into his Greater Manchester Police Force standard-issue mug. He raised the coffee pot in Detective Sergeant Corrigan's direction, but Corrigan declined.

Graham had been hoping for some support tonight. But DI Chinn's youngest child was ill, and rather disappointingly he'd chosen to go home. He was a smart and dedicated Officer, was Chinn, but this sort of thing would probably cost him a promotion or two down the line, thought Daley. And DI Pitt had a long-standing engagement with the in-laws, so had also vanished come seven o'clock. Lightweights, the pair of them.

Daley would have to brief Corrigan on his own. He was a sly character in Graham's estimation, and not one he ever felt completely comfortable around. He had no idea if Corrigan was a 'bad apple', as the press liked to call them, but he wouldn't be surprised if something underhand was going on with him. He had an untrustworthy moustache.

"Right" Daley said, glancing at his handwritten notes as he sat back down. "You're doing this one with DI Chinn, Terry. I'll be in bed."

DS Corrigan nodded his assent.

Daley carried on. "Here's where we're at. Four hours from now, at six a.m. Eight Detectives, Conference Room One. Overtime has been approved. Two objectives, both highly time-sensitive. One – arrest the four remaining members of Peter Garton's gang as soon as is humanly possible."

"For what?" asked Corrigan.

Daley was incredulous. He was exhausted and frustrated, and it was starting to tell. He was becoming cantankerous.

"What do you mean?"

"That's what my Officers will ask me in the briefing" Corrigan said, as if this represented the height of sophisticated professionalism on the part of the men and women under him. "What are we nicking them for?"

"Because they're fucking drug dealers, Terry."

"Yeah, we all know that, but the reason we didn't nick them yesterday, or the day before that, is we've not got enough on any of them, have we? It's got to stick, or they'll be back home in two days."

Daley responded extremely slowly, with a forced quietness.

"At this stage of the game, Terry, I give not a single shit what they're charged with. Tax evasion. Cruelty to animals. Urinating in a public place.

Just get them nicked."

Corrigan was unconvinced, and his expression indicated as much.

"Second" continued Daley. "Find Arjan Marku and however many of his fucking bandidos he's brought over with him. We're liaising with Belfast on that. They know all about him over there."

Marku had profitable operations running in Belfast, Liverpool and Cardiff already. Manchester was just the latest location in a growing portfolio. But Daley was determined not to allow him a foothold here.

On the desk, Daley's phone lit up. As ever, he'd kept it on silent after ten o'clock, so it didn't disturb his wife. No chance of that this evening – she was fifteen miles away under a lovely 16-TOG duvet.

Graham didn't recognise the number.

He had a maxim he liked to live by. A phrase he'd used a good many times in the last few years since his kids had become teenagers: 'Nothing good happens after two a.m'.

He looked at the clock on his phone's display. 2.06.

DI Daley looked at DS Corrigan as he picked the handset up.

"What's the betting this is bad news?"

23

There is a breed of dyed-in-the-wool Mancunian whose senses are finely attuned to the city's vibrations. Those few thousand of these pure-bloods, raised on hotpot and Eccles cakes, are somehow plugged into the veins of the place. They divine subliminal messages from the warehouses and hedgerows and alleyways around them, as if they'd left the radio on all night and absorbed its output while sleeping. While this may be happening nightly in any city you'd care to name, Manchester has its own, peculiar frequency.

These born-and-bred would have woken that morning with a preternatural awareness of there having been much industry overnight. There had been an urgency about the City before the sun rose. But a quiet one – Police vehicles had raced around its arteries siren-less, two-way radios were connected to earpieces, and spotters along the main roads were hunkered down in silence, hidden from view. The traces of this activity oscillated on the breeze that floated in from the neighbouring hills.

Now, in the weak sunlight of 7am, Leonard Watts stared out of the floor-to-ceiling window of his office at the theme park of Victoriana below him. He loved this place, and he hated it.

If he had his way right now, he'd lock down the entire City, from Heaton Park to Didsbury, Trafford to Stockport. He wanted to freeze it in amber, immobilising everything within its boundaries.

But instead, a couple of hundred of his Officers were – fruitlessly thus far – chasing an invisible quarry. Scouring the city for a ghost.

Careers were shipwrecked over this kind of thing. The sheer profile of the incident – the perception that those in charge of law and order were unable to keep the rest of the population safe from the likes of Peter Garton – could tarnish reputations beyond repair.

Watts had begun to doubt his senior Officers. Perhaps the likes of Daley, Chinn and Pitt were lacking in strategic nous when big operations like this were required.

There were concerns about the rank-and-file too. How could this man, Garton – notorious, recognisable and dangerous – simply walk out of a Category A facility and vaporise? Where were the ears to the ground? The informal intelligence networks, the stoolies willing to talk for a few quid? So much of Community Policing operated on a nod-and-a-wink. Had his force become too centralised? Had it lost touch with those it was meant to serve?

These were not issues that could be resolved quickly. Watts would throw every resource at his disposal behind the hunt for Peter Garton, and leave the post-mortems to a later date.

≈

Hours earlier, an unremarkable Kia had meandered along the A-roads that connected East Manchester to the Derbyshire market town of Glossop.

By three o'clock in the morning, the car was tucked away in a long-stay car park on the outskirts of the town, stationed with its windscreen facing a dense copse. Given the darkish tint on the rest of the windows, this meant nobody could see into the vehicle's interior from any angle.

Peter Garton lay across the collapsed rear seats. Was there any feasible way he could have been tracked? How could the Police possibly know his whereabouts? He wished he'd been made aware of how good Keiron Stafford was years ago – the young man appeared to be a born deceiver, and Peter could have utilised his enterprising mind in a dozen different ways.

Even this location was perfect. The town was sleepy, and an unlikely destination for an escaped convict. They were a healthy distance from the centre of Manchester, but not too far away. It would only be a twenty-minute drive to Oldham this evening.

In the meantime, he would sleep, consume the energy bars provided for him by his new Lieutenant, and utilise the waterproof duffle bag he'd been given for use as a toilet. These would not be the most exciting hours of his life, or the most comfortable. But he would savour every minute.

Strangeways was a memory, and he would spend every ounce of effort he could muster to ensure he wouldn't be returning.

≈

Shaun Mullin had spent more than a decade trying to give up smoking. In his late forties, he gave up giving up and settled instead for tighter regulation. The frequency of his cigarettes was now under control – three roll-ups a day, on most days. The meagre risks associated with this were preferable to the slow-drip torture of a nicotine-less bloodstream, so he had now settled on part-time smoker status. In relation to cigarettes, he was a tourist.

In fact, he was proud of his restraint with tobacco. Smoking had been a powerful habit in his younger years, when the span of time between actions and their consequences was so wide as to be irrelevant.

Shaun stood at the bottom of the garden at Bluebell Farm, a skinny handmade smoke wedged between his lips. He wore an old dressing gown he'd found in a bedroom at the cottage – one he'd had as a teenager. The flannel had long since lost its bounce, and now hung limply from his body.

There was some trace of a hangover from the previous evening. Ben da Silva had called round with chocolates and a bottle of wine. Aware of the strength of the pharmaceuticals in his body, Shaun had stuck to two small glasses of red – and capsized in the armchair at about half past nine. Ben had departed soundlessly sometime after that, and Shaun hadn't come round until four o'clock this morning.

Shaun remembered their conversation – centred largely around the events on Saddleworth Moor a week previously – and wondered if it had been wise to bring Ben into the fold. The key, the cottage, Emlyn's passport – would Ben talk if the Police began to bend his ear and his arm?

On balance, Shaun felt he wouldn't. Ben had become a more agreeable acquaintance the more time the two of them spent together. But he vowed to be more circumspect in future with the details of his abduction.

He looked out at the surrounding moorland as he leaned on the four-foot-high fence that enclosed this mother's property. This fence had always seemed pointless to Shaun, separating as it did the moorland further off from the moorland that ran right up to the back door of the cottage. The terrain on both sides of it was identical. There had been no turfing over or scaping in Emer's garden. No beds dug out or ornamental features installed. Given that much of the land surrounding the garden belonged to Bluebell Farm, the delineation created by the fence was totally spurious.

Or perhaps city-dwellers needed the sensation of enclosure. They felt more secure when constricted. And when they moved into the open spaces surrounding the city, they needed to draw artificial boundaries to restore balance.

As he pulled a draught of silver-blue smoke from his roll-up, Shaun wondered how he had got here. He had been, somewhere in the murk of yesteryear, a ten-year-old who hand-wrote his own weekly school newsletter and photocopied it at the library for distribution in the playground. It contained cartoons featuring unpopular teachers doing inexcusable things, and scathing reviews of the Head's assembly speeches.

And now, in the blink of an eye, here stood a clapped-out eccentric with the best days of his career well behind him, recuperating from an abduction brought about by his own idiocy.

He had been at best naïve to entertain any sort of allegiance to Emlyn Parry. This was all his own fault.

It occurred to Shaun now, for the first time, that his professional qualities and predilections were as much about his weaknesses as they were about his natural gifts. His inability to let things go. The almost vindictive impulse to self-destruction. Impatience. A prickly nature. Excessive introspection.

Maybe he should have been a Detective.

Christ, no. Imagine working with coppers every day.

He had probably followed the right path in life, he thought. He'd been successful and fulfilled, mostly. It had all, broadly speaking, 'worked out'.

So why the hollowness in him now suddenly? What was this creeping sensation of time having passed too quickly without being spent as wisely as it could have been?

There had been a path not taken, an alternative life running in parallel alongside his own. One that featured Madeleine March. The Editorship of a political magazine perhaps. Maybe kids.

He had, this morning, confronted his mutilated finger for the first time. Unwrapping the bandages and gauze that had been wadded up inside, he saw little more than a shortened digit and a black crust of scabs. It had been ugly, but not especially alarming. Perhaps this is what had set his current mood in train. Could one grieve for half an inch of missing flesh and bone?

It would pass. Everything did.

Shaun took a deep breath and flicked the end of his fag over the fence.

As he turned to go back inside, he was confronted by the sight of two uniformed Officers standing on the path beside the house. They had come around to the side of the cottage and were about to step into the back garden.

PC Kylie Charles was accompanied by a square-jawed youngster called Rowbotham. Both had on uniforms that still bore an obvious newness.

"We did ring the bell, Mister Mullin" said Kylie.

Emer was out at the shops. And Shaun had been lost in his thoughts at the foot of the garden.

"Would it be OK if we had a word? Can we go inside?" asked PC Rowbotham.

"I'll get dressed. Give me five minutes" responded Shaun.

≈

Given how preoccupied the majority of the Manchester Force currently was with tracking down the escaped Garton, it had fallen to PCs Charles and Rowbotham to deliver Shaun the bad news. They were both determined to be diligent and personable Officers, and this was an early test of that commitment.

As the trio settled in around the kitchen table, Kylie Charles began.

"We've found Emlyn Parry's body, Shaun."

Shaun's immediate reaction to hearing the news was surprise that Graham hadn't come. Maybe it wasn't his shift. Or perhaps he'd moved on from this particular adventure and was now entwined in some other matter.

"We wanted to let you know. Obviously we'll have further details at some point soon."

The Officers had been instructed to make no mention of Garton. The news of his escape wasn't yet public, and Greater Manchester Police were keen to eke out as many hours as they could before it became known. Informing the populace of these things usually complicated matters.

Shaun nodded. He was impressed by how Kylie Charles had broken the news. She was only a kid, really, but she had already mastered the right tone for imparting unwelcome developments. It had been a bit 'training course', but she was clearly empathetic in nature.

The confirmation of Emlyn's death fell surprisingly flat for Shaun. He had assumed the worst since his escape into the woods on Saddleworth Moor, and to have his hunch ratified left him emotionless. Shaun had no questions. And if he had, the two Bobbies probably wouldn't have had any answers.

Charles and Rowbotham were at Bluebell Farm for less than ten minutes. As instructed, they raced back to Manchester Central Station to put their shoulders to the wheel in the hunt for Peter Garton.

≈

By midday, DI Graham Daley was able to confirm to the Chief Commissioner that the lightning roundup of Peter Garton's old associates – now in the pay of Arjan Marku – had been completed successfully.

Michael Rossi was dragged from a bed in his step-brother's spare room and had barely hauled on a pair of tracksuit bottoms before he was manhandled into the back of an unmarked Mercedes.

Bobby Yardley and Karim Kerimoglu were apprehended together at a greasy spoon off Piccadilly, both of them only a couple mouthfuls into their eggs and bacon. Two rogues with one stone.

Dmitri Barber had been traced to Platt Fields where he was walking Red, his whippet. The dog outsprinted DI Lee's BMW comfortably, but his owner did not. Barber was pinned to the ground just a few yards from the Wilmslow Road, flailing and spitting and cursing.

Thank God they hadn't needed to arrest Craig Phillipson, thought Daley. It would have been an unpleasant encounter for whichever unfortunate Officer had come across him. The four men now in custody had, in contrast, been brought in with relatively little fuss. Daley would now discover how deep their allegiances to Arjan Marku really ran.

Kerimoglu was interviewed first, as the perceived junior in the group. He dutifully offered up more details about Garton's operation than he'd expected to, wooed by promises of leniency if he co-operated.

As Daley probed and prodded for answers, he became transfixed by Kerimoglu's nose. It had a kink halfway down which created a sort of shelf. Above the break it was sleek and aquiline, but below it the flesh was bulbous and malformed. Nobody was born with that nose. It had been comprehensively rearranged at some point in the past. Looking at it suggested a particular hinterland to this young man – if you were stood next to him at the fish and chip shop counter, you'd give him an extra couple of feet to himself, just in case.

As well as confirming some of the long-held suspicions of the Officers present, Karim Kerimoglu offered up a few surprises. Graham Daley felt rather chipper as the conversation was concluded – if each of them were this free and easy in interview, Garton would be banged up for a decent stretch. If they could find him, of course.

Daley reminded himself that these men had been part of the Albanian outfit for months. Did his obsession with Garton mean he'd neglected intelligence-gathering on Arjan Marku? He attempted now to redress the balance. Unsurprisingly, this topic of conversation was tougher going.

Kerimoglu remained tight-lipped about the Albanians. Perhaps, thought Daley, there just wasn't much to say. As relative newcomers, these men probably knew very little about the workings of the Albanian operation at this point in time.

Michael Rossi was, frustratingly, almost completely silent on any topic whatsoever, as was Bobby Yardley. Dmitri Barber was sullen and monosyllabic, but not completely uncooperative. He corroborated some of the new intelligence gleaned earlier from Kerimoglu, but didn't offer up much more than that. Certainly nothing new.

The four interviews were completed by 3pm.

At 3.44 the forger Eugene O'Hare joined the quartet of dealers in the custody suite, having been identified by Karim Kerimoglu as a significant associate. From DI Daley's perspective, it was O'Hare that shone the brightest light on the who, what and how of Peter Garton's operation as well as the comings and goings of the Albanian newcomers.

He seemed to revel in informing Daley of, among other things, a back office at a snooker club somewhere around Altrincham, utilised as a base by Arjan Marku and his accomplices.

O'Hare was a tangential figure to both gangs, which meant his bonds were not firmly established with either.

He was a logical thinker. He'd known his goose was cooked from the moment four officers barged into his shop barking instructions like Sergeant Majors. Their approach was not indicative of a polite enquiry, and O'Hare had resigned himself to a spell under lock and key at once.

So he immediately focused on one thing – how to engineer the lightest sentence he could for himself. This meant full co-operation with the Police. Everyone else could go hang for all he cared.

During the conversation with O'Hare, it occurred to Graham Daley that he had never felt more jaded than he did right now. He had always tried to resist the cynicism that enveloped so many of the Detectives he'd known, and remain open-minded and diligent. But now, listening to this lowlife exchanging everything he knew for a few months off his sentence, Graham felt despair at the moral vacuum at the centre of all these people.

He knew this was a one-dimensional response, an unthinking one. Empathy meant insight, in his experience. And blanket condemnation was, in a Detective, the quickest route to mediocrity.

The watch-mender revealed everything he knew about Garton, and even gave the Officers a few ideas on where he might be hiding out. Graham Daley knew these wouldn't be fruitful leads – Peter Garton was too thorough and too cautious to head for a known safe-house.

It was O'Hare's final revelation that shook Daley out of his introspection. He spoke about a visitor to his shop, who had come on behalf of the dead man Emlyn Parry. The man had used a pseudonym that O'Hare had seen straight through. He knew perfectly well who the man was. Surely everyone in Manchester did?

Daley strode out of Interview Room Four after speaking to Eugene O'Hare for close to seventy minutes. As a colleague approached him, he hoped for a moment to be informed of the news of Peter Garton's recapture. Instead he was informed that his colleagues were focusing on Mandley Park as a potential destination for the grey Ford Focus Garton had escaped in. Not much of a development. Commissioner Watts would be turning puce by now, the preening old poser.

As Daley filled a plastic cup with water from a communal dispenser, DI Chinn sidled over to him.

"What did you get out of O'Hare?"

Graham Daley smirked.

"Plenty" he replied. "I need a car to take me over to Oldham. And a couple of Officers."

DI Chinn suspected he knew what this development meant, and allowed himself the beginnings of a smile at the news. The pursuit of Garton and Marku was growing legs. Lines were being drawn between hitherto unconnected individuals, and one illicit enterprise now seemed to overlap with the next. It was in danger of turning into a comprehensive trawl of every reprobate in Manchester.

≈

Graham Daley knocked on the door of Bluebell Farm shortly before five pm. It was Emer who answered. She invited him in, along with the two uniforms stood behind him. She fully expected to be putting the kettle on imminently for the nice Mr Daley and his strapping young lads, but the convivial visit she was anticipating didn't come to pass.

Shaun came downstairs on hearing Daley's voice in the hallway. He looked at Daley, expecting to see a reprise of the kindness that had been evident on his face during the chat they'd had at the hospital. There was no trace of it. Instead, Daley's expression was a mask of hostility.

"Shaun Mullin" said Daley. "We'd like you to attend an interview under caution, in relation to a suspected crime committed under Section 4 of the Criminal Law Act 1967."

Emer's face fell, and she raised a hand to her mouth.

Shaun racked his brain for meaning.

Section Four. What the hell's in Section Four?

It was information he knew he'd once possessed but could no longer locate.

Daley continued. There was not a trace of compassion in him.

"We'd like you to come to Manchester Central with us now, please Shaun. You do not have to say anything. But it may harm your defence if you do not mention…"

Shaun knew the rest. His brain didn't have the space to absorb the remainder of this statement. It was racing in a dozen other directions.

Section Four…

Do they know about me and Emlyn?

Who have they spoken to?

Why now?

What the fuck is Section Four?

He knew he didn't have to go, interviews under caution being voluntary, but was aware that declining them simply deferred whatever bother one was in. Best confront it, and now. It showed willing, apart from anything else.

Shaun was hustled from his mother's house within a minute of the Officers' arrival, and escorted to a waiting car.

24

Shaun Mullin had heard the phrase many times: 'My Solicitor'. He'd always found it rather an alien concept, having one's own legal representative that could be referenced whenever it suited, as if they were kept in a bottom drawer in the spare room.

Given that most people only bought three or four houses in their lifetime, and were very rarely troubled by any sort of legal squabble, what would 'my Solicitor' be for, exactly? Perhaps the rest of the population spent its time contesting random wills or constantly trying to sue neighbours over the height of their shrubberies.

Shaun, obviously, didn't have a Solicitor.

The Officer in charge of processing him at Manchester Central had called a number and requested a Duty Solicitor, for which Shaun wouldn't have to pay. This seemed to Shaun like a very good deal indeed. In the twenty minutes he waited for this woman (a Ms. Nissanka) to appear, Shaun was informed of Peter Garton's escape.

The news was a relief. Maybe Daley had brought him in because of his visit to Strangeways, which had in fact been entirely innocent. Greater Manchester Police may have drawn inferences from the contact between he and Garton. If that were the case, this would be done with soon, and Shaun would be very keen on an apology from the mouth of DI Daley.

Then Shaun remembered what Section 4 of the Criminal Law Act was.

Assisting an offender.

Specifically, aiding a known criminal in evading the Police.

The passport. They know about the passport.

This would be an altogether tougher rap to beat.

Why hadn't he simply shut the door when Emlyn called? What was it about, this perverse desire to become enmeshed in intrigue? Shaun had told himself that helping Emlyn had been the decent thing to do. A morally upright imperative. He was a good guy who did the right thing.

But he now saw through his own deceit. The truth was, he'd been drawn to the adventure in it, through boredom or a misplaced machismo, or both. It had made him feel relevant. Still in the game.

What a crock of shit.

You're an idiot, Shaun.

He could still extricate himself. There was a line he could hold that might suffice. And if it did, there could be no more of this behaviour. At his age, dignity was everything. It would become one of the measures by which others judged him in his advancing years. And sitting here, on the plastic chairs of Manchester Central Police Station waiting for a free brief to rock up, was hardly dignified.

$$\approx$$

Ms. Nissanka's arrival gave him an immediate boost. On walking through the door, she shot DS Corrigan a well-honed look of pure disdain. A lesser character would surely have shrivelled, but this was day-in, day-out hostility to the Detective Sergeant. Nissanka's appearance, in a creaseless dark suit, tied back hair and flat shoes, gave her an air of authority belying her youth.

"Mister Mullin" she said, "I'm Thusita Nissanka, your Solicitor. Try not to worry."

The two of them were escorted in silence to a private room on the first floor of the custody suite. It could not have been less welcoming. Two plastic stools and a slab of Formica with uneven legs.

Once they were sat together and Ms. Nissanka had been through a few preliminaries, Shaun began to tumble through his version of events, from Emlyn's unexpected appearance at 44 Church Street to the abduction at Clayton Vale. He told the truth with one exception, claiming not to have known what was in the packet Emlyn Parry had given him, or what was supposed to be in the envelope he'd received from O'Hare in return.

The Solicitor had been around the block with this sort of offence. She suspected Shaun was entwined in some way with a few less-than-upright characters, but he probably wasn't an out-and-out lawbreaker.

Once Shaun had finished, she offered her perspective on the interview he was about to undertake.

"Right Shaun. I'm not really one of the 'say nothing' brigade. A bit of honest information can help your cause a great deal, actually. But be cautious. Think before you speak. And if you're not sure about anything, just look at me. OK?"

Shaun was feeling better about the prospect of being interviewed now that this pocket powerhouse had appeared. She was very good news.

They stood and walked over to the door. Thusita Nissanka knocked, and the Officer stationed on the other side turned the key in the lock.

≈

Sergeant Corrigan accompanied DI Daley into Interview Room One. Both men were immediately scrutinized by Nissanka, who sat next to Shaun on one side of the interview room table. As Daley completed a text message and placed his phone on the table, he eyeballed Shaun and sat.

"This is Detective Sergeant Corrigan, Shaun. He'll be conducting the interview with me today. Obviously we're recording our conversation, and anything on that recording can be used against you in a Court of Law."

Shaun nodded his understanding.

"I'll level with you Shaun. Today is somewhat frenetic. So if you're amenable, let's get going."

Thusita Nissanka interjected with a forceful "no".

Daley looked her way.

"I don't think we're quite ready, are we Graham?" she asked.

"I'm sorry Ms. Nissanka. This is a formal interview. I'd prefer you to address me as Detective Inspector Daley".

He then added, with palpable sarcasm, "If that's alright".

"Oh, you *are* a DI, are you? Given the number of errors you've made already, I thought you might have wandered in off the street."

"Errors, Ms. Nissanka?"

"First of all, this interview needs to be conducted in a room that is comfortable, at an appropriate temperature, and aptly lit. I would argue that two of those three criteria are not being met in here. Also, my client is free to leave whenever he desires, and you need to inform him of that."

Daley attempted to counter.

"He knows full well – "

"On the record. With his legal representative in attendance. Thirdly, your mobile phone is not switched off, which is contrary to your own Force's interviewing guidelines."

"Right. Fine" said Daley.

"I've got more" said Thusita.

"I'm sure you have."

Daley powered down his phone. He then stood, marched over to a panel on the wall and brought up the lighting by several degrees of brightness.

Although Shaun was enjoying this exemplary display of pure shit-housery, he did wonder whether antagonizing Daley to this extent was advisable. Perhaps Ms. Nissanka was drawing fire away from her client, ensuring she was the biggest problem in the room and not him.

"Conduct the interview like a DI, and I'll address you as one" Thusita suggested.

Graham Daley turned to face Shaun, almost in the hope of some sympathy. Shaun grinned. For a split second, no more than a blink, it seemed to Shaun that Daley might knock his lights out.

DI Daley looked, to Shaun at least, exhausted. His naturally flinty eyes were rheumy, and their light seemed to have dimmed. Shaun knew the drill here. When men reach a certain age, the sheer energy of younger, keener minds can tie them in knots. One can't raise one's own level to meet what's incoming, and the barrage is overwhelming.

These were the dynamics of ageing – the rapid, scattergun minds of the young eventually morphing into a more sluggish but precise mode of operation. Vigour begetting wisdom, slowly but surely.

It seemed Thusita Nissanka understood precisely what she was doing – draining Daley's resources of patience and concentration before the main event had even begun. She was making light work of him so far, and Shaun was beginning to think she was extremely canny.

Once the minutiae were all in order – which only took five minutes or so but felt chronically punitive – Daley began the interview in earnest.

Item one on the agenda was, unsurprisingly, Emlyn Parry.

Graham began by delivering a deliberate shock to his interviewee. He hoped this might scramble Shaun's thinking a little. To loosen his resolve, and prompt a more open interview, in spite of Ms. Nissanka's presence.

"Shaun" he began, "are you aware that Emlyn Parry was very likely responsible for the death of Carl Wilks?"

Shaun did well not to flinch. At least not externally.

Daley continued.

"Yes. That lad you found was killed – we think – by your mate Emlyn."

"Mate is a bit strong" deflected Shaun.

According to Daley, the boy whose body Shaun had discovered was in fact one of Emlyn's runners. He'd been skimming cash off the top of his takings, and getting away with it by adding weight to the drugs he was selling. Baking powder was the favourite method. So, at Peter Garton's insistence, Parry had Wilks held down while he administered to the lad a fatal dose of opiates.

Daley hoped that this news, however distressing it might be, might put a proper perspective on whatever kinship Shaun may have felt towards Emlyn. Parry was no 'lost soul', he stressed to Shaun. No hapless hanger-on, easily led. He was a savage, just like the rest of them. The world wouldn't give Parry a second thought now he was gone, and neither should Shaun.

The picture was complete. Wilks to Parry to Garton, and back again. Dots on a map.

"So you told us previously that you bumped into Emlyn at Clayton Vale purely by chance. Didn't you?" enquired Daley.

Shaun nodded.

"And was that true?"

Daley knew it wasn't by now. He must do, thought Shaun, or this interview wouldn't even be taking place. Thusita raised her eyebrows as Shaun looked over to her, as if to suggest an honest response might not be the worst way to go. Within reason.

"No. That was a lie. I arranged to meet him to give him a package."

"A passport."

"I've no idea what it was. Emlyn asked me to take something over to a man called O'Hare, and then wait for a package in return a few days later."

"Ah yes. Our friend Eugene O'Hare" said Daley. "I had a good natter with him earlier today."

It then emerged that O'Hare had identified Shaun as the emissary from Emlyn. 'Mister Fleetwood' had been a pointless alias. Shaun was relieved he'd copped to transporting the package – there was solid evidence of it having happened anyway, and a denial would have been disastrous.

Daley shifted in his seat, and changed tack.

"What do you know about Emlyn's plan to go to Belgium?"

Shaun paused, genuinely non-plussed.

"Belgium? No. He mentioned he might want to go to Spain for a bit, to get away from Arjan Marku."

DI Daley smiled.

"He knew we were onto him about Carl Wilks. Makes more sense, doesn't it, to be hiding from us and not some random Albanians?"

It does.

"In Belgium?" asked Shaun.

"He bought a one-way Eurostar ticket to Brussels using a false identity. Presumably the one that was in his fake passport. But he used his own credit card, so luckily we didn't require the services of Sherlock Holmes to get to the bottom of that one."

"That's a dickhead move, to be fair" said Shaun.

"Yup."

"But Brussels is the hub, isn't it? For the Eurostar. He could've been going on to anywhere from there."

"There's two nights in a hotel. Same credit card."

Bloody hell Emlyn, you might as well have emailed the Police your itinerary.

Daley continued.

"Apart from this key Emlyn had in his possession, Marku didn't give a toss about him. If he'd handed the key over he'd've been in no danger."

"I don't know anything about a key" said Shaun.

Daley gave him a look that indicated very clearly his scepticism. Shaun didn't waver. He would hold to the lie that he knew nothing about the key.

There was silence.

Don't fill the gap. Don't speak next.

"Alright then Shaun" exhaled Daley, eventually. "As I think you've been informed, Peter Garton has managed to extricate himself from prison. There was a tiger kidnap last night, which is where – "

"Yeah I know what it is" snapped Shaun impatiently.

"Course you do. Well-versed in the language of crime, aren't you?"

Thusita Nissanka took exception to this.

"I'm sorry, what are you implying by that?"

Daley looked to Corrigan, then folded his arms.

"My client has zero information about Peter Garton's escape, and I'd really rather we didn't embark on a fishing trip for information on every crime committed in the last six months" barked Thusita.

Graham Daley smiled. There was little point in a confrontation with this woman. She could start a fight in a phone box.

"That seems fair, Ms. Nissanka" he conceded. "Let's talk about our friend Arjan Marku instead then."

Shaun was relieved at this change of subject. Answering questions about

Marku would require far less subterfuge. He was much less likely to contradict himself or expose any previous statements as untruths.

"Have you ever been to the Altrincham and Hale Snooker Club?"

Oh FUCK.

Shaun tried to maintain a well-moderated exterior. They couldn't possibly know about the encounter with Marku in Hale. Could they? And what if they did? What inferences might they have drawn from it?

Tell as much of the truth as you can, Shaun. Only change the facts that need to be changed.

"I have, actually" Shaun said. "My mate Ben plays snooker there. I went with him a few weeks ago."

"Was Arjan Marku there?"

"I dunno. I wouldn't have recognised him from a bar of soap at that point. Barman's Albanian though. Don't know if that's of any use to you."

By offering up this little investigative tit-bit, Shaun felt he'd thrown Daley far enough off the scent.

Thusita now interjected.

"We did like a fifteen-minute break please."

Daley glared at her. These people always did this just as things were beginning to move in the right direction.

"As stipulated in Greater Manchester Police's interview guidelines, obviously."

"Obviously" said Daley.

≈

Once Shaun and his brief were enveloped once again in the privacy of their tiny conference room, Thusita Nissanka got to work.

"Right Shaun. I'm surprised by that to be honest. I fully expected they'd have had you nailed before bringing you in, but in terms of a Section Four offence they have got absolutely diddly-squat."

Relief.

"They'd have to prove you knew Parry was evading arrest. Which they can't do, because you didn't. They've just said as much. They might be able to cook something else up from here if they're really determined to, but whatever it is will be very minor compared to a Section Four offence."

"Good. Right" said Shaun. "So what are we looking at?"

Ms. Nissanka replied briskly.

"I would imagine a suspended sentence at worst, but maybe not even that, depending on the charge. I'm not sure if they can pin anything on you at all, if I'm honest."

Thank Christ.

"So we're going to change our tactic when we go back in. They have nothing, so we're going to make sure it stays like that. Yes and no answers only, wherever you can. Alright?"

Shaun nodded. His gratitude to this woman was currently unbounded. She had shown herself to be courageous and not a little muscular in the presence of two senior Police Officers.

Already, he found it hard to imagine coming through this without her.

"Could I employ you, Thusita? Is that possible?"

The slight pause that followed suggested this offer needed clarifying.

"I'd like you to follow me around one day a week, and have a proper pop at everybody" Shaun continued.

"Bit busy with the law stuff" she replied, with a smile.

"Well let's stick to that then. How much are you?"

"Only the usual outlandish amount."

The two of them shook on it. As Shaun returned to Interview Suite One to resume his interview with Daley and Corrigan, he reflected on one of the few positives that had come out of today.

From this day forth, he'd be able to use the phrase 'my Solicitor.'

PART THREE

Nine Tenths of the Law

25

There had been very few moments in his life when Shaun Mullin had wished he could drive a car. Generally, he'd gotten about fine over the years with a combination of taxis, trains, buses and shoe leather – or 'Shanks Pony', as his father had liked to call it. As a kid, Shaun had no idea who Shanks was, and still didn't now.

Men in particular seemed aghast when he informed them he didn't have a driver's licence at the age of fifty-three, but it was a perfectly normal circumstance to Shaun's mind. Cars were a luxury, he felt. He didn't have a swimming pool either, and nobody commented on that.

Brits had a tendency to fetishise their vehicles. Men utilised them as conversational filler whenever they met someone new at a barbecue or in the pub. Car chat was dull but ubiquitous. Men were, on the whole, gigantic dorks beneath their manly facades, and talking about cars was a desperate 'go-to' in the absence of social fluency.

Teenage epilepsy had scuppered Shaun's youthful ambitions to be a driver. Half a dozen fits at age sixteen meant a two-year medical embargo on his getting behind the wheel, and by the time his condition had faded away he was into his early twenties and a student in London. By then, nothing would have convinced him to take on the intricate thoroughfares of the capital and the bull-headed wankers traversing them. A student's income made it a practical impossibility anyway. And there was the Underground, home to the most eclectic grouping of every type of folk imaginable, and a far more entertaining mode of transportation.

But now, at close to 8pm on the last day of May, standing in the car park of Manchester Central Police Station, Shaun wished he had a car. He'd always imagined driving to offer solitude. Thinking time. Space. Silence. And how he needed those things now.

Instead, he waited for the taxi he had ordered five minutes previously, having been released on Police bail and instructed to report back to the Station in three days' time.

Thusita Nissanka had driven here in a newish Volkswagen, but Shaun reckoned a lift was probably beyond the call of duty. She had done more than enough for him in the last hour and a half.

The white Skoda pulled up, and the driver's side window was lowered.

"Shaun? For Oldham?"

"Ta."

Shaun got in, eager to put some miles between himself and Graham Daley's all-knowing voice. Despite Thusita's extremely effective counter-punches during the interview, he felt assailed. Diminished and exposed.

He wanted, right now, nothing to do with anything or anyone. He needed to escape to the desert island in his head, and simply count the grains of sand.

What he absolutely didn't need was a garrulous taxi driver asking him if he'd been a 'naughty boy', then embarking on an interminable monologue about the overpopulation of 'this country' by Asians.

'This country'. Do fuck off. As if there's anything worthwhile left here anyway, you cretin.

Instantly angry, Shaun tuned out as soon as this nonsense began.

He found himself wishing for an anonymous existence somewhere remote. A place in which he was a stranger to everyone, free of the obligations that come with citizenship. Perhaps he'd end up that way eventually – a hermit in a cabin, with a dog and a vegetable patch. The local kids would glimpse him from afar, feeding birds, solitary and unknowable. They'd create lurid myths about him and pass them down to their little brothers and sisters.

An unusual aspiration perhaps. But one he hoped to make real, and never more determinedly than right now.

Leave it all behind.

This wasn't his first brush with the desire for permanent solitude. He recalled a few years ago, at the end of this time at *The Mirror*, searching the internet for lighthouse-keeper jobs. He was only half-joking. But it seemed the UK's lighthouses were all automated now, and the job no longer existed.

If only.

≈

As the taxi rounded the bend that led to the driveway to Bluebell Farm, Shaun noticed the unmarked Police car had gone. Police protection was dependent, apparently, on him keeping his nose clean with DI Daley. The emerging bond between them – surely preferable to the years of antagonism that had preceded it – had been broken. Shaun was now exposed to the elements once again.

In truth, he felt no fear, really. Marku would either have Peter Garton's key in his possession by now, or have moved on to another method of tracing it. He couldn't possibly still think Shaun knew of its whereabouts, given how obvious the 'trip-to-Salford' ruse had been. And he was far too focused a man to be distracted by grudges or allow his ego to enact petty revenges. He may have been fond of his dog, as far as Shaun knew, but she was simply collateral damage. There would be no reciprocal price for her death. Arjan Marku was unsentimental about the fate of others.

So Shaun, on balance, felt safe.

He was relieved to discover that his mother had gone to bed by the time he'd unlocked the door and crept into the hallway. He'd rung her from the Station to assure her he was in fact coming home again and wasn't being shipped off to Alcatraz for the next twenty-five years.

After her initial relief on the phone, she'd been annoyed that Shaun had forgotten to take his Saint Christopher necklace with him to the station. Her assumption was that this small silver disc depicting a tall, bearded fellow carrying a child across a river would have had a material effect on the outcome of his interview. Such was the banality of faith.

The truth was that Shaun wore the necklace only when visiting his mother, and for no reason other than to avoid the conversation he'd had to have earlier that evening on the phone. Certain hypocrisies were justified. The Lord would forgive him, after all, the old softie.

As he walked into the kitchen in step with the rhythm of the old clock in the hallway, he remembered how quiet this place had been when he was growing up. How he had lain in bed and heard cars approaching from a mile away; further, when the wind prevailed. The amplification of any small noise at night – wooden beams contracting or a window lock rattling.

It occurred to him that perhaps this house was the model for his cabin in the middle of nowhere. This was his hermitage. Or at least, this is where that particular dream had been formulated, years ago.

Shaun sat at the kitchen table and, for the first time since leaving Manchester Central, checked his phone. Five missed calls from Ben da Silva, and a text message: *"Heard you've had an interesting evening! Let me know when they let you out. Hope all is OK."*

His mother would have rung work. Let's face it, she'd've likely rung her entire address book in the time he'd been gone. There was no more choice gossip for the Irish than a transgression in the family, after all.

Shaun typed a concise reply to Ben:

"Back now. Knackered. All fine."

No details. Not now.

The kettle boiled, and Shaun decided he couldn't even be bothered with a cup of tea.

The kettle that was too familiar. The limp teabags in their banal little tin. This house and the memories it held had begun to seep into him. He'd been here for almost a week, and was slowly falling under an unwelcome spell. Something akin to regret, buried inside of him somewhere. A lifelong melancholy exuding from these walls and into his cells.

Gripped by a strong impulse to take action and quell these feelings, Shaun stood. He had to get out, if only to tramp the moors for a while. He could make his way to the pond he used to fish in, if he could remember the way. He used to bunk Sunday School and run up there with his Woolworths fishing rod and a Tupperware container of worms from the garden.

There would still be gudgeon and sticklebacks there, he hoped, flitting their tails just beneath the surface.

≈

The air had lost its springtime chill in the last week or so, Shaun noted as he trudged up the driveway. It wasn't exactly balmy – that was not a word often associated with the outskirts of Oldham – but the longer days were bringing warmth. He was glad he'd opted for a jacket and not a coat.

He made to turn left at the top of the driveway as it met the road. The little pond he'd spent so many hours messing around at was somewhere over the rise behind Bluebell Farm. He looked right to check for traffic and was about to set off when something caught his eye.

Fifty yards or so further off there was a single light shining. It was a tangerine colour, filtered as it was through stained glass. It came from The Church of Saint Anthony.

Shaun stopped for a second. The light coming from Saint Anthony's was a beautiful hue. It cast a beatific orange onto the plants and trees in the church grounds.

He'd not been inside the church since the eighties, when his attendance had been framed as compulsory under pain of damnation. He had shunned it as soon as was practically possible, at seventeen or so. The rituals and the strictures and the language – the sheer *slowness* of it – were stultifying to him. By his late teens he had been moving through life at speed to get wherever he was going as soon as he could, and all of this felt like stasis.

But it welcomed him now, dispensing its warming tint in his direction, ever-forgiving, still lucid in its old age.

He couldn't go in, could he? The apostate Shaun Mullin, the man who abandoned his faith the minute he was out of his mother's sight?

You've done with all that, Shaun. Years ago.

He still admired much of the pastoral and community work these parish churches did. The material stuff that sidestepped God and went to the populace direct. Food and shelter. Solace. He wanted The Catholic Church preserved for this, if for nothing else.

Shaun tilted his head and took a breath. He felt the weight of each of his fifty-three years, and the burden of the concrete block in his brain that let nothing pass.

If there was ever a moment, ever a feeling, ever a need to be met, it was now. The pull to turn right and bask in the radiance emitted by Saint Anthony's was subtle, but real.

I'll just go for a quick swizz round, see if it's changed.

≈

The latch kicked up at the rear of the heavy timber door, and Shaun strode inside.

Apart from some natural dilapidation, it hadn't changed at all. The same green, vinyl-covered hassocks, the tiled floor running all the way to the apse at one end, and the mock-velvet drapery. All of it a little less vivid than he'd remembered it. A muted facsimile of his memories.

He made his way further onto the church's nave, and looked up at the ceiling. Its nooks were still familiar. His voice had risen up into these old beams on dozens of Sundays, as he joined his mother in singing *Agnus Dei* and *Abide with Me*.

"Fast falls the eventide…"

It really bloody does.

The thirty-six years he'd spent between visits felt like nothing. Bookends on an empty shelf.

He sat on a second-row pew, facing the altar on the lectern side. This was his mother's favoured spot.

The opening of a door somewhere in front of him echoed against the stone walls. Shaun suddenly found himself hoping he wasn't intruding. Surely he was permitted to be here at this hour? The door had been open after all, and he was – in the broadest sense at least – still a Catholic.

A priest emerged from an office room off the transept. He walked with a gait that was instantly familiar. He was stooped even further than in Shaun's remembrance of him, and his beard was now grey.

Bloody hell, look who it is...

"Father Hillier" said Shaun, almost involuntarily. He was surprised to note the excitement in his voice.

The priest approached. He hadn't recognised this interloper yet.

"Good evening" said Hillier. "Have we met?"

Shaun could feel his face flushing now. How unexpected it was to feel this emotional, this enthusiastic for someone he'd dispensed with so readily from his life.

"We certainly have."

Shaun smiled. He would wait for the moment of recognition.

Father Hillier was close enough to see his features now, and sure enough, a light came to his eyes as he got closer.

"You're not Shaun Mullin, surely?

"I'm afraid I am."

There was self-effacement in this. The trace of an apology for all the things he had and had not been.

The priest took Shaun by the shoulders and assured him it was a pleasure to see him again. There was no hint of the disappointment he must have felt at Shaun's sudden flight from the Lord's side three-and-a-half decades ago.

Shaun remembered now. How could he have erased the fact from his mind so easily? Father Hillier had always been, quite simply, a lovely man.

They were side by side now in the second row of pews, Shaun trotting out a potted history of his life since nineteen-eighty-seven. All of which Father Hillier already knew, thanks to Emer's weekly bulletins.

Shaun began reliving a few of the lowlights of his Catholic years at Saint Anthony's, as a sort of unofficial penance – flicking rubber bands at the choir, singing hymns in a Chinese accent, and changing the words of prayers (meaning he was saved from the clutches of Santa and delivered from Yeovil, amongst other things).

"Oh, I remember the elastic bands" said Father Hillier. "I had to pick them all up afterwards."

The door at the front of the church opened. Father Hillier turned to face it, half in expectation of another long-lost lamb returning to his flock.

But the new arrival was as far from that as could be imagined.

An imposing frame was silhouetted against the night outside.

"Hello Father. Hello Shaun" said Peter Garton.

26

Peter Garton ambled across the nave of Saint Anthony's, taking in the architecture and antiquities it held within. It's hard to do anything else in a church, of course – our instinct is to absorb every inch of it immediately, so alien are the details to the rest of our lives.

Eyes wide at Peter Garton's sudden appearance in this semi-rural backwater, Shaun held his breath. It looked as if Garton could have been casing the joint, had his criminal instincts been baser ones.

He's found me.

Father Hillier – working off Shaun's obvious alarm in reaction to the man – stood up instinctively, preparing to defend his small piece of the Lord's realm from whatever looming threat this person represented.

He's come here for me.

There could be no other explanation for Peter Garton's presence on the outskirts of Oldham. The most wanted man in Britain tonight was stood six feet away, taking in a detail of seventeenth-century craftsmanship.

"Beautiful marquetry on the back of these pews, Father" said Garton.

Father Hillier did not respond.

Garton eased himself into the pew, beside Shaun.

"Shaun. Nice to see you. How's the finger?"

Shaun responded quietly, and as calmly as he could, trying to keep any trace of apprehension out of his voice.

"Peter, I can't help you. There's no plot to rob you, or whatever else you might have cooked up in your head. Your letter was bullshit. Leave me alone."

Garton absorbed this, before nodding genially enough.

He stood again and approached Father Hillier.

"Father, I wonder if you might give me a moment with Mister Mullin?"

As Garton came closer, the priest gasped.

"I know who you are" he exclaimed.

"Unfortunately, most people do now."

"I am calling the Police immediately" spluttered the priest.

Garton nodded once more, matter-of-factly.

With that, Father Hillier turned on his heels and marched with some purpose back towards his office.

"Father" said Garton, strongly.

The priest turned, as if commanded by a force from above.

"I wouldn't be picking up the phone just yet" warned Garton. "I've something to attend to first. Once I've gone, you can do as you wish."

Father Hillier responded with a fierce righteousness.

"You do not deserve your liberty, Mister Garton."

Garton strode briskly towards Hillier, every inch of him filled with intent. Hillier took a couple of steps backwards, but the hulking escapee was on him too quickly. Garton grabbed him by the throat, exerting just enough pressure to force the buckling of the priest's knees.

"Take my word for it. I have fucked up better men than you, priests or no. You do as you're told, and we needn't have a problem, me and you."

Father Hillier wrestled himself free of Garton's grip – although in truth, Garton was prepared to let him go – and stood defiantly before him. He spoke with a rare vehemence, steely-eyed, possessed.

"Mister Garton. I am eighty years old. In my time I have heard the most abysmal things in that confessional over there. I have buried more children than I care to remember, and given rites to countless of the dying."

He paused – rather melodramatically, thought Shaun. The two men locked eyes.

"Do not take me for weak man, or a man easily scared. I shall not be coerced by a degenerate like you."

Careful, Father.

Shaun interjected. The moment had to be defused.

"Father" Shaun said, "give me five minutes with him. Please. Then he'll leave."

A hiatus. The three men stood in silence for a moment, before Garton broke the spell. He looked at Father Hillier and smiled, adopting once more a pleasant countenance towards the man as if a switch had been flicked.

"If you're amenable to that, Father, come with me."

He took Father Hillier by the arm and led him up the nave and across the pulpit, to the confessional box at the back of the church. There, he opened the priest-side door and invited the old man to enter.

Shaun considered bolting. Sprinting for the door and hurling himself out into the street. But what would be the point? He couldn't leave the priest here with a desperate fugitive, and the thought of this encounter continuing around his mother's kitchen table was distinctly unwelcome.

Calm. He'll be gone soon. Breathe.

Hillier was shut into the confessional booth, away from any subsequent conversation. Garton came back over to Shaun.

"Still here?" he asked, as if he'd read Shaun's mind when it had urged him to run a moment ago. "Jolly good."

Shaun now registered something. One of Peter Garton's tricks was to encroach, just slightly, on personal space, as an intimidatory tactic. There was an accepted distance people kept between one another. It was mutually understood. Peter Garton had mastered the minimal invasion of this unspoken boundary. He'd done it when addressing Father Hillier, and now with Shaun too. It was surprisingly unsettling to be on the end of.

Garton sat, and continued.

"Now then Shaun. I find myself in a bit of a tight spot, if I'm honest. I'd like you to do something for me."

"You need to hand yourself in, Peter" said Shaun, plain and flat.

"Oh, I assumed you'd have a better imagination than that, Shaun."

Shaun's response was loaded with the guilt he felt over Emlyn Parry, the

223

shock of his torture, and the reckoning he had been put through at Manchester Central Station. He wouldn't subject himself to any of it again.

"I can't help. I don't know anything."

It was a plea, of sorts.

Forget my name.

I don't exist.

Just leave.

Garton registered the complexity in Shaun's refusal, and adjusted his line of negotiation accordingly.

Softly, he said "I get it Shaun. You're uncomfortable."

Shaun stared dead ahead. He didn't move.

Garton continued.

"You're not a natural, are you, at breaking the rules? But we've got a few things in common, haven't we, me and you? Not much, but a bit."

Oh here we go.

"I'm sorry Peter, if this is the bit where you tell me your really Robin Hood, I might lose my shit."

Peter Garton laughed at this, open and throaty. His mirth boomed around the cavernous church.

"Hardly" he grinned. "I rob from the poor, for starters."

Peddling drugs was an exploitation of the neediest. Garton knew it and couldn't care less. He seemed to find this amusing too.

"Peter. You can skip all this. I'm not going to help you. Not in any way."

This man's reappearance in Shaun's life felt egregiously unfair. This is what Garton did – he dragged people, kicking and screaming, to do his bidding. Parry, Kerimoglu and the rest of them, and now Shaun.

Peter Garton thought for a moment, before sitting next to Shaun once again. He took a deep breath.

Shaun leaned forward, his forearms now resting on his legs. Strangely enough, he felt in no immediate danger from Peter Garton. Trouble would come from elsewhere – in uniform – if he didn't maintain his position of non-compliance.

"Listen" said Garton, "my old man earned a living from intimidating people. Bailiff. Doorman. He had five convictions for crimes of violence. Fists like anvils. He used them on my mum fairly regularly. She got taken young. The Catholic curse. Booze."

There really isn't a violin small enough -

"So it's not really in my DNA, all this. Church, career, behaving myself. I could've been a good boy, worked my bollocks off, put my trust in the ways of the world. But do you know what I'd have right now, if I'd been made that way? Absolutely fuck all. Hard work counts for nothing when you come from nowt. The world tends to piss on you from a great height regardless."

Shaun wasn't taking any more of this. It was about to become a repulsive piece of revisionism that would no doubt cast the speaker as some sort of anti-hero. The vanity in it was astounding. Enraging.

He stood.

"The things you've done, my God. You're not a man with no options, Peter, and you never were. You choose to hurt people."

Garton responded with control.

"So what? I'm not other people, am I? I don't live in someone else's body. In someone else's mind. I live in mine. So I come first. We're all the same, Shaun."

Shaun quelled the urge to take this up a notch.

It occurred to him just in time that he would be speaking from panic if he did. From desperation. The pressure of this man's very presence, coupled with a speech he'd found provocative, could easily have drawn him into a clash he wouldn't win. The need in him to escape the orbit of this malevolent individual was immense.

Stop.

He shouldn't let this move any further towards conflict.

For God's sake don't.

Shaun began to pace across the nave, silently now, wanting desperately to be alone again with the gentle Father Hiller, discussing childhood things.

Garton began to smile. And, eventually, helped bring Shaun down from his perch with a mollifying statement.

"I suppose it's all a question of degrees. Self-interest, I mean."

Shaun's voice was powerful and earnest.

"I won't help you. I'm sorry. I won't. That's it".

Something seemed to change in the fugitive now, so convincing was Shaun's refusal.

Garton took a mobile phone out of his coat pocket. The screen lit up.

"Do you do Facebook, Shaun?" he asked, trying to disguise his anger.

What?

"No" Shaun replied.

"I wondered why I couldn't find you on there" Garton responded. "Your niece uses it though, doesn't she?"

Shaun looked at Garton.

He flipped the phone around so that the screen faced Shaun.

Claire's Facebook profile was open. There were images of her on various nights out, memes and daft YouTube videos, family stuff. The typical social media page of an outgoing young woman.

Garton scrolled down. Shaun now saw three images of Claire sitting next to a young man he didn't recognise. Nothing unusual in that – Claire had become involved with more new blokes in the last two years than Shaun had had haircuts. Good-looking boy, this one. But there was a definite touch of the rogue about him. They were in a pub, quite possibly the Crosskeys in Failsworth, judging by the carpet. They were drunk and they seemed comfortable with one another.

"That lad there, sat next to Claire. He works for me."

Shaun's skin went cold. He felt his heart leap into a sudden thud.

Bastard. You fucking bastard.

"They met last night, in the boozer. Small world" grinned Peter.

Third-party victims were a bit of a favourite of Garton's it seemed, after the tiger kidnap of Adam Wickens' fiancée. A tried and trusted strategy.

"His dad was in Strangeways with me. Bit of a face in my line of work. Or he used to be, anyroad. Underneath that cheeky grin, the lad's a nasty piece of shit, just like his old feller."

Garton had him by the balls, Shaun knew. For now, there could be no satisfactory riposte to whatever Garton wanted him to do. He was outflanked by a more devious mind, a mind that belonged to a man who was prepared to go to lengths Shaun could never entertain. Shaun was dealing with a different animal, one with sharp teeth and a hunter's instinct.

There wasn't enough thinking time, not enough air in here, not enough space in his brain for any of this to come together properly. He would have to nod his agreement and fashion a way out as soon as he could.

≈

Peter Garton laid out Shaun's task simply. There was no need to labour something this straightforward.

There had been a key in Emlyn Parry's possession, made of brass and engraved on its hilt with the number seventy-one. It belonged to Garton, and he needed it brought to him before Arjan Marku got hold of it. There was the beginning and end of the job, and Shaun was to carry it out.

Shaun protested that he had no knowledge of the key's whereabouts.

"Bollocks" said Garton. "Emlyn had it. Now you've got it. Haven't you."

"Why have I?" Shaun protested.

"Come off it Shaun, You were in thick, the pair of you."

"We absolutely were not, Peter. I hardly knew Emlyn. And I know fuck all about your key."

Garton wasn't sure he believed him, but it seemed a peripheral concern anyway. A logistical inconvenience. He regarded Shaun as more than resourceful enough to locate the key, especially given his recent proximity to Emlyn and whatever business he was at when he died. Shaun was clever. He'd figure something out. There would have been clues in Emlyn's behaviour and conversation in his final few days. Shaun would piece it together, given the right level of motivation to do so.

There was no word between the two men about the repercussions of failure. All the time Claire was knocking around with Keiron Stafford, oblivious to his darker proclivities, threats need not be spoken aloud. Their voice was in the photos of Keiron and Claire. Shaun felt a sudden anger at this wickedness, this unscrupulous leveraging of the guiltless.

Shaun sunk deeper into the pew, his chin dropping to his chest. He was trapped in another man's narrative. He was enmired in all of this. Garton, Marku, Parry, the Police. Violence, lawlessness, lies.

How? Had he asked for all of this? Was his familiarity with the criminal world over the years the root cause of a disastrous complacency? When did the observer become a participant?

If you lie down with wolves, you're one of the pack.

He'd been reckless. He should never have gone to Strangeways to visit Garton. He should have shut the door on Emlyn Parry. Not gone to O'Hare for the passport. Told DI Daley the truth. Taken greater care – far, far greater care – of himself and others.

For how much longer would it take before he could shake off Garton, the Albanians, and Graham Daley? Would these few weeks define his life? Is this who he was now, a gangster's bagman? A permanent suspect? The prospect of that was appalling.

The first port of call – a point-blank refusal – was no longer an option. Shaun couldn't handle the potential consequences of that. Given Claire's unwitting involvement, he wouldn't survive the stress of it. It would surely cause some sort of irrevocable collapse in his brain.

Play along. Just for now.

And get out of here.

Garton was delighted Shaun had changed his mind and seen sense. Funny what the mention of someone's nearest and dearest could achieve.

He would give Shaun three days. He'd be in touch on Sunday morning and expected to be notified of significant progress at that point.

"And what happens then?" Shaun asked, flatly. "Is that the end of it?"

"I can promise you Shaun, you get that key into my hands and you will never hear from me again" swore Garton.

Shaun responded with a look of scepticism. He wouldn't trust this villain as far as he could spit him.

Garton opened his arms and indicated their surroundings.

"Wouldn't lie to you in here, Shaun. House of the Lord, mate."

"I get hold of this key somehow, and then you waltz off with it to Belgium, is that right?"

As intended, this was a curveball for Garton. He froze momentarily, before his chin rose a few inches. He regarded Shaun down the line of his nose now and his eyes narrowed.

"Who the fuck told you that?"

"Nobody" Shaun replied.

This was a minor victory in context, but one he would enjoy nevertheless.

"Emlyn told me he wanted to go to Spain, but the Police mentioned he'd bought a one-way ticket to Brussels on the Eurostar" he continued.

Garton sounded almost defensive.

"What's that got to do with me?"

Shaun smiled.

"Emlyn had ordered a fake passport. He had a key to what I'm guessing is a safety deposit box, and a ticket to the country with the loosest money laundering regulations in Europe. A picture does start to form, doesn't it?"

"You don't know what you're fucking talking about" Garton snapped.

Shaun paused for a moment and met Garton's eyes with his own. It wasn't fear he could see in them, but perhaps a measure of concern. An uncertainty, for the first time.

"Parry was going to Belgium, was he?" asked Garton.

Shaun nodded. He saw a flash of loathing in Peter's eyes for a second as he registered the double-cross that Emlyn Parry had been planning.

Garton snarled "Wanker."

Yeah, you're definitely going to Brussels, Pete.

Shaun's wrong-footing of Garton was momentary and changed nothing.

He had pledged allegiance to this man and would now have to figure out how to break that bond with as little risk to himself as he could.

≈

At the same moment Peter Garton delivered his instructions to Shaun Mullin from the second row of pews at Saint Anthony's church, Detective Inspector Graham Daley strode confidently into the Altrincham and Hale Social Club. He was dutifully followed by three other officers.

The joint wasn't exactly buzzing. A couple of middle-aged men in Post Office uniforms supped from nobbled pint jugs at the snooker table furthest from the door. And that was the entirety of the club's current clientele.

A wizened pensioner attended the bar. This must be the man they'd come to see. Daley was on his way over to him when the old man's Slavic voice said "Very sorry, closing now."

Daley – aware that this was something of a cheesy move but enjoying it all the same – dug into his jacket pocket and flashed his badge. This was the universal language of "You're not closing to me, sunshine".

"Graham Daley, Manchester Central. Can I talk to you about some of your customers, Dardan?"

DI Daley noted with interest that the man seemed to wither in front of him, becoming even smaller than before.

"We'd rather not do it here, if that's alright? Maybe you could come with us, once you've locked up?" suggested Daley.

Dardan was wide-eyed with surprise, and clearly reluctant.

"We'll wait" said Daley.

≈

By the time Shaun had closed the church door behind him, Peter Garton had long dissolved into the black hills of Saddleworth Moor.

God knows where he's sleeping tonight.

Under a rock with the other insects.

He'd squared away the previous ten minutes' drama with Father Hillier, who had been released from his own confessional box unscathed. Shaun had suggested that the priest not alert the Police – or anyone else – to Peter Garton's presence in his church. Being a well-meaning citizen wasn't always in everyone's best interests, Shaun maintained. A public spirit would only bring further trouble on this occasion.

And, he explained, that trouble would likely fall upon his niece Claire, who was entirely uninvolved with any of it. Father Hiller thought he remembered Claire from last year's Easter Service. He described her as having a 'bit of a wild air about her'.

Yeah, that's her.

The authorities would catch Garton anyway, Shaun had assured him, so the canniest course of action was to forget it had ever happened.

Father Hiller suggested Shaun pray with him for a few moments, and Shaun didn't feel he could refuse. So he went through the motions, his heart thumping in his chest and his mind spinning.

As Shaun ran back towards Bluebell Farm, he was already mapping out his cleanest, quickest route away from Peter Garton.

He'd made the reasonable assumption that Garton was avoiding Manchester altogether, given his fugitive status and the sheer number of Officers tasked with finding him. So Manchester was where Shaun would go. Back home. He'd hunker down there and think of a way to make it all disappear.

Pack your things.

Don't wake your mother.

Call Ben.

27

*B*en da Silva's antique Renault hauled itself out of the steep drive from Bluebell Farm and onto Abbey Hills Road, wheezing like a fun-runner suddenly tasked with the ascent of Ben Nevis.

The car's two occupants had travelled no more than a hundred yards together, but were already in the midst of a vigorous discussion.

Ben had been offered snatches of the evening's encounter at Saint Anthony's by means of a few hurried text messages. He had far too many questions to ask, and they tumbled from his mouth in a random order.

He'd've made a terrible investigator, thought Shaun. No logical progression, no development of a line of thought.

"You're sure it was him?" asked Ben.

"Fucking hell Ben, I've just had a fifteen-minute chat with the bloke."

"What the hell's he doing round here?"

The vocal register of both men was rising with every exclamation.

Shaun replied "Right. It's complicated. I'll tell you when we get to mine. Just get me out of fucking Oldham."

Ben swerved to avoid the kerb on his right-hand side. His focus was almost entirely on his passenger, at the expense of the road ahead.

"Don't fucking crash" yelled Shaun, "I will lose it if you crash this car."

Ben had never seen Shaun this tightly wound.

"There's a Police Station in Oldham isn't there? By the leisure cent – "

Shaun shut his colleague down before he could even finish the thought.

"No. No Police. We're keeping our traps shut about this unless I say otherwise, alright?"

Ben protested with the full expectation it would be futile.

"You're joking. Have you seen the centre of Manchester? There's squad cars roaring up and down left, right and centre. You tell them where Garton is, they'll give you a bloody medal."

Exasperated, Shaun snorted.

"Or, scenario B, they've released me from Manchester Central at half eight, and by quarter to ten I'm having a nice little chinwag with public enemy number one. What d'you think that looks like?"

The two of them sped towards the outskirts of the city, bickering at one another, Shaun unloading all of his fear and self-loathing onto Ben.

"What did he want?"

In the seat next to Ben, Shaun sighed, and crumpled.

"Shaun, what did he want with you?"

"He's asked me to do something for him" said Shaun.

Ben turned, eyes wide, almost running the car off the road again.

"What's he asked you to do?"

Shaun couldn't explain it. This was all too complex for the passenger seat of a careering Renault. He needed to be under his own roof, calm and quiet, to formulate any coherent thought.

"You're not going to fucking do it, are you?" asked Ben.

Shaun gave the best answer he could, for now.

"I hope not."

As Ben continued to dig for details, clearly aghast at this development, Shaun was surprised to discover he'd begun to cry. Not the heaving, sobbing kind, but silent tears borne of some profound sadness in him.

It felt like he'd left himself behind in Oldham somewhere. Or maybe in that shack on the Moors, or in Interview Room One at Manchester Central. He couldn't locate his own centre any longer, and this had brought a deep anguish.

He was bent over now, head in hands, as if he were trying to fold himself into the footwell.

Ben saw his boss rocking to and from beside him, his face covered with his hands.

The landscape had begun to change, as suburban Manchester beckoned them towards the city's core.

Ben fell silent.

≈

It was ten forty-five when Graham Daley began his interview with the licensee of the Altrincham and Hale Social Club, Dardan Rexha.

Even DI Pitt – not famed for his parsing of human expressions – had commented to Daley that the man looked terrified. Pitt asked what Daley had threatened him with. Nothing, as it happened – he'd been relatively pleasant to the old man. Daley conjectured that perhaps Rexha was in the UK illegally. That would explain his seeming reluctance to engage. Or perhaps he knew far more about the Marku gang than he was letting on.

They would uncover the truth beneath the stark strip lights in an interview room, Daley was sure of that.

As they'd entered the station, The Chief Commissioner was doing the rounds. Watts was showing his face at a time of great crisis which, he thought, exhibited strong leadership. In fact, it made rank-and-file Officers tighten up to the point of being unable to function freely. This wasn't the night for being on best behaviour, Daley had thought. Watts should piss off and let these diligent men and women get on with it.

During an interview that was shorter than Daley had anticipated, Dardan proved a tough nut to crack. Daley couldn't quite determine how big a language barrier there actually was. It seemed to be a good tactic, were someone so inclined, to 'misunderstand' things. Rexha was taciturn anyway, and being interviewed in a second language did little to oil his vocal chords.

Still, after thirty minutes they had gleaned this much: Arjan Marku and his associates had turned up at the Club fairly often for three months or so. They had moved a couple of computers into a back room and set up a sort of office in there - unsanctioned by Rexha. But what could he do?

The office wasn't a hive of activity, but it was an unofficial base nevertheless.

The old man claimed not to have seen his compatriots for a week or so, but reckoned Thursday night was the most likely time to find them there.

Thursday was tomorrow.

Graham Daley steeled himself for a frantic twenty-four hours. Greater Manchester Police needed to get its finger out.

≈

Ben swung his motor off the Oldham Road and into Ten Acres Lane. Five more minutes, and they'd be safe behind Shaun Mullin's front door at 44 North Road.

The closer the car had got to Clayton, the more Shaun's physicality had seemed to loosen. There were now several miles between him and the site of his encounter with Peter Garton.

There had been silence for the last few minutes. Ben could feel the synapses fizzing in the capacious brain next to him, and decided to let Shaun work through whatever thoughts were occupying him so intensely.

They turned into North Road at the eastern end, and drove past the landmarks of Shaun's daily life – Goldman's Pharmacy, the brightly painted playschool on the corner, Asif's General Store.

Ben had almost drawn up to Shaun's front door as the car passed the Clayton Amateur Boxing Club. Shaun saw immediately that something about its façade was out of place. He gawped at the frontage and said "What the hell's gone on there?".

Ben slowed almost to a stop and looked. Two large windows at the front of the building had been boarded up.

"Kids I expect" said Ben.

Shaun's investigative mind was already at work. This club was fully embedded in the community around here. Almost all of the local youths had been members at some point. They respected the place, and would be justifiably wary of getting on the wrong side of the men running it. Vandalism or burglary would never have been condoned by anyone local.

This was where Shaun had met Emlyn Parry. Emlyn was in the building on an almost daily basis, whacking heavy bags that hung from the ceiling and skipping with ropes.

Why would anyone break in? The building contained little of value.

The car came to a stop outside number 44, and the two men got out. Ben was clearly keen on accompanying Shaun inside, which was a bit of a surprise. Shaun had wanted to collect his suitcase from the boot and shut the door on the outside world as soon as possible.

But he couldn't object to making Ben a cup of tea, given the mercy dash he'd just made on Shaun's behalf.

Once inside, the men continued to discuss Shaun's predicament, albeit more calmly and agreeably than before. Ben understood the need for careful thought now - Claire's precarious situation decreed it. And Shaun was probably right to assume a less-than-enthusiastic reaction from Greater Manchester Police. Ben assured him he wouldn't breathe a word to anyone.

As a second cup of tea was poured and the biscuits ran out, the conversation turned to Peter Garton himself.

Ben understood the fascination Shaun had with Garton. He was an unusual criminal. He lacked the showmanship or egomaniacal excesses of most other violent men, and could easily have come across to his neighbours as a factory foreman or sales rep. He was fastidious in presenting himself as an ordinary Joe, and therein lay his success.

Shaun related the conversation he'd had with Garton during his visit to Strangeways. The clever manipulating by Garton of the dynamic between them. His instinctive controlling of the conversation.

"Why did you go in the first place? For the sake of a bloody article?" asked Ben.

"Actually, between you and me, I wanted to write a book."

"On Garton?"

Ben shook his head in dismay. This was a dangerous notion with a criminal of Garton's hue. Shaun at his self-destructive best.

"But why couldn't you just write it?

Shaun tilted his head.

"You knew plenty about Garton, and he knew bugger all about you. You could've just written the book without having to bloody well introduce yourself to him first" said Ben.

"Our job is all context. It's about how we frame things."

With few exceptions, career criminals were not monsters. Shaun could think of only a handful he'd encountered over the years that had not a single redeeming feature within their make-up. Or at least something interesting – a psychological hook to hang their criminal intent from.

Harold Shipman had an impressive intellect. Dale Cregan – a violent psychopath and the first man to murder a female Police Officer in the UK – was a proper charmer if you could forget for a moment what he was capable of. Men like these were in so many ways irredeemable, of course. But they had attributes that might, in someone else, be admirable.

But the general public didn't like to entertain this particular nuance. And the nation's press didn't ask them to.

We are, it seemed to Shaun, only able to process evil acts when they are perpetrated by savages – semi-humans, nothing whatsoever like us; strangers to love or empathy or laughter.

That notion is wide of the mark, Shaun knew.

"Myra Hindley was obsessed with badminton. Did you know that?"

Ben looked back at Shaun quizzically.

Serial rapist Mark Hancock had published a book about the history of the Spanish guitar. Patrick Baynes grew oranges in his greenhouse and made marmalade with them. And one of Strangeways' most recent admissions, arsonist Matthew Thompson, had more than a dozen karaoke trophies on his mantelpiece at home. These were the everyday interests and achievements of people like you and me. Anyone and everyone.

In the context of people like these, the ordinary was extraordinary, the most mundane details a source of great fascination.

"It's the difference between being a reporter and being a journalist, Ben" said Shaun. "If my job was relaying facts, I'd've jacked it in years ago."

Shaun insisted that Ben should always be looking for an inversion of norms, a duality, or a unique connection. The very best stories took their readers by surprise, at least a little. Real journalists had a knack for it.

After an hour or so of conversation, a half-empty bottle of whisky made an appearance from the cupboard above the sink in the kitchen. Perhaps a couple of tots might restore some equilibrium for Shaun. It was augmented by a double dose of Sertraline from his bedside table and a Tramadol from his suitcase. God knows what demon this particular cocktail might create in his head, but it couldn't be worse than what was living there at the moment. He rejected the idea of a beta blocker, half a dozen of which were still in the bathroom cabinet somewhere.

The conversation began to ramble as the evening progressed. Ben, righteously, had by now switched to tonic water.

Shaun was eventually obliged to outline Peter Garton's demand – to track down a small, brass object that Shaun had no lead on whatsoever. But it couldn't hurt to kick around various potential solutions with Ben. At around midnight, somewhat emboldened by the booze, he seemed to have fixated on one plan in particular: take Claire on a holiday abroad. There were echoes of poor Emlyn Parry in this, he recognised, and that felt appropriate. She couldn't be hurt if she wasn't here.

This was, he knew deep down, one of those ideas that wouldn't stand up to sunlight or sobriety, but it had quelled the storm in his mind for now.

Soon after midnight, the opening of a second bottle of whisky had become an absolute necessity. Ben stuck around, acting the watchdog to a man whose sanity had been tested in the severest manner for the last six days.

Shaun would remember nothing much about what happened after 2am, by which time Ben da Silva was sleeping, mouth agape, in the armchair by the window.

28

*E*leanor Brake of The Manchester Herald had always suspected she would've made a very good politician. She was, in her own regard at least, a confident communicator unafraid to dive into detail and tackle the tough stuff.

The major bar to her ever following that line of employment had been her lack of conviction in anything particular. She'd never been swept away by a movement or a principle. She didn't really 'stand' for anything much. And surely a career in politics required that.

She saw life in varying shades of grey rather than in black-and-white terms. She didn't deal in absolutes – there was always a qualifying factor or a caveat to be found in anything, she believed.

This view of the world had practical ramifications – thoughts become behaviours, and behaviours become character. And not all of the aspects of her character were generally regarded as desirable.

One of her least appealing traits was a lack of loyalty. Almost a total absence of it, in fact. She didn't, in any real sense, know what it was. Her best guess would be an irritational inclination towards someone based on fresh air. Eleanor tended to stay on the fence about people, and judged them only by their most recent actions. Any history that existed was moot, and she never felt as if she owed anyone anything.

This, of course, made her highly adept at making employees redundant, sacking off unworthy boyfriends, and cutting ties with tedious acquaintances. She did all of these things often, and guiltlessly.

Perhaps, she thought, her preparedness to cast adrift the unwanted might be in play again at some point in the next few weeks.

DI Simon Chinn, who she didn't believe she'd met before, was in her office. He claimed to have been 'just passing' and had come in for a chat.

"Passing to where?" Eleanor had asked, sceptical. "The canal??"

Her joke fell immediately flat. Chinn did explain that sometimes they did have cause to do just that, which made sense when Eleanor considered his line of work. There was the occasional bloated corpse dragged out of there, to be fair.

The Detective Inspector had come to talk to her about her employee Shaun Mullin. And he hadn't showered him with praise. Shaun was under investigation for some transgressions connected to the Manchester drugs trade, and Chinn felt it his public duty to inform his employer.

This description of the situation was deliberately provocative. Chinn had revelled in making Shaun's involvement, whatever it may have been, sound worse than it probably was. He couldn't care less. The arrogant prick had needed a lesson for years.

"We felt you needed to know what was going on. You'll speak to him yourself, obviously. Just don't let him pull the wool over your eyes."

"He's not managed that yet" Eleanor assured him.

He was an odd man, she thought. And this had been an odd conversation. She had suspected early on that Simon Chinn was over-egging things, but the policy of 'letting Shaun be Shaun' may have to be revisited, nevertheless. Reputation and propriety had to be considered.

But she wouldn't bring it up with him until he was fully recovered. He'd be back in a week or two, she supposed. She'd park in until then.

≈

Ben da Silva stirred in the armchair and opened his eyes. He knew at once it was later than he wanted it to be – it was a warm, cloudless morning and the position of the sun in the sky gave away the lateness of the hour.

His phone confirmed his suspicions. He was already twenty minutes late for work. Mind you, his boss was unconscious on the settee in front of him, so punitive measures seemed unlikely.

Ben decided to leave Shaun as he was. The man had consumed the best part of three-quarters of a bottle of Scotch last night, and he deserved as much oblivion as he could get away with this morning. Ben himself felt fine, if a little jaded. In moments like this he was thankful for having found the continued strength to avoid alcohol.

He lifted his coat from the armchair and crept towards the front door.

As he reached the hallway, he heard a familiar voice.

"Oi."

He turned. Shaun had one eye open, just about, and frowned as the consequences of the previous evening became evident.

"Christ" he said. "I'm hanging."

"Indeed" returned Ben, trying to keep the judgment out of his voice.

Once he was upright, Shaun suggested breakfast at Luigi's café, a couple of hundred yards down the road. It was a simple establishment that served boilerplate breakfasts, and that's what was required right now.

"It's half nine, Shaun. I'm late for work" said Ben.

"So what? Eleanor won't do Jack. You're my responsibility, and that's that."

His superior having spoken, Ben was happy to comply.

The pair walked out into the bright sunshine – wasted on a suburban landscape, Shaun always felt – and trudged down the street in the direction of bacon and eggs.

There was a van parked outside the Clayton Amateur Boxing Club. It had a sort of frame on the side of it that held secure various sizes of panes of glass. A man in grey overalls was erecting a ladder at the front of the building.

There had been a faint preoccupation in Shaun's mind since he'd seen the broken windows the previous night. Not a clear enough thought to be voiced out loud, but a vague suspicion that had lingered.

Emlyn had been a member of the boxing club. People were looking for him and for the key in his possession. Were the broken windows something other than a coincidence?

Maybe. It was feasible.

Count it out.

Strike it off the list.

He was already crossing the road towards the club when he spoke.

"Let's go in. Come on."

"What for?"

"Just a hunch."

≈

The gymnasium area of the boxing club was already fetid with sweat, as half a dozen muscular young men slapped and thwacked at various inanimate objects. This was an immediate reminder to Shaun just how basic boxing was as an activity. See object, punch object. It was almost embarrassing, really.

He'd found, during his brief flirtation with the sport, a useful kind of release in its utter obviousness. That was until he'd first pulled on a headguard and been properly sconned by a left hook from a man called Jed Farlow. With some experiences in life, once was enough. Fuck that.

But he'd always enjoyed the bustle of the place. It was focused and industrious, and there was a supportive attitude from the boxers here, beneath the blatant machismo.

In the boxing ring that took pride of place in the main hall, there was a tiny young man – no more than eight or nine stone, Shaun judged – who ducked and weaved a non-stop volley of left and right jabs from his coach. It may not be the most subtle of sports, thought Shaun, but there was real skill in this. Month after month of dedication, fine-tuning and technique.

The boy was incredibly nimble. He seemed to be teleporting from one position in the ring to another with no extraneous movement, his eyes locked on the flurry of incoming fists – not one of which made contact.

Shaun noted the surprise on Ben's face. The nondescript façade to the building offered no clue to the busy and serious interior.

After Shaun and Ben had stood for a couple of minutes watching the display in the ring, the coach, in singlet and shorts, noticed his visitors. He immediately dropped his hands and stepped away from the crouched boxer in front of him.

"Shaun!" exclaimed Wayne Ablett, with a wide grin. "Back for more punishment?"

Shaun chuckled.

"I think you and me both know that's not happening, Wayne."

Ablett was a Yorkshireman who'd found his calling on the wrong side of The Pennines, and revelled in his status as an emigre. He had short legs and a proud pigeon chest.

Shaun had quickly discerned on meeting Wayne that he was stunningly ill-informed about the world, and was prone to repeating the most ridiculous fictions as if they were common knowledge. He'd once told Shaun that ninety per-cent of all the actors in Hollywood were Freemasons. 'Everybody' knew it, apparently.

Shaun didn't judge him for his intellectual poverty - there was nothing in the world more irritating than an educated Yorkshireman, after all.

Wayne clambered down from the ring, slipping off his boxing gloves.

"In t'wars?" he asked Shaun, nodding at the bandage on his left hand.

"Oh, no big deal" Shaun said.

Now that Ablett was close, Shaun was reassured to see that he was in his natural state - dripping with sweat. Either this man lived in a state of permanent dehydration, or he drank an awful lot of water every day.

Wayne nodded backwards towards the ring.

"Raymond is at the ABAs next month, the lickle legend" beamed Ablett.

Shaun had no idea what this meant, but assumed by the look on Wayne's face it was a good thing.

Wayne now introduced Shaun to Ray Burns, the youngster in the ring.

"Ray. This is Shaun Mullin. Worst boxer I've ever seen" he scoffed.

Shaun turned and addressed Ray.

"I was hoping Wayne might make a man of me. Didn't happen" he shrugged.

"Nowt to do wi' me. Boxers are born, mate. You've not got worrit takes."

That's because I have a brain worth preserving, Wayne.

Ablett changed tack.

"I tekk it you've heard nowt from Emlyn?"

Oh God. He doesn't know.

Ben shifted uncomfortably from one foot to another at Shaun's side.

You could say what you liked about Greater Manchester Police, but they could keep a secret. Word of Emlyn Parry's death had, extraordinarily, not yet reached the network of his friends and acquaintances.

"No. Heard nothing."

This wasn't the time for unpalatable facts. Breaking the news to Wayne Ablett and sparking up the bush telegraph wasn't what they were here for.

"Would you tell us what's happened with your windows?" enquired Ben, in an oddly formal manner Shaun didn't quite understand.

Ablett looked at him, then back to Shaun.

"Who's this?"

"This is Ben, he's –"

Ben's intervention stopped Shaun from finishing the introduction. Ben had been playing catch-up since they entered the building, but had now fallen in with Shaun's line of thinking. He was on board with the hunch.

It was time for a bold gambit.

"I'm a private detective" he said, with an amount of confidence that surprised even him.

You're a fucking WHAT??

Ablett took a step backwards, uncomfortable, and glared at Shaun.

Oh Jesus.

Shaun shot Wayne a mollifying look in response. He was too stunned by Ben's improvised roleplay to speak.

Ben continued.

"Shaun's asked me to have a look into Emlyn's disappearance, and we thought you guys might be able to help."

That was actually a very good piece of framing, thought Shaun. He could see Wayne Ablett easing at once.

"Right" said Wayne.

Looking at Shaun, he said "You vouching for this feller, are you?"

Shaun nodded. "A hundred per cent."

"Was it a break-in you had?" asked Ben.

"Yeah. Last week" said Ablett. "Come on, I'll shurr yer."

The coach led them further into the building, to a rear door down a dim corridor. As Shaun followed Ablett, he glared across to Ben and mouthed "…the fuck?".

Ben responded with a shake of the head and a concentrated look that suggested Shaun go with it.

The back door of the boxing club bore evidence of having been forced – the wood had begun to split in its frame, and the door itself had caved inwards a little where the lock was positioned.

"They tried to get in here, but they couldn't force the door. So they went round t'front and did the windows in" said Wayne. "Police never came. Couldn't give a toss."

"Yeah" said Shaun, "I gather they've been a bit preoccupied."

"Anything taken?" asked Ben the private detective.

"No, not really. They trashed some of the lockers, made a mess. But that wor about it."

Ben nodded along sagely to this.

"That's common" he judged, with a bogus look of expertise on his face.

Shaun intervened now.

"Could we have a look at the lockers, Wayne?" he asked.

Ben and Shaun were led to the changing rooms, a tiled bath-house style area with showers at one end and twenty-four metal lockers at the other. The middle column of lockers had clearly been subject to a concerted assault – their doors were out of shape and some of the locks had been smashed out of their fixings.

Ben's next question was, Shaun knew, the nub of the matter. The

245

epicentre of the hunch that had brought them inside.

"Wayne. Were any of these lockers used by Emlyn?"

Wayne stepped forward and touched the open door of a locker in the middle column.

"This one. Number fifteen. Most of t'lads just use a random locker whenever they come in, but there's a few regulars who've gorra permanent one. Number fifteen wor Emlyn's."

Shaun now pushed the door of locker fifteen open a little further and looked inside. It was empty.

He asked "Whatever was in that locker might have been stolen, then?"

"No" said Ablett. "I cleared it aaht a couple of days before the break-in. We're tight on numbers, and as Emlyn hadn't been in for a while…"

He trailed off, suddenly embarrassed by how clinical this sounded.

"So where's his stuff?" asked Shaun.

"Black bin bag. My office" responded Wayne.

≈

In Wayne's office – little more than a cupboard with a window, really – the pair sifted through a bin liner containing the contents of locker fifteen.

The early items Ben produced were not promising: a pair of Bolton Wanderers football socks, two old copies of Ring Magazine, a parking ticket, thirty-eight pence in coins. Then an empty Snickers wrapper (why Ablett would keep hold of that was anyone's guess) and a water bottle. Two postcards with photos of heavyweight champion Tyson Fury on the front, which had apparently been Blu-Tacked to the inside of the locker door. Some receipts from the corner shop across the way.

And then, and the bottom of the bag, a folded sheet of A4. It had been partially stained by what looked like Lucozade.

Ben unfolded the piece of paper part-way. It was enough to reveal a printed letterhead and, beneath that, the word 'INVOICE'.

Shaun, pulling rank, took the paper from him and opened it further. He read its full contents, with Ben at his shoulder.

The document revealed that Emlyn Parry had, at the end of September last year, paid a twelve-month lease on a static home north of Manchester. The invoice, from the Chadderton Fold Caravan Park, was dated three days before Emlyn was last seen by his friends and associates.

Shaun put the paper back, and suggested to Wayne there wasn't much of interest in the bag, but thanks anyway.

Ben tried to maintain an outward calm as he bade goodbye to Wayne Ablett, thanking him for his co-operation. In truth, he couldn't wait to get out of there and back to Shaun's place.

Sod breakfast.

Once the two men were clear of the Clayton Amateur Boxing Club, they scuttled back towards number 44.

Shaun opened the conversation with "What the hell was that?"

"What?" asked Ben.

"Fucking Poirot in there, you dick."

"It worked, didn't it?"

"Depends what you were trying to achieve."

Ben's mouth opened and, for a moment, nothing emerged. He couldn't believe this. Through his own ingenuity, he'd led Shaun to a potential resolution of the Emlyn Parry business. A feasible explanation of his whereabouts since the autumn.

"We found the invoice. That's where he was hiding all that time. Chadderton Fold" said Ben.

It did make all kinds of sense, thought his boss, without saying as much. But that wasn't the point.

They reached Shaun's front door in less than twenty seconds and were about to go in when a voice rang out across the street.

"Alright Shaun?"

He turned and saw four young men sat on a low garden wall on the other side of the road. Each of them wore standard-issue hooded sweatshirts, giving them the look of rather cliched ne'er-do-wells. Whatever effect they were striving for, they were trying a little too hard.

One of these lads was grinning in Shaun's direction. He gave a little wave as Shaun tried to work out who it was he was looking at.

The hood came down. Shaun recognised him at once as the man he'd seen in Claire's Facebook photographs. Garton's hired thug.

So this was how Garton would be staying in touch. Sentries. Eyes on Shaun's front door at all times. There were four of them, they could work round the clock in pairs. Peter Garton would know of Shaun's every move.

The lads now appeared to Shaun as sinister birds. Diabolical crows, perched next to one another awaiting the sight of carrion. He had no doubt they would swoop should there be orders to that effect.

"Who's that?" Ben asked.

"Don't know. Get inside" urged Shaun, turning the key in the door.

Shaun rounded on Ben in the hallway the second the door had closed. His temperature had risen further by panic at the sight of Keiron Stafford on his doorstep.

"Don't ever do that again. You try that in the wrong company at the wrong time, and you don't pull it off, you'll end up with a broken nose, minimum. Do not fuck about."

"Oh don't be dramatic. I made a judgment. Wayne's not a psychopath, he wouldn't have —"

"No, *he* probably wouldn't. But he is personally acquainted with at least twenty men who would. Fucking *think*."

With that, Shaun marched into his living room and fell onto the sofa. Anger didn't suit him. He could never quite pull it off without coming over as petulant.

Ben eventually followed Shaun into the living room.

He stood there for a moment, hands in pockets, awkward.

"I take your point" he said.

"Good" replied Shaun, more reasonably now.

In the subsequent silence, it occurred to Shaun that there was no awkwardness between himself and Ben any longer. They didn't need time to adjust to one another these days. Perhaps that's what friendship was. Ease.

Shaun eventually looked in Ben's direction.

"You know what I'm thinking. You're thinking it as well."

"Ben, we're not going to –"

"But what if the key's there? It could be the end of it. You could be done with all of it, Shaun."

"Forget it. Go to work. And do not do *anything* that doesn't directly involve journalism, alright?"

≈

Ben's drive into the centre of the city was no more focused than his journey from Oldham had been the previous night. He skipped at least one red light, and just by the University made a false turn into a one-way street, having missed the signage.

He was consumed by the Emlyn Parry conundrum. There was surely a reasonable chance that the missing key was at Chadderton Fold. If it was, therein lay an escape for his beleaguered boss. The Police would eventually retrieve it if Ben didn't. And where did that leave Shaun Mullin?

There were variables left-right and centre. Should he defy Shaun's orders and consider trying to retrieve the key? Probably not. But he felt the temptation of it – the pull towards a heroic resolution. Vindication in the eyes of his boss forever.

And perhaps the key wouldn't be there, in which case nobody was any the better off. What were the risks? Few, as far as he could discern.

He continued turning over a seemingly endless list of questions all the way up the three flights of stairs to the office of *The Manchester Herald*. He wouldn't be getting very much work done today, he suspected. Events in Clayton had become all-consuming.

His first act once at his desk was to search the Internet for Chadderton Fold Caravan Park.

The resulting images showed a series of unkempt fields connected by paths through woodland. From above it looked like a neglected golf links.

Ben recognised the entrance to the site, off Haigh Lane. He'd met a girl a few times up that way, in a pub called the Horton Arms.

According to the park's website, one of the fields was available for weekend camping. Another was designated to mobile caravan bays – holidaymakers would come and go for a week at a time. But the majority of the area of the park was allocated to semi-permanent static homes. Some of these were Portakabin-style premises perched on a concrete base, others wooden chalets or huts. This was what Emlyn had rented.

Ben began to think about how he might go about locating the property that was in Emlyn's name. Devising a plan didn't mean he necessarily had to implement it, after all. But if he did manage to bring Shaun round to his way of thinking, he needed to be ready to roll.

He'd been in his seat for no more than ten minutes when Eleanor opened the door to her office and called him in. This was a rarity. She dealt largely with Shaun in the event of any issue with the writers. He stood and made his way over to her.

"How are you mate?" she asked.

The word 'mate' never felt right coming from Eleanor. She conclusively didn't have mates at work, and at times Ben wondered if there were any outside of it either. She was just a little too dry for genuine friendships, it seemed to him.

He sat in the designated chair across from her desk.

"How's Shaun?"

What did that mean? How's Shaun doing after his stay in hospital? Or how's Shaun this morning after two pints of Irish whisky?

"Yeah" replied Ben, too timidly to be convincing. "As far as I know…"

Eleanor knew he was being evasive. And Ben knew she knew.

"I take it you're aware of his brush with the law this week?" she asked.

"I am, yes. He's helping them with the Peter Garton business."

"Not the story I got" exhaled Eleanor. "He's under caution. What for, they won't say. And I know I won't get a straight answer from him, so…"

She looked at him rather forlornly, he felt, as if she needed help. She never needed help. It was a ploy.

Ben didn't quite know which way to turn. He opted for the most obvious response.

"I could try and find out, if you like?"

"That would be great. And listen, Ben, I know you two are quite close, so this will stay between us I hope…."

Eleanor paused, carefully formulating her next utterance.

"Be your own man."

"What d'you mean?"

Eleanor hesitated again. This was tricky territory.

"We all follow in someone's footsteps in this business. It's just the way it works. It's important to… to realise when that sort of relationship may not be of value any longer."

And so ended a confounding conversation. It left Ben with a sinking feeling on Shaun's behalf. It felt very much like Eleanor might be weighing up the risk and reward of keeping her senior reporter around.

He hoped he'd misjudged it. He hoped he was wrong.

29

In the United Kingdom, there is a formal process to be undergone before a Police Officer can take a loaded weapon into a public space. There are exceptions – Officers at airports and in the City of London for example – but the Manchester Force was not exempt, day-to-day.

Leonard Watts had just signed off on a Special Case Emergency Firearms Warrant for only the fourth time in his long career.

Graham Daley thanked him for pulling the necessary strings to get the permit issued so quickly. Tonight would represent a vital window of opportunity, and if ever there was a 'special case', this was it.

At the gathering of the Firearms Team at Manchester Central, Daley, Chinn and Pitt held court. They'd settled a few moments earlier on the name Operation Crucible for tonight's activities. The snooker reference, which Chinn had thought extremely clever, seemed lost on the room.

Officers who have never seen a shooting up close find this kind of operation exciting. But those in the room who'd had cause to fire their weapons during their careers did not. It was an alarming and psychologically complex form of justice. Nothing good happened when guns were involved, and the Officers would rather avoid using them if at all possible.

So there was a tonal mismatch between the two groups assembled in Conference Room Four; Daley and his men were upbeat in anticipation of a headline-grabbing arrest, and in contrast the Firearms Officers seemed downcast and introspective.

DI Pitt revealed a large, printed schema of the Altrincham and Hale Social Club and surrounding streets on a wall-mounted board. He had positioned green Post-It notes at various spots to indicate lay-up points in advance of the operation. There would be Officers hidden from view at six points in a triangle around the building.

Daley suggested everyone be in place by 4pm. It was almost eleven now.

The Firearms Team became itchy immediately, exchanging dark glances with one another. They needed time to sign out their kit, prepare and test, and run through the standard drills.

They were released at 12.15. Graham Daley turned to his colleagues with a look of satisfaction. This was feeling like it might be a decent job.

It had better be.

Chief Commissioner Watts had avoided his eye more than once today, Daley had noticed. This was not a good sign. He needed tonight to go well.

≈

Ben da Silva had a standing appointment with his parents on the first Thursday of each month – a family dinner at 6 Tatford Close in Blackburn, with his mum and dad and whichever of his cousins were in favour that week. This diary date was non-negotiable. Ben may as well try to move the Pennines to Essex than rearrange family dinner.

He'd long suspected that this uncancellable obligation was designed by the forces of nature to inconvenience him. It fell on very much the 'wrong' night with an uncanny frequency.

Ben was not an enthusiastic socialiser. He didn't do much most weeks other than snooker on a Monday and the cinema at the weekend. But he had, since the turn of the year, turned down numerous social invitations - a ticket to see Bruce Springsteen in Liverpool, a good friend's birthday drinks as well as the climax of the First Test on television in the pub. He'd also needed to wriggle out of a work function at the Town Hall with Shaun and Eleanor. The universe didn't seem to know that these kinds of events shouldn't be scheduled on a first Thursday.

He could make tonight's clash work, however. Snooping was done better after dark, and it would be light tonight until gone nine o'clock.

Dinner was a restless experience. Ben felt a nagging ache in his lower back, which caused him to shift in his seat almost continually. He was distracted – almost absent at times – to an extent that drew comment from his father Joao.

"Something going on with you, Benny?"

"No. Sorry. Tired."

Dad would have to make do with a regulation brush-off. He was used to it by now.

Ben's cousins Maria and Bruno had been diverting enough after dinner, sparking off one another in a debate about the current events in EastEnders, which Ben didn't watch. Maria could be very funny when she was irked.

As he drained his second ginger ale, Ben glanced at his watch. Eight forty. He'd need to hang on for another thirty minutes or so, but that would be an acceptable departure point. Chadderton Fold was three-quarters of an hour's drive from here.

He felt a shudder of anticipation, a frisson that ran up his spine and into his neck.

The adventure he had planned for tonight would be a lot more fun than reporting on new traffic schemes or civic initiatives. And once he'd completed his mission without incident, Shaun would be appreciative of it, he knew.

≈

Five unmarked cars and a white van had been in position by the Altrincham and Hale Social Club for five-and-a-half hours. In addition to the ten armed officers in these vehicles, another ten uniforms had been stationed inside an auto-parts warehouse in the street that ran down the side of the club. DI Daley hadn't left himself short of numbers.

Dardan Rexha had arrived at 4.30 and unlocked the place, entering through the front door and down the stairs. He was oblivious to the many pairs of eyes watching him as he did so.

Nothing much else had occurred other than four drunk lads arriving and going again within the hour.

The chat over the Police radios had been typically banal. Lying almost flat in the passenger seat of a nondescript Toyota saloon, Daley listened in. He was always impressed by these Officers' endless patience and good humour in these circumstances.

"Indigo Three, I can hear your stomach rumbling from the other side of the road. Over."

"Thanks Charlie Two. I've been staring at the front of a curry house since four o'clock. Big test of discipline."

"Charlie Two – the bhajis in there are unreal."

"Yeah, I assumed you'd know, Victor One. Over."

This kind of low exchange sparked up every five or ten minutes. It was important that everyone stayed on their toes, which was hard when not moving from a set position for hours on end. Regular check-ins ensured continued engagement. They kept minds moving.

The tone of these chats belied the tension inside each of the vehicles. As time crept forward and the sunlight began to wane on Hale, each Officer knew the chances of a contact were increasing by the minute.

Graham Daley had given instructions. If Marku and his cronies approached the building, they should be allowed to enter. Six Officers would then station themselves at the rear door that led into the kitchens. Once they were in position, ten others would follow the target group into the club and down the stairway, armed Officers first. There were no other exits bar these two – anyone inside at that point had zero chance of evading contact.

At seven minutes to nine o'clock, there was a heads-up across the radio network – one of many in the last few hours.

"Charlie One, this is Indigo Three. Male approaching from the west of the building. Over."

"Got him Indigo Three. Eyes on. Over."

The man in question wore a black hoodie and a rucksack. He strode with some purpose along Hale Road in the direction of the club.

DI Daley, watching on from the Toyota, raised his head to catch sight of the approaching figure. In an instant, his years of experience coalesced into an instinct – this was no innocent passer-by. Perhaps it was the weight of whatever was in the rucksack, evident from how it pulled down on its straps. It could have been the slightly hunched shoulders or fixed head position. But there was an energy about this figure that was 'off'.

Daley picked up his radio.

"All units. This is Alpha. I'm getting vibes off this character. Wits about you please."

"Same, Alpha. That rucksack weighs a ton by the look of it."

With this, the hooded figure dipped down the side street that ran alongside the club.

"Where's he going?" asked Daley, of nobody.

He soon had an answer. The figure stepped around the rear of the club, into the employees' car park and to the rear door. The radio was suddenly alive again.

"Alpha this is Charlie Two – subject at rear entrance."

"Alpha, request to intercept. Over."

Daley spoke to his Officers once more.

"No. Do not intercept."

The man they were tracking was too short to be Arjan Marku. He had the look of a scally about him – the swagger as he walked. His clothing. In other words, Daley had a strong hunch he was local.

The reply came.

"Roger that Alpha. All units hold. As you were."

"Can anyone see what he's doing back there?" asked Daley.

Nobody could. The man was largely hidden behind two tall bins on wheels at the back of the property, adjacent to the rear entrance.

Daley began to doubt himself. Was this figure just an irritation that needed to be removed from the scene with as little fuss as possible? Or was there some connection to the Albanians that they should let play out?

He thought about sending in two Officers. Low-key, no drama, put this lad under caution and move him on.

Before he could make the decision, the man moved away from the back door of the club and back into the side road.

"Still eyes on the subject, Alpha. Now back in the street."

"Roger that" Daley responded.

The youth – which is what Graham Daley could now see he was – rounded the corner back onto Hale Road and walked to the front of the club.

"This is Alpha. All units still hold. If he wants to go in, let him."

The man pulled the door open and disappeared inside.

There was silence from the Officers watching on. Was this the start of something, or an entirely innocent occurrence? Whatever had happened at the rear of the building was odd, but no specific threat had yet been identified.

In ten seconds' time, the threat would be all too evident.

Halfway down the stairwell of the Altrincham and Hale Social Club, unseen by the posse of Officers on the other side of the door, the man stopped. He let his rucksack drop from his back, opened it up, and unscrewed the top from a plastic container within. The container held six litres of petrol.

The liquid was poured down the stairwell and thrown up the walls until the container was empty. Then the rucksack was hurled to the foot of the stairs, where there was a second door that led into the snooker hall itself.

The Officers outside observed the door opening again and the man in black coming back out.

"Rucksack's gone" said one of the Officers on the radio.

The youth held the door open and produced from his pocket a Zippo lighter. The flint was actioned and a small flame flickered from the wick.

Daley just had time to aim an expletive at his radio before the lighter was hurled down the stairs and the door slammed shut.

When accelerants such as petrol are used to start fires, the initial 'catch' of flame to the fuel can cause the blaze to expand at an extremely rapid rate.

This speed creates great force in a concentrated area. This effect is more succinctly known as an explosion.

The culprit, now stood outside the door to the Altrincham and Hale Social Club, was clearly no scientist. The door blew out of its frame within a second of having been shut, and knocked flat the figure in black, before skidding noisily halfway across the street.

There was no need for radio contact. Officers poured out of vehicles and towards the club, instinctively heading for the unconscious perpetrator who lay face down on the pavement. Daley's initial assessment was that the man in black could easily be dead. The edge of the door had slammed into his skull with sickening force.

Flames now leapt from the entrance to the club. Officers ran towards the unconscious man and hauled him away from the site of the blaze he had started.

Once he was lifted out of harm's way and set down further along the pavement, one Officer urged his colleague to retrieve the man's wallet so he could be identified. DI Daley said there was no need. Now he was up close, he could assure the Officer that this character was well known to the Police.

His name was Keiron Stafford.

≈

A white Renault drew into the car park of the Chadderton Fold Caravan Park at just before ten o'clock. The very last smatterings of deep orange could be seen over the hills beyond. It was now all but night.

Once parked, Ben sat in the car and took stock of what lay beyond the fence in front of him. From here, he could see perhaps a third of the Park's static caravans, the remainder being situated further off into the gloom or beyond the thicket of trees sixty yards away. The Park's wooden reception building was locked up, as could be expected at this hour.

He sat up straight in the driver's seat and centred himself, then got out of his car and walked towards the gated entrance.

It was oddly quiet out here, and the noise of the gravel under Ben's feet as he made for the interior of the park made him feel conspicuous. He was an intruder, and he felt like one.

Ben had examined the map of this place for a good thirty minutes during his lunch break at work. He'd narrowed down the likely site of Emlyn's rental considerably.

There were two sizes of static home here; four bedroomed 'luxury' rentals and smaller, two-bedroomed units. The larger properties were the most visible – to other inhabitants as well as anyone who might happen to be driving past on the main road. The smaller abodes, beyond the trees, were more secluded.

Given Emlyn's need for anonymity at the time of his absconding, and the fact that was presumably hiding here alone, he would surely have rented one of the smaller units. Ben was heading for them straight away. He would aim to narrow the field of potentials even further once he got there.

As he emerged through the far side of a small copse that separated the two halves of the caravan park, he saw the lights of the Horton Arms a mile or so distant. He recalled the two awkward dates he'd had in there with an Indian girl, Sunam. What had happened to her in the intervening two years, he wondered? She'd be with someone worthy of her, Ben hoped.

Laid out before Ben were twenty-two cabins, almost identical in size and exterior decor. He reckoned Emlyn's would be among this group. Fourteen of them had lights on inside, which meant they were occupied. He could strike these from the list of candidates.

Of the eight remaining, two were obviously not in a state to be rented out – one was held up with scaffolding poles where the hard standing beneath it had broken up; the other had blue tarp instead of windows.

That left six cabins as feasible options. There were no features that distinguished one from the next. Not at this distance, at least.

Ben would have to investigate each in turn.

As he walked the path in front of the cabins, two of the six were counted out immediately. One housed a loud and obvious snorer, and the other had a clothesline outside on which were pegged various kids' clothes.

So four were left.

Ben would have to be extremely careful the moment he strayed from the communal pathways that connected these cabins. He couldn't be seen peering into windows at night, off the beaten track, and expect to go unchallenged.

He decided to move to the far end of the park so that he could evaluate the properties from the rear. Perhaps that would provide him with more information that he had gleaned from the front.

Crouching down a little to stay beneath the line of the top of a hedge, Ben studied the first caravan left. The curtains at the rear bedroom window were open, which he supposed was a sign that nobody was asleep in it.

Could he risk it?

Ben wasn't prepared to consider coming all this way to do half a job. He crept in from the hedge, across the grass towards the window. On arriving there, he peeked inside the caravan, and initially could see almost nothing.

He pulled his phone from his pocket and shone its torchlight through the window. His assumption had been correct – the bedroom was unoccupied. Clothes were strewn across the floor and the bed, and among them was a dark coloured singlet.

On it, Ben could make out the typeface of the shirt's brand, emblazoned across the front.

Lonsdale.

Boxing equipment.

At the very least, this was now an excellent candidate for Emlyn Parry's erstwhile hideout.

Ben moved around to the door at the side of the caravan. As he expected, it was firmly locked.

He returned to the rear and looked at the sealing along the bottom of the window, where it joined the frame. There was a rubberized border all the way around, which held the glass in place. Up close, Ben noticed it had deteriorated in a few places, and was dangerously thin at points.

He began to pull at the window's rubber surround, and hadn't been at it for very long before a sizeable section of it came away completely. This caused the entire pane of glass to slip out of place, dislodge itself from the window frame and hit the concrete standing at Ben's feet.

The sound created by the windowpane as it shattered into a thousand fragments could be heard several fields over. It seemed to bounce around Chadderton Fold for an eternity, glancing off the treetops and cannoning off the sides of the caravans. Ben may as well have set off an air raid siren.

Should he run? Or would that be worse?

Ben crouched, motionless, barely breathing until silence settled in again.

Nothing for a moment. Then a light came on in the next caravan along. A flabby man with ungoverned wisps of hair escaping his cranium appeared at a window. He peered blearily into the gloom for a few seconds, then scratched his naked belly and disappeared again.

Ben didn't move a hair for five full minutes. He was ready to sprint for the treeline at any moment should he be discovered.

Eventually, he rose from his haunches and peeked around the side of the caravan. Nothing was moving in his field of vision. And if the shattering of a window hadn't brought the neighbours out with torches and kitchen knives, nothing would.

Ben threw his left leg through the vacant window frame and hauled himself over the sill.

≈

Graham Daley dumped his coat on the back of his office chair and sat down. He tried to rub the exhaustion from his face, but it wouldn't shift.

Operation Crucible had taken a highly unexpected turn.

He had stayed until the conflagration was extinguished by the Fire Service. A rum bunch, fireman, he had thought. Bit too full of themselves, bowling about with their chests puffed out. A little bit of humility wouldn't hurt. Public servants, after all.

He then checked in on the arrestee Stafford, who was now conscious again despite a fractured skull, and handcuffed to a hospital bed.

Daley needed a minute to evaluate where things were at. Clarity had been at a premium for the last forty-eight hours, and his brain was full.

The bottom line was this: no Marku, no Garton. That would be the diagnosis from Leonard Watts.

How exhausting this all was, the constant showing of one's workings and the results-driven culture that had emerged since he began on the Force as a callow graduate. It was perfectly possible to run an operation like this superbly, have everything go as planned, and still not come away with a result.

Equally, some of the biggest clusterfucks he could recall had resulted in arrests, despite the Force's efforts and not because of them.

But there wasn't space for that sort of nuance in the modern Force. The only criterion that mattered was what could be read on a spreadsheet.

It occurred to DI Daley that this line of thought was somewhat self-indulgent, given the bustle that was still going on around him at three in the morning. His colleagues had maintained their fierce determination to catch either or both of their targets well into a second day.

Should he get some sleep? Or do the rounds to gauge the status of things?

Before he could answer that question, Sergeant Corrigan bowled onto the office floor from the corridor, looking surprisingly energised.

"Graham…" he bellowed across the office.

No "evening sir", or "tough night?". Corrigan had something to say.

"Can you join us in Conference Room Four? We've had a tip-off from a copper in Preston. You'll want to hear this."

Daley straightened in his chair. He prayed this was bona fide good news and not a dead end. It was common for exhausted Officers to exaggerate the importance of intel when they were becoming desperate. Daley would come at it as objectively as he could.

He stood, weary, and went over to join Corrigan by the doorway.

Perhaps – just maybe – tonight wouldn't be a total write off after all.

30

As dawn broke on Friday morning, Shaun Mullin lay on his back, eyes wide open.

Californian Dave had failed him last night, offering the usual soothing ruminations but to no practical effect. Shaun hadn't slept a single moment.

And now, as the sun crept up into view and the corners of his bedroom were revealed once again, he realised the opportunity for sleep had probably gone. He would likely stagger through the day with sore eyes and a chainsaw running in his forehead until mid-afternoon, when he'd capsize on the settee. That's how it usually went from here.

He blearily pulled a curtain aside, which he could do from his bed, and checked the street for Peter Garton's hired urchins. He hadn't seen them since yesterday afternoon.

They'd be back.

Shaun made yet another attempt to assuage his anxious state of mind. He was troubled on three fronts.

He hoped to God Ben hadn't done anything reckless.

Tomorrow was the designated day of his return to Manchester Central Police Station.

And the day after that was Garton's deadline day.

These were all, of course, aspects of the same situation, and Shaun had spent six hours in complete silence attempting to resolve each to the satisfaction of the others.

He could of course spill everything he knew to Graham Daley and take whatever punishment there was coming from the law. But then, Peter Garton would remain unsatisfied, and that was a chilling prospect.

What if he did try to locate the key, starting at Chadderton Fold? How could he, in all conscience, simply capitulate to a vile character like Garton? Who was he, if he did this man's bidding? Morally, that wouldn't do either.

And if Ben had found the key – or even tried to find it – Shaun would feel a great weight of responsibility for any repercussions. Ben was simply too artless, too inexperienced, to have hidden his own footsteps well enough.

He got up and pulled on a vintage Morrissey t-shirt he'd bought in the nineties. Shaun had gone off the bloke in recent years but couldn't countenance ever disposing of this item of clothing. It was threadbare now, and had a growing hole in the armpit, but it was nonetheless a welcome link to simpler, freer times.

As he descended the stairs, he compiled a to-do list for the day. He should speak to Thusita about his second interview tomorrow. He'd no idea what to expect. Was this the point at which things fizzled out and he could relax a little, or would the screws be turned and charges made?

He needed to check in on Ben.

His finger needed re-dressing.

And he should probably ring his mum to explain fully his sudden exit from Bluebell Farm two nights ago.

Shaun reached the bottom stair and noticed a package in the hallway – a small bubble-wrap envelope with tape wound around it. He took a small detour to collect it from the doormat and went into the kitchen.

As the kettle went on, Shaun opened the parcel.

A small, metallic object fell out of it and clanged on the tiled floor.

≈

Peter Garton was awake too, but in rather less comfortable surroundings. He slouched in the back of the Kia rented by Keiron Stafford, wondering where the hell his accomplice had got to.

Had he bottled it – the job at the snooker club designed to incinerate Arjan Marku – and done a runner? Or had something gone wrong?

Garton would wait. He had no choice. He stared out through the front windscreen of the vehicle. There was a thoroughly depressing vista afforded by his position on level four of a multi-storey in Stalybridge.

Perhaps he should contact Shaun ahead of time. Get things moving.

No.

He had one burner phone, and without Stafford in tow he wouldn't be able to purchase another without showing his face on the street. He needed to use the one he had judiciously, and dispose of it within an hour of its use, as planned.

Mullin wouldn't have found anything yet. Garton wasn't sure he ever would, but he'd keep the screws on the dickhead for as long as he could.

He lay back on the floor of the van and tried to keep some perspective on Keiron Stafford. He might yet return. And if he didn't, Garton told himself there would be a way forward. There always was.

≈

Shaun's early morning had shifted in a second from a rather dilatory one to a frenzied whirl of activity. A key had been posted through his letterbox in a padded envelope, almost certainly by Ben da Silva, and Shaun knew viscerally that he simply could not have this object remain in the house. He had recoiled from it as he saw it skitter across the kitchen floor, as if it were emitting radioactivity. It needed to be taken away.

What the hell had Ben done? And how had he done it? Clumsily, guilelessly, and traceably, Shaun had to assume.

Shaun muttered various theories and judgments to himself as he ransacked his kitchen drawers, looking for a specific implement. He had no garden at number 44, and therefore no gardening tools, so he had decided on a cake slice instead. That would serve his immediate need.

He'd have to pump up his bicycle tires and cross his fingers they'd stay inflated long enough to get done what he needed to do.

≈

Father Norman Hillier was stirring a pan of tinned soup on his stove at the back of Saint Anthony's Church – cream of vegetable, of course, it being a Friday and therefore the day of abstaining from meat. He'd debated vegetarianism his entire adult life, weighing up the ethical difficulty of eating God's creatures against the clear physiological evidence that humans were designed to eat flesh, and it was therefore His will. Abstinence Fridays were a boon – the decision had been made for him by Catholic tradition, and so his mind could rest easy on the matter.

He dropped a couple of slices of wholemeal onto a plate. And as Sod's Law would have it, the back doorbell rang just as his soup came to the boil.

He muttered a forceful 'drat' to himself (which was as strong as it got for Father Hillier) and turned off the heat beneath the pan.

At the rear door to the church stood Shaun Mullin.

Hillier noticed immediately the dirt on his face and on his hands. There was a rucksack on his back, and he was breathing heavily.

"Shaun" he exclaimed. "How are you?"

With a nod, Shaun replied breathlessly "Bit out of practice on the old bike, Father."

The priest bade him in and offered him soup. Shaun accepted some, which seemed to please the old man. It indicated that Shaun didn't feel the restrictions of propriety, and was relaxed here.

They sat opposite one another at the table. Shaun was aware of the dirt about his person and on his hands and face, and was thankful Father Hillier hadn't brought it up.

"I wanted to apologize for the other night, Father" said Shaun. "You shouldn't have to deal with people like Peter Garton under your own roof."

"None of it was down to you, Shaun" Hillier replied. "I leave the door open at all times, day and night. What comes through it..."

Hillier shrugged.

Shaun couldn't quite formulate what he wanted to say, but knew he'd come here for reasons other than forgiveness. Hillier saw Shaun wrestling with his mind for a moment, before speaking with a quizzical tone.

"Garton's done awful things. Unforgivable. And I should acknowledge him as a terrible man. But… I don't think I can" said the guest, with a spoonful of soup hanging in mid-air. "Is that wrong?"

"Others are unknowable, Shaun. There are infinite possibilities within each of us. Our judgments say as much about us as they do other people."

"But you judged him. The other night. You called him a degenerate."

"I was afraid. Fear is a moral weakness, like so many we are subject to" admitted the priest.

Shaun sat back in the kitchen chair.

Hillier felt the impulse to push a little. To help uncover whatever trouble Shaun was preoccupied with.

They spoke around the houses for a while, with Hillier getting the distinct impression Shaun was waiting for an opportunity to unburden himself of what was really on his mind.

It came eventually. Shaun was wrestling with a moral conundrum. The details were scant, which Father Hillier understood, but there seemed to be a moral core to the problem.

"What is it you want in this situation you're in, Shaun?" he asked.

"What do *I* want?"

"Of course."

Shaun paused.

"I want to be safe. Which feels selfish."

"Why?"

"There are other concerns. Other people."

"It's not selfish at all" said Hillier. "It's a very basic need."

The conversation rambled, almost dying at times, then resurrecting itself with a new thought. Shaun's inability to provide specifics meant the priest couldn't be as helpful as he wanted to be.

"There will be a solution, Shaun. Don't assume defeat" he said. "If God is anywhere, He is in the powers he has given us. Superior beings, and all that. There is a way out."

≈

Saturday morning came. But unfortunately for Peter Garton, Keiron

Stafford did not. Peter was hungry – there were only so many oatcakes and nut bars a man could take – and deeply uncomfortable splayed out on the floor of the Kia. Twenty-four hours until he would contact Shaun Mullin. It made no sense to factor Keiron into any further activities. He knew in his heart he must see this through alone. Take risks. Wing it.

Not his preferred modus operandi, but his situation was bordering on desperate. He would need a touch of good fortune to come through this a free man.

≈

Shaun's face was buried in a pile of plastic bags at the bottom of his wardrobe. He'd slept well, and a little too long, and now had to hurry to be ready for his Solicitor's arrival.

There had been a release last night from his considerable penury, after his meeting with Father Hillier at Saint Anthony's. Shaun had come to a simplified equation as a basis for solving his problem:

The primary aim was safety, for him and for Claire. That wasn't negotiable. So how could he ensure it, without aiding and abetting an established criminal?

A plan had formed between 10pm and midnight, and he'd relayed it to his legal representative via email at 1am. There was work to be done to bring the plan home, but it was a feasible escape. He had felt the heaviness seep from his shoulders as he powered his laptop down and headed for bed.

Thusita Nissanka had agreed to a meeting at 44 North Road before she and her client left for Manchester Central at 11am. This would afford her the opportunity to get across the significant developments Shaun had outlined to her the previous evening. The interview with Daley and his colleagues this morning would be taking on an unexpected hue, that was for sure.

Having delved about in his wardrobe for a couple of minutes, Shaun stood abruptly, and clutched a blue necktie in triumph. He hadn't seen it for three years, since a wedding he went to in Crewe. It might be a good look, he thought, for an interrogation.

On her arrival, Thusita disagreed.

"Are you going out of your way to look like the accused?" she said.

Shaun hadn't thought of that. It was a bit 'sheepishly stood in the dock'. The tie came off.

Shaun made coffee. Thusita declined.

"We need to be really clear about what we're trying to achieve this morning, Shaun. They'll want to drive the agenda. If we're going to derail that we've got to be careful."

"I've got something they want" rationed Shaun, contradicting Thusita's rather pessimistic interpretation of the circumstances.

"Don't get carried away" she said. "You're about to introduce a good deal of uncertainty to the conversation, and that makes things unpredictable."

"What are the chances they might charge me with something at the moment, d'you reckon?"

Thusita considered her response carefully.

"Fifty-fifty. You're not helped by the big, fat blanks they've drawn everywhere else to be honest. They'll be looking for an entry in the plus column at this point."

"But we can leverage what I've got, can't we?"

Thusita nodded.

"In theory, yes" she said.

≈

Ben da Silva hadn't heard from Shaun in the day-and-a-half since pushing a padded envelope through his front door. He had discovered in that time the great frustration of investigative work – you couldn't share it with anyone. He would love to have recounted his story of the expedition to Chadderton Fold, but there was nobody he could tell it to.

He suspected Shaun was probably furious with him. But that was OK, it wouldn't last. He hoped there might be some admiration there, eventually. Perhaps even a touch of gratitude.

Ben had almost rung Shaun on three or four occasions the previous day, but the prospect of his call being declined or shifted to voicemail was too much to handle. He had done what he'd done for Shaun and only for Shaun, and needed to maintain his faith that his actions would be acknowledged as brave and selfless in time.

Tomorrow would be the watershed, when Shaun would speak to Garton or one of his emissaries. A small, brass key would, all things being right, release the considerable pressure his boss was under.

≈

"Before we start, my client would like to share some information with you" said Ms. Nissanka, with the clarity and boldness of the town crier.

Graham Daley and his colleagues Pitt and Corrigan all raised their eyebrows in unison. Was the journalist about to fess up to something, and disguise it as useful intel to lessen the blow? They'd seen this move before.

Thusita continued, "It should not be misinterpreted as any kind of attempt at mitigation, as there is nothing to mitigate. He maintains his non-involvement in any crime. He is divulging certain information to you now solely because it's the right thing to do."

Daley wasn't buying it. There was some subterfuge at work here.

DI Pitt had everything crossed for an admission of guilt from Mullin in some roundabout fashion – conspiracy to help Emlyn Parry flee the country on a hooky passport would be a prison sentence.

DS Corrigan eyeballed Shaun, looking for flags in his body language.

"Interesting" said Daley. "Why now, Shaun?"

"The information I've got only came to light very recently" Shaun said.

"Oh, how very timely" Daley said sarcastically.

Funny how often that happened. Daley sat back in his chair and crossed his arms, aping Pitt's posture. Shaun found himself looking at the human rendition of a brick wall.

"We're all ears, Shaun" chipped in DI Pitt. "Off you go".

Shaun began. He tried to remember what his Solicitor had told him in the car about the need for methodical thought at this moment, but things suddenly felt overwhelmingly intense, and he gabbled it a bit.

"I know where Peter Garton is going to be at some point in the next few days" he said. "An actual address."

Silence. Shaun knew only too well that he shouldn't fill it. Daley or Pitt had to be the next to speak.

It was the former.

"Care to elaborate?"

"Certainly" said Shaun, before Thusita intervened.

"On two conditions" she said.

Pitt muttered "Oh here we go..."

Daley interjected with a practised air of weariness.

"Well we'd certainly be prepared to hear these conditions, Ms. Nissanka. Go on."

"Firstly, my client will be subject to no charges relating to the activities of Peter Garton or Emlyn Parry. Mister Mullin maintains his position that all of his behaviours in relation to the two men were lawful. He would like that recognised by Greater Manchester Police and to not be persecuted any longer."

That was an odd choice of word, thought Daley. Incendiary, at this point. And Ms. Nissanka was forensic about every syllable that came from her mouth, he knew that much.

'Persecuted' was a deliberate gambit, an escalation of terms. She was letting him know she'd be happy to follow a 'Police harassment' line, if it came to it. Objectively, she might have enough to make that stick, it occurred to him. They'd been tinkering around the edges of Mullin's liberty on and off for some while.

Daley nodded. Pitt snorted.

"Secondly, my client's identity is to be kept out of all evidentiary materials, particularly around documents required for any trial that might occur. He doesn't wish to be associated publicly with the case in any manner."

"You're scared" sneered Pitt, at Shaun. "Garton's given you the heebie-jeebies."

Daley frowned. He didn't appreciate this sort of imprecise language in interviews. And Pitt's goading manner was unlikely to foster a cooperative atmosphere.

"We're all weak in our own way, aren't we Detective?" said Shaun, borrowing from Father Hillier's liturgy of self-effacement.

DI Pitt had no idea what Shaun was getting at. It was a typically oblique comment. You could never get a straight answer from this arsehole.

"And this is straight up is it, Shaun?" asked Daley. "Concrete intel?"

Shaun nodded.

"Because if you're fucking us about…"

Daley and Pitt excused themselves from the interview, citing the need for a recess to discuss the demands Thusita had made. As the door closed behind them, Shaun glanced across at her. She was a picture of self-containment, perfectly controlled. He felt better for having seen her implacable face, her unbreachable superiority.

They hardly spoke a word for the eleven minutes they were left alone with DS Corrigan. There was nothing that could be helpfully said. Corrigan sighed a couple of times, scanning the two faces opposite him for a sign of something. But the faces remained slab-like, inexpressive.

When Daley returned, it was without DI Pitt. As he sat back down, Thusita suspected Pitt had been jettisoned. He was an oaf, and men like him were a risk in nuanced circumstances like these.

He was replaced at the table by the glowering DI Chinn.

"OK Shaun" said Graham. "On the basis this is actual intelligence we can use, we can agree not to charge you with any of the potential crimes we've discussed with you to date. Any new ones that emerge, however, are outside of that agreement. And we can anonymise you in the paperwork, no problem."

Nissanka looks across at Shaun. There was the faintest trace of a smile.

"Over to you" said Daley.

So far so good.

Take your time.

Shaun began at the beginning.

"So, Peter Garton has been looking for a key. It's the reason he escaped from prison in the first place."

"Right" said Daley, with an encouraging tone. "The key we spoke to you about in your previous interview."

"Exactly."

Before Shaun could continue Graham Daley stepped in.

"Do you know where this key is, Shaun?"

There was a beat, in which Shaun caught Daley's eye.

"Yes."

Daley leaned forward.

"Ok, Shaun, listen to me. We need that key".

Thusita intervened again.

"No you don't. You need the key *and* Peter Garton".

Daley totally ignored the Solicitor and rounded on his interviewee.

"Where's the key, Shaun?"

"I buried it."

"You mean it's been in your possession?"

"Yes."

"Fucking hell Shaun."

Daley could scarcely believe the sheer front of this man.

"Where is it buried?" he demanded.

"No comment" said Shaun.

Daley could cheerfully have kicked Mullin halfway down the corridor. This was the central piece of evidence in the prosecution of Peter Garton, and he was having to negotiate to find out its whereabouts. He should do this prick for obstruction of justice.

Thusita Nissanka had to smooth this over. Daley had become too heated for anyone's good.

"Detective Inspector" said Thusita, "we believe there is a strategy that secures both the key and Garton at the same time. In the midst of a criminal act, too. If you'll just hear my client out, he'd be happy to explain it."

Daley composed himself, remembering just how many Officers were looking on from the control room.

He would give Shaun the benefit of the doubt for now. This proposal was intriguing enough, and his silence prompted Shaun to continue his line of thought.

"You cannot arrest Garton in the UK. That's not negotiable. The arrest will take place overseas" said Shaun.

Daley's brow furrowed. There was that word again.

"Not negotiable? Sorry Shaun, that's pretty bold for someone who's being interviewed for perverting the course of justice. What makes you think you can tell me where I can and can't arrest someone?"

Shaun poured petrol on the flames. He couldn't help himself.

"Take it or leave it Graham."

"Do you know what it takes for us to be able to nick people abroad? It's a fucking minefield."

"Sounds like a 'you' problem" replied the interviewee.

It looked to Shaun as if Daley might explode.

Beneath the table, Thusita placed her hand on Shaun's arm. Shaun needed to placate him a little.

"If you nick him in the UK, he'll know I've grassed on him" he said.

Thusita tried to interject. "Detective Insp –"

"So fucking what? He'll be nicked won't he? What are you worried about?"

Shaun resented this. Daley was pursuing a line that was obtuse. He knew this was far too simplistic.

He took the volume up a notch now.

"He has associates, Graham. Fucking dozens of them, all over Manchester. Four of them stationed, by the way, outside my fucking house right now. It's what he does. He gets other people to do terrible things on his behalf. It's his entire business model".

This last sentence was especially vehement, Daley having chosen to ignore Garton's well-known methods for the sake of convenience.

Shaun now transferred his attention to DI Chinn.

"Yes, DI Chinn, your colleague was right. I am afraid of Peter Garton, and so would you be in my shoes. I will not spend the rest of my days waking up in the night at the slightest sound. Taking the long way home after dark. Avoiding certain pubs and clubs and streets. Why should I live like that?"

Shaun's outburst hung in the air.

He had needed that. And the Officers had needed to hear it.

Shaun spoke again, more softly now.

"The safety of myself and my family is paramount. There is no deal if that is not assured. If Peter Garton is arrested, it cannot look as if it involved me in any way. I will not live waiting for some scrote in a hoodie to fucking shiv me. End of."

Graham Daley wore a complex expression. He'd always respected Shaun's intelligence, and what he'd said in defence of his stance on Garton was accurate and logical.

But he was stunningly arrogant. Who comes in shouting the odds like that at their own police interview? Who did he think was in charge, for God's sake? How would he look to his colleagues on the other side of the one-way glass if he let himself be bullied by a suspect, in his own Station?

Thusita spoke.

"If Mister Mullin could continue? I think you'll be satisfied with the resolution. We're looking for something that works for all parties."

Daley sighed.

"Fuckinell. Right. Go on."

Shaun looked at Thusita, who opened her briefcase and began retrieving a large, folded sheet of paper from it.

"Garton told me the key has the number 71 engraved on it, and that's the one I buried. So it's definitely his. It doesn't take a genius to work out what it's for, right? It's likely a safe deposit somewhere."

Daley nodded along.

Thusita unfolded a printed sheet of A2 on the table. It took up most of the surface area, forcing Chinn to collect up his notes and stow them on his lap.

It was the map of a city.

Daley craned his neck to read some of the street names and landmarks. "Brussels" he said.

Shaun nodded. He waited. This was the moment of no return. He was about to hand over his sole bargaining chip.

DI Daley provided the push he needed.

"You have my commitment, on this tape, that your demands have been agreed to."

Shaun glanced at Thusita Nissanka. Her eyebrows flicked upwards just the merest touch in a signal of assent.

Do it.

"Garton is on his way to Brussels early next week. With the key."

"How?" asked Daley. "How's he getting there?"

"Your guess is as good as mine. The boot of a car, the back of a lorry. P&O ferry. Who knows."

Thusita handed Shaun four drawing pins, each with coloured heads. He now planted each of these at a different location on the map, with an accuracy borne of obsession.

"There are four safety deposit facilities in Brussels open to foreign nationals. It could be any of these, of course. But the first one…" Shaun placed his forefinger on a pin situated next to the Gresham Belson Hotel.

"The first one, here, has by far the strictest criteria for opening an account. National Insurance number or whatever the regional equivalent is, two forms of photo ID, proof of address, tax number. All sorts. I don't think someone like Garton, doing what Garton's been doing, would take that on to be honest."

He looked at Daley. Daley didn't disagree.

"Now, this one…"

Shaun moved his finger to a second pin in the map, this time located by the Royal Bruxelles Yacht Club.

"Here, it's a small facility. A high-end, boutique bank. And they only have forty-eight deposit boxes. So it doesn't make a lot of sense to number one of them seventy-one, does it?"

"Number three." Shaun's finger switched to the far north of the city, to a pin placed near a hospital on the riverbank.

"This one is miles out of town. An arse-ache to get to. And to be honest, judging by the website, it's a bit of a grubby operation. Crappy old building and what not. Shabby. I think Mister Garton would want a little bit more spec than that, don't you?"

Daley raised his eyebrows.

"Which leaves us with one candidate, by a process of elimination."

"Yes, and…" said Shaun. "…number four has a lot going for it. It's the only facility with a fully English version of its website. It's the nearest of the four to the Eurostar terminal. And it's bang in the middle of the jewellery district.

Daley smiled. Trinkets. Bracelets, chains and watches. Very Peter Garton.

"Sixty-three Rue Breydel, Brussels" said Shaun. "I'm going to tell Peter Garton where his key is buried. He is going to collect it. And once he gets to Belgium in a few days' time, you can collect him."

It was an odd enterprise, thought Daley. And an awkward one to set in motion from here. But everything Shaun had said made perfect sense.

Shaun sat back, awaiting any kind of response. Graham Daley was deep in thought. DI Chinn's expression hadn't changed a jot - he still had the same look of scepticism on his face, tinged with distaste.

There would be cross-border difficulties. Language problems. Budgetary issues. Selling it to Leonard Watts would be tough. And it would produce a horrible admin burden for his staff.

But it wasn't impossible.

"That's very interesting, Shaun" he said, eventually. "Leave it with me. I'll have to talk to my boss."

Epilogue

*A*rjan Marku was forty miles *from the Altrincham and Hale Social Club when it went up in flames. He was at the time in an Air BnB holiday rental outside Preston, having presented himself to the owners as a Bulgarian engineer visiting Manchester for a conference.*

Marku was apprehended there four hours after the fire in Hale began. The network of Police Forces in Lancashire had been well briefed – a simple tip-off from a beat Bobby (via a petrol station checkout worker) proved his undoing.

As I write this, the authorities are still compiling the growing list of offences they intend to hang around Marku's neck. That list might eventually cover almost every serious crime on the statute.

The gentle Dardan Rexha, the club's proprietor, died in the Hale blaze. The rear door to the premises, which led into the kitchen, had been padlocked from the outside by Keiron Stafford. This left one available route out of the basement, and that was the burning staircase – a no-go within a few seconds of ignition.

Rexha was found asphyxiated in the fetal position beneath one of his snooker tables. Not a death I would wish on anyone, let alone a man whose only crime was timidity in the face of extreme malice.

As for Keiron Stafford, he is to stand trial in the spring of next year. Conspiracy, kidnap, arson and murder, in that order. He'll be away for some time, one would hope. Like father, like son, and on it goes.

And so to the main event. Peter Garton.

Garton was nicked within a week of our last contact. Belgian Police were waiting for him at a deposit box facility in the Rue Breydel in central

Brussels. They held their nerve until he'd emptied his safe deposit box of –
wait for it – eighty-six wristwatches with a value of about four million quid.
Was there ever a clearer symbol of pathological acquisitiveness than that?

The arrest was a triumph of cross-border collaboration – long assumed
to have been impossible since the UK's departure from the European Union
– and became a career-making feather in the cap for Graham Daley.

By the end of my first encounter with Peter Garton in Strangeways, I
knew he wasn't the one-dimensional villain he'd been painted. There were
complexities to him. But I couldn't quite figure out who he was, in his
essence.

At our second meeting at Saint Anthony's in Oldham, however, he
revealed himself a little more clearly. I got to the bottom of him – to my
own satisfaction at least – soon after that.

To my mind, Peter views himself as a sort of avenger. Not in relation to
an individual, but to an entire society. For him, each criminal act, self-
serving decision and call to violence represents a kicking back against (as he
sees it) the forces of oppression. He views his criminality as entirely
justified.

He was born, he has told himself, into a particular band of citizens who
were pre-ordained to fail. It had been decreed by those that had plenty, that
he should have nothing, and for Garton, that could not stand.

His underclass status became his mentality day-to-day, and that in turn
developed into a key aspect of his personality. He has long viewed the world
through the eyes of the aggrieved, and allied his own plight with that of
notorious rebels from history. Freedom fighters, in his mind.

It takes a great deal to rouse a Brit to violent protest. We are by nature a
race of doormats, unless there are highly exceptional circumstances. But
Manchester does have a rebellious streak. We are, round here, not averse to
delivering a swift kick in the balls to authority, and various of us have paid a
heavy price for it over the decades.

I am in agreement with Garton, I would assume, that the majority of social uprisings have had right on their side. Were the Peterloo protestors 'right'? Yes. The Salford chapter of Suffragettes? The Moss Side rioters in '81? Yes and yes, to my mind. And to Peter Garton's, it can be reasonably assumed.

Therefore, according to his own internal logic, Garton is 'right' too. His is the same fight, against the same enemy. It is the battle for prosperity and self-determination against the forces that have subjugated 'his people' for centuries.

After his arrest, Peter Garton did not return to Strangeways. He now inhabits a cell at the country's most secure penal establishment – Belmarsh, in London. He won't be leaving there until he's carried out in a box. I shall never set eyes on him again.

My mutilated pinkie gave me some discomfort for probably three or four months before healing completely. I now have half a nail bed beneath the amputated section. I place a rubber sewing thimble over the stump when typing so that I can reach the Q, W, A and S on the keyboard as easily as I used to. I'm not sure it makes much of a material difference, but I enjoy it as an affectation. And it annoys Ben.

I make a point of visiting Father Hillier twice a month. I am by no means 'back in the fold' by the way – I see him on any day other than a Sunday, as that would feel like religion, and I'm sworn off that for good.

But I am a better man for his company, and his wisdom, and his guidance.

Whatever he may mean to each of us, God doesn't discriminate, it seems to me. He affords grace to the ugly as equally as ugliness to the gracious. Humankind is unfathomably rich, contradictory and random. All we can rely on is our own unpredictability.

That extends, of course, to the Gartons and the Markus of the world. Consider their contexts. These are, it can be argued, two men as much corrupted as corrupters, who have suffered misfortunes (personal and ancestral) equal to those they have created.

That statement will be viewed as contentious by some, I know. But those *folk will have written me off as bleeding heart long before now anyway.*

It seems unarguable to me, however, that the slow drip of poverty kills the soul. It wastes lives. And souls with a bit of fight in them, a bit of chip... well, they're not going to sit idly by, are they? There will always be those who refuse to accept the circumstances of their birth. And some part of me will always be cheering them on in doing so.

Other people are indeed unknowable, as Father Hillier said to me over soup at Saint Anthony's. As such, they are not to be quantified by their eccentricities. There is no true yardstick for good and evil, in the end.

If the Christian concept of forgiveness means one thing, to me it is this:

We are none of us above sin, cruelty or selfishness. And each of us has the resources for love, compassion and bravery.

And we get to choose which of these we want. How we want to live. Neither is our birthright or our fate.

Let's be kinder to each other, in the hope that the latter qualities begin to outweigh the former.

From

'NO GOOD DEED:
ME AND THE MANCHESTER MOB'
By Shaun Mullin

Acknowledgements

ANNE COTTON

EVE McCABE-EAGER

FIONA BLAKE

EMMY ASCROFT

DANIEL ASCROFT

PAUL DAVIS

KATHRYN FLEET

JASON CHEATER

IAN MOORE

If you've enjoyed the first of the series featuring Shaun Mullin, you can find out more at:

www.shaunmullin.co.uk

The series will contain five books, which are:

THE FIGHT IN THE DOG
THE PATRON SAINT OF NOWHERE
TRUE NORTH
THE LOST LANGUAGE OF CROWS
PALE HORSE

Printed in Great Britain
by Amazon

28968935R00162